The Chaos Circus

Five trials. One prize.
One mad adventure.

To Georgie

you Are The
Fire

R. Dugan

THE CHAOS CIRCUS

Copyright © 2020 by R. Dugan

For information contact :

R. Dugan

PO Box 1265

Martinsville, IN 46151

www.reneeduganwriting.com

Book and Cover design by Maja Kopunovic

ISBN: 978-1-7339255-3-2

Second Edition: March 2020

10 9 8 7 6 5 4 3 2 1

DEDICATION

To the Almighty One who gave me the gift.
It's all for You. Always for You.
(Proverbs 3:9)

CHAPTER ONE

*J*know I ought not to think this way, but I could swear the air is flaked with sizzles of golden power that shimmer between the buildings as we pass them. It glints on the curve of my necklace and the heels of the dark revolvers and polished knives on the hips of the watchmen ahead of us. I cannot look away from their weapons as we go along to watch them arrest the most dangerous mass-murderer Barrow Island has seen in a century.

Part of me wishes I did not have to go along for this, following the renowned reporter Charles Metters with his crumbling cigar and faithful notetaking pad through the dark streets of Barrow Downs, the seediest district of our island-wide city. But I am the youngest and newest of all the reporters at Morrow Daily and the unpleasant assignments always fall to me. For Mister Metters, it isn't so unpleasant. He loves the thrill of the story, and I can hardly begin to imagine what favors were called and debts were created to make this evening possible. Us, on assignment with the night watch themselves for the arrest of such a killer.

The notion raises my hair, perhaps for different reasons than why Mister Metters is strutting like a peacock.

A lonely coach lumbers past, the horses whinnying in quiet unease. Fog from the industrial district clenches tightly around us as we conquer Center Street with brisk strides that suggest we belong here, and the thick shroud both muffles and magnifies our footsteps. I feel I'm more fog than person, my arms slick with sweat from the long walk and the anticipation, and I know that with my dark skin and dark coat, I blend even more into dusk.

But perhaps that's for the best, because I'm not keen to draw this murderer's attention tonight. Mostly because this coat, which is the only winterwear I have, emphasizes my smallness. Not in a dainty way, like the glass dolls Nan loved to collect when I was a child, not small and charming like a girl not yet grown into womanhood, but small like a burned wad of paper all crumbled in on itself, embers nibbling its edges even after the fire has gone out.

I push that thought away. There I go, rambling again.

No, it's good I'm here. Where else would I be but in my apartment, barely wide enough to pace across—which I do often, though I wish I wouldn't—a graveyard of milk bottles and empty wafer containers on the stained counters, and the sofa where I sleep when I can? At least I'm earning a wage tonight, and if I'm fortunate I may even have my name in tiny script under Mister Metters' on tomorrow's headline, and maybe someone with a monocle the size of their face will actually be able to read it and then I'll be noticed in a good way, for once.

I shouldn't have thought that.

Mister Metters slows and through the fogbank, I see that the watchmen have halted. We've come to the front of a very plain-looking confectionary, the sign over the door gilded in peppermint twists and faux powdered sugar flocking that almost looks edible. *The Alibi Shop,* reads the whimsical script. It looks like any other sweets shop, but according to a reliable tip to the Morrow Daily, it's a speakeasy—one of many to follow the prohibition when the residents of Barrow Downs refused to pay liquor taxes on imports from the mainland.

Mister Metters reads the sign and snorts. "Trite."

"It's a carnival term," I offer. "Something about…their excuses for why no one ever wins their games…"

The look he gives me is so chilling even my coat can't defend against it. I snap my mouth shut and look around while the watchmen quietly discuss how they will go about this arrest. As the fog begins to settle, new shapes take form through it, and I'm convinced all the buildings nearby have edged closer to hear my brief outburst and the whispers; the steepled clock tower reading ten minutes precisely until midnight, the complex homes and apartments on the wide boulevard, and the wizened signposts at the corner of every street seem to press in. I read the nearest sign and suddenly my heart thunders so loudly, I'm certain everyone can hear it.

We're only one street away from the Splendor House.

Clamminess licks the centers of my palms, and no amount of rubbing on my thighs sends it away. A sprig of curls bounces in the corner of my eye, flashing like a human hand, and I flinch at the thought of fingers reaching around to grab me from behind. I seize the familiar shape of the tethered balloon around my neck and chafe it along its cord while I fight to steady my breathing. As usual, that simple touch calms me a bit, and I remind myself that the Splendor House is sleeping at this hour. The curfew, after all, is sundown, no matter the season. The patients can't curse and gnash at me for my release while they sit in those pristine rooms and look out through those barred windows that were once my prison, too.

But I swear I can feel their eyes just the same.

"Tessa LaRoche!" Mister Metters barks, and I let go of my necklace, swiveling away from the mist-streaked street that whispers my name. His cold look from before has turned frigid, and I remember how closely he's watching me, how many times he's warned me that I'm a probationary reporter, less than a novice, until he's certain I won't go mad again.

Mad Tessa, always strumming that necklace. Mad Tessa with one freckle on her cheeks for every outburst that first put her in confinement. Mad Tessa who can't recall more than a few shadows of memory from before her stay in the Splendor House.

The watchmen don't seem aware of the coolness that stretches between my mentor and me. One puts a hand to his baton and says, "Here's how this will go. You'll keep your distance. Ask all the questions you like, but do nothing that will interfere with our arrest. And under no regards are you to touch this man. Do you understand?"

Mister Metters looks at me, and I nod. I have no intention of touching anything that came through a Rift, one of the gaping black wounds that joins our Mortal Lands to the fantastical Mirror Lands—a parallel world of bizarre fey creatures and stunning dangers from which this murderer allegedly sprang. I don't know why we call it Mirror or what the Lands were like before the Rifts opened up, but I'm certain Mirror Folk are not to be trifled with, and never to be touched. In the Splendor House and beyond, I heard tales of how, with one graze of the skin, they could change the course of mortal future, plunging their victims toward an inexorable and horrific end.

When we've both nodded, the watchmen stroll into *The Alibi Shop.* I fumble my notepad free and follow them, with Mister Metters behind me.

It's clear at once that this is no confectionary. The long, tall shop is too dark, and its ceiling drips with amethyst fabric in bunches and tendrils reminiscent of the jellyfish that wash up on Barrow Beach every now and then. Pearl booths line the room, and under every fabric bunch is a table of lacquered sangria wood to match the walls. Few occupants are here tonight. One could almost believe this has all been planned just for us.

The speakeasy's owner pauses at our arrival. Tallish, balding, with a cleft deep in his brow like one of his own bottles scoured him, he eyes us as the head of the watch ambles up to him.

"Easy, friend, we aren't here for you," the watchman says, and I am reminded that, prohibition notwithstanding, some of the town watch still knows of places like these and allows them to keep their doors open for a small fee traded beneath those dark tables. It's one of the stories everyone knows, and no one reports. There is a list of them that Mister Metters gave me the day I hired onto the Morrow Daily. If anyone writes a story about these illicit activities among the watch, they'll wash up on the beach with the jellyfish before the ink is dry.

It seems the keeper knows it, too. His smile is like a rat's, toothy and filthy, and he confers briefly with the watchman before pointing a subtle finger to one of the few occupied tables. I am already tense before the watchman returns to us, fingering first his baton, then a knife, as if he relishes the chance to use either. "That's our man."

I shift my hood aside to catch a glimpse of the accused at the table: black hair, olive-bronze skin, and a strong jaw. His locks swirl against his high, round cheekbones and the ends curl thickly at the nape of his neck, badly in need of a cut. He sprawls in a deceptively casual way, white shirt undone to the fourth button, hands settled lazily over his belt. Though his wrists are almost too thin for the rest of him, power pulses from the sinews of his arms.

This is no ordinary Mirror Folk, but he doesn't look like a murderer to me. Not in that languid sprawl, not with those eyes. But then, who am I of all people to judge if someone is deranged or ill in the head?

Whatever else he is, I realize he's looking right at me. And then he says, "I've been waiting for you."

My armpits grow damp at once. I shrink behind Mister Metters and the watchmen as we approach the table. I'm here only to observe, to take notes for the paper. He shouldn't be looking at me.

The head of the watch touches the brim of his hat with two fingers. "Evening, Mister—?"

"Call me Nicolai." The accused drags his eyes from me and taps his brow with the same two fingers, and I strangle the urge to giggle.

This is not funny. Nothing he does is funny. There are twenty people dead in a short year because of him. But that gesture is simply so absurd from someone so refined that the laughter nearly escapes me.

Oh, I hope Mister Metters didn't see me bite back that smile.

"Mister Nicolai, you are under arrest on charges of murder," the head of the watch says. "Twenty counts, to be precise."

He whistles lowly. "That's quite a large number, isn't it? Apparently, I've been very busy."

"Mister *Nicolai*," Mister Metters barges into this exchange as he does every other: pen in hand, eyes as sharp as his tongue. "You were seen fleeing the last crime scene."

"Was I?"

"An eyewitness placed you there." Dogged, Mister Metters places pen to notepad. "Why did you choose a hanging as your method? Was this personal? Did you hope to see the victims struggle? And why these people? What was their—?"

"Mister Metters!" A watchman grips his shoulder. "Not until we've done our part." He turns to Mister Nicolai. "You're aware that the Accord between our Lands forbids Mirror Folk from laying hands on a mortal here?"

"Oh, I'm aware." Mister Nicolai smiles, all teeth. "To do that, we must tempt them into *our* Land."

My heart kicks coltishly at the notion of walking through one of the

Rifts scattered across Barrow Island. How anyone could do something so absurd, so utterly *mad*, so abnormal is beyond me. But our island survives on the certainty that the mainland tourists will do just that. But such an action is something the residents of Barrow Island laugh at, and something we no longer do ourselves. The mere thought is absurd anymore.

I know personally that the last resident of Barrow Island to go through a Rift never came back. And that was the end of that.

"Then you're also aware that you've broken the Accord," the watchman continues, "which makes you subject to mortal law and punishment."

Mister Nicolai's eyes shift shade, like cream swirled into coffee. "I would be, if I had been the one to murder those people. As it happens, I'm here for the very reason you are: tracking the real killer."

A fizzle of shock burns in my veins. I had expected to encounter a man proud of his actions after all the glamor and glitz at the fine houses where the dead have been found in the last twelve months. I'd followed the case so closely even before I was a reporter, because it was all the talk in the streets from the moment I left the Splendor House. Curiosity at his denial pushes me forward like a hand in the small of my back, my pen and notepad ready as I take the fore. "What proof do you have that it wasn't your doing?"

His eyes lock onto mine, and the fizzle turns to flame. From this close, and with the jellyfish lights right above us now, I can see they're the color of crushed coffee with flickers of thought lighting their depths.

I've never met one of the Mirror Folk before—at least, I don't remember if I have—and there is certainly something immortal in that look.

The chill from the street returns. My pen wobbles on the paper.

"Hello," Mister Nicolai breathes, "you must be the junior reporter of Morrow Daily I've heard so much about."

I suddenly remember that I hadn't wanted to draw his attention, but now I have, and it seems there's no escaping it. If I shy away now, Mister Metters will think I'm unworthy of anything but fetching coffees and teas in the mornings. "Mister Nicolai—"

"Just Nicolai," he says with a rakish wink. I want to fold my notepad shut and hit him over the head, and where did *that* absurd urge come from?

He's one of the Mirror Folk and I was just thinking of his immortal stare—and now this!

Mad Tessa, thinking of hitting men who could break her in half. But that's half the population of Barrow Downs, anyway. "Nicolai, then. Where's your proof? What evidence could you offer of your innocence in these grisly killings?"

"I could tell you that the real murderer is in this speakeasy, that it's the very thing that's brought me here—would you believe that?"

"Proof," I repeat. He grins.

"I wasn't aware you were a prosecutor as well as a *probationary* reporter, Miss LaRoche," Mister Metters says stiffly.

The chill spreads all across my body. I've embarrassed him. I've bitten into the baitings of a murderer. Oh, what am I doing here? I shut my notepad, and Nicolai sits up straighter. "How do you like your job at the Morrow Daily, Miss LaRoche?"

I stare at him. Is he making casual conversation with me about my occupation during his own arrest? *He's* the mad one!

"Between you and me and the gatepost, it suits you, if you *must* have a profession," he adds. "To answer your question, I don't have a shred of proof. Yet. But then, neither do your watchmen, except for a few glimpses around street bends and one report from a witness who vanished like smoke afterward. They just can't help themselves out of wanting to arrest Mirror Folk."

Mister Metters laughs downright nastily. "Don't insult our intelligence. These boys did their job perfectly. The clues led to this speakeasy. The killer is here, and he's you."

"Right on all counts but one." Nicolai's eyes are riveted on me. "When that clock chimes midnight, the murderer is going to leap from his chair, cross this room, and make his escape through the door. Unfortunately, he won't be able to escape without bloodying his hands."

The head of the watch fingers his revolver now, and I know things have just taken a very serious turn. "Is that a threat?"

"No. But it is the truth."

"And how can you know?"

"I see more than you mortals do."

That flash again, a spill of light through his eyes, and I comprehend it just as the others do. We all jerk back as one when Nicolai stands.

"You're one of the Deathless!" Mister Metters growls.

"Correct."

I want to clutch my heart into my chest. *Deathless.* The most dangerous of all Mirror Folk, the ones with immortal power to match their immortal looks. I have a sudden memory of Nan tucking me into bed at night, telling me stories about the Deathless who feed on the power of the Mirror Lands, growing so strong that their flesh can hardly contain it. Men and women who can wipe whole clusters of stars from the sky, who can turn night to day with only a thought, who can make the impossible as real as the breath in your lungs. I think of how Nan used to send me to sleep with a doll on my bedside table, an effigy from her collection of Deathless so that if they came hunting for mortals to tempt through the Rifts that evening, they would pass me by.

A Deathless, here, and *murdering...*

Nicolai shifts forward, and with a gasp, I finally lay a hand to my collarbone—brushing bare skin.

My necklace is gone.

No, no—it's in Nicolai's hand. I didn't even see him move! But there is my necklace twirling around his fist, then dangling loose, then whipping around the other way. He turns it casually, again and again.

That flame he awakened in my blood with his strange stare waxes hotter. I take a step toward him. "Give me that necklace."

My voice shakes. He sends the necklace on another revolution. "Come and take it. If you can."

How *dare* he tease me, how dare he *taunt* me with my most precious possession stolen right from around my neck? I shift, and Mister Metters shouts, "Don't you take another step, Tessa LaRoche!"

"Come away, Miss!" The head of the watch fumbles for something, a knife, his revolver, and I am between him and the murderer. But all I can see is that necklace, and I feel the empty space where it is not, over my heart. My fingers flex, desperate for the comfort of the skin-heated metal against my palm.

"Please," I say, and find myself taking another step.

Gong! The clock tower chimes, setting my teeth on edge.

"Tessa," Mister Metters howls. "Tessa!"

The necklace stops turning. Nicolai's enigmatic eyes alight fully on me, and I can hear my heart hurtling into my ears. "I am begging you, please, *please*. Give it back to me."

A strange look crosses his face. He offers his hand, offers the necklace coiled in his palm. Against those deep grooves, it resembles a glittering silver serpent coiled to strike. "Take it. Just take it from me."

"Tessa! Don't you touch him!"

I know I shouldn't. I should be behind the men, I certainly should *not* be standing here between their revolvers and this murderer. This is madness, utter madness, and I can *feel* how mad I seem to them, ignoring their orders, taking another step forward. I can feel the walls pressing in, and the Splendor House shambling closer, its great front door open to devour me.

Gong!

But without my necklace's comforting weight shackling me to sanity, to the truth of the world around me, I am already lost. I am lightheaded and not at all myself, I am almost floating above me, watching this girl with a coffee-grain dusting of freckles across the bridge of her twitching nose scenting the air for danger like a frightened rabbit as she takes another step, as she reaches out.

"Miss!" howls the head of the watch.

"Take it." The challenge is low, strange, and I almost hear the strum of music in Nicolai's words.

I will never know if it is desperation or that dare in his voice that brings my fingers to his, closing over the necklace.

Gong!

"Tessa, you little fool!" Mister Metters will tear his throat with how much he's shouting. The entire watch goes tense all over, all at once, like someone has jerked a string and made them stiffen. "The House will hear about this! You're finished at the Daily! This is the end of you!"

Gong!

"Tessa! *Tessa LaRoche*, come back here!"

But I don't. Because just then, Nicolai clenches my fingers like a handshake. And he smiles.

Gong.

A flurry of movement erupts from one of the curved pearl booths. A figure springs across the glossy table and comes straight toward us, shooting like a bullet—just as Nicolai predicted. I scream, and Nicolai jerks me against his chest, but my weight surprises him. We slam into and over his chair, and the impact with the hardwood floor disorients me. I come to my hands and knees, scrambling for my necklace, but the figure from the booth reaches it first.

In his gloved hands, it becomes a weapon. It slashes down one watchman's face, and blood slaps the floor. The man screams and falls. Mister Metters trips over his own curses and collapses into one of the booths, sheltering around its side. The attacker hesitates, holding my necklace aloft, staring at it with a cocked head. I see the bearded line of his jaw twitch as his mouth curves down at one corner.

By the time I lurch onto my feet, the man has fled with my necklace in hand, the speakeasy door creaking shut behind him.

"Give that back!" I scream, and chase after him.

This is not at all like me, I think as I splash through oily puddles, my dull boots disturbing their opalescent skin. I don't chase after thieves. There are watchmen and procedures for that. But he has my necklace, the only thing in the world that really feels like it's mine, the charm that has bitten into my palm through so many sleepless nights. The thought of those polished gloves clutching it makes me want to sob.

So I sprint after him, past the Splendor House, down a dozen twisting cobblestone streets until my breath sears in my lungs. But I find I can keep going.

Where did this stamina come from? I've never run this far or this fast before, and yet my muscles seem to know exactly what to do, how to stretch, my lungs know how to pace themselves through pulls of air despite my panic.

There is no time to question it. I can only see the man's path through frosted flirts of immaculate cloth around darker corners. I don't know what I will do if I catch him, but I remember that I wanted to bludgeon Nicolai with my notebook and think that I will start there.

The way levels out suddenly, and I see a signpost suspended across the gutted street, the word *Danger* faded and repainted countless times over a century. My heart stutters and my stride slows.

I know what he is running toward. Of course. Because he is Mirror

Folk, too.

And now I can see him clearly, the size and shape of a man barreling toward a slit in the very fabric of the world, a pulsing black fathom between buildings. I can only imagine what the occupants of these now-abandoned apartments thought the day this gap opened in their midst, bringing the perpetual, choking smell of forge-metal to the air, a tang of power that I can taste as I stagger to a halt.

The thief does not slow at all. He lunges into the Rift, and just like that, he's gone. My last scream at him is worthless, not even touching his heels as he vanishes.

The Rift's inborn wind rakes at my curls. The breeze blows toward it, not from it, as if it's sucking the Mortal Lands into its maw. I shake my head, but I don't back away. I can't.

That necklace—that piece of me—

Something detonates at the mouth of the street. I jolt at the sound of ricocheting metal and realize that the watchmen are approaching, firing blindly down the alley, firing at a figure racing one step ahead of their aim.

Nicolai. It's him they're shooting at, but they don't seem to mind at all if a stray bullet hits me—and one nearly does. But Nicolai flashes up his arm and I see he's wearing a cloak like mine, but sleeker, and when he spreads it out the bullet bounces harmlessly away. Had it not, I would be bleeding on the cobblestones now.

It's the last thought I have before I hear a pin unlatch, and realize they are going to hurl a grenade at him. At *us.*

Then his arms engulf me, and I'm punched with the scent of foreign spice and sweat and something strange that makes me think of golden power flaking the air. The force of the collision barrels us into the hungry wind—or perhaps that's the burst of the grenade. Perhaps I will never know.

And we fall through the Rift.

CHAPTER TWO

*T*he air tastes different when I come back to myself—mulled with a heat that has nothing to do with sunlight. It ought to be winter, anyway. But the atmosphere is downright humid as I struggle back to consciousness, battering off a shivering half-dream of the Splendor House. I feel at once that I am soaked, that I'm lying on something quite unpleasantly hard, but at least I'm alive. My throat burns with salt, and I'm reminded of swimming in Barrow Harbor and nearly drowning. How old was I then—six, perhaps seven? It's hazy, as all my remaining memories are.

I crack my eyes open and wish I hadn't.

Nicolai is standing further up the shore, shirtless and wringing out his clothes. So, the Rift almost certainly dropped us into water. I've never conceived of the Mirror Lands having bodies of water, but now I can hear one licking the shore, and as I slowly sit up I'm greeted by a long stretch of dark rock—the source of my discomfort—mopped with foam from an equally black tide. This must be a lake of sorts, washed in moonlight. And from somewhere behind us, I hear distant, tinny music and delighted shrieks.

And then it hits me that I am *here*, I am in the Mirror Lands where no Barrow Island native ought to go, where stories tell of Deathless luring us like gentle lambs to slaughter. Mister Metters saw me go, and even before that, he told me I was finished. Is he even now marching to the Splendor House, to Missus Fiona Chambers who oversees my case?

Though we seem to be far from the Rift that spat us out, I can suddenly feel its hungry winds pulling at me. I can feel the orderlies in their pressed white uniforms closing in, can taste the starch on their collars as I bite and kick like a crazy person, like an animal, struggling to get away. I can hear them telling me I'm ill and my own voice saying I'm not, I'm not, I'm not, I want something, I want, I want, until their medicines lull me to sleep.

But maybe I *am* ill. I chased after a thief—no, a murderer, if Nicolai is to be believed. The real murderer who was lurking in that pearl booth, leaping to escape at the chime of midnight. But even before that, the watch and Mister Metters saw me act out in sheer madness, reach for Nicolai, touch one of the Deathless.

"Tessa?"

I freeze, realizing only then that I'm standing now, dripping and shaking, and that has alerted Nicolai to my waking. He turns to face me, shirt still half-wrung in his hands, and he measures me with the same cagey regard as Mister Metters did. I want to scream. I reach for my throat, but my fingers brush an ever-broadening gap where my pendant always hung. It might as well be a wound ripped wide open.

"They'll send me back," I choke. "What have I done, how could I be so foolish, so, so—"

So mad.

But I don't want to say that, because if I admit to such a truth, I might as well march to the door of the Splendor House and submit myself to it. Missus Fiona told me I could always come back if I felt like I was slipping, and they would set me straight again.

Right now, I feel I'm slipping. I stumble a few steps up the shore, and suddenly Nicolai is in front of me, hands splayed. "You don't want to go that way, fey beasts prowl in those woods. Unless your intent is to get eaten, in which case you have a remarkable sense of direction."

I smack his hands out of the way. "Do you have any inkling what they'll do to me when I go back, what I've just done to myself? Missus Fiona must be sending out searches even *now*...it won't be your arrest in the Morrow Daily first thing, it will be all this odd behavior of mine!"

His smile is infuriatingly arrogant. "I hardly thought your display in the *Shop* was fodder for front page gossip, Miss LaRoche."

"You don't understand! They've been watching me!" I shout. "Waiting for the smallest incentive to take me back to the Splendor House. No one ever believed I was cured, and now…" Now, by chasing a thief like some reckless vigilante, by ignoring the orders of the watch and my supervisor, I've just proved it to them all.

"Then don't go back," Nicolai says. As if it's the simplest thing in the world that I could *stay* here. In the Mirror Lands!

"I *must* go back, I'm mortal, it's where I belong!" I sit down hard again and cradle my head in my hands. "This is a disaster."

I feel so empty. My collar feels empty. I am fighting not to cry.

Nicolai clears his throat. I'm sure he has very, very little experience with comforting almost-crying girls on dark shores in the dead of night. Well, I have just as little sympathy for him. If he had come along quietly with the watch instead of stealing my necklace in the first place…

I jolt, dropping my hands to look up at him, and something in my face sets him back on his heels. "*You.* This is all *your* fault."

"Hardly," he begins.

"If you hadn't stolen my necklace, that other thief couldn't have stolen it either!" I lurch back to my feet, staggering toward him. "Do you know what you've done to me? That necklace was my greatest possession, it was all I had with me in the Splendor House, it was—it was—"

It was my only friend, but dare I add to the measure of my absurdity by saying that? What sort of girl, even one a year fresh from the asylum, has no friends but a necklace that makes her feel courageous? I know how silly it sounds, but I feel as empty as when Nan disappeared and never came back. As empty as when we took word my parents had died.

I stand there, fisting and unclenching my hands, because I want to hit this Deathless and that is perhaps the maddest of all the things I've considered tonight.

Nicolai's strong jaw works, chewing over a particularly difficult problem. "I never intended your necklace to be stolen by the likes of him."

There's an odd intimacy to his choice of words, something that eases my anger like a placated carthorse. "Him. You knew who he was, that…that blackguard?"

His lips tip, but there is no amusement there. "Just that he's one of the Deathless, and that he's the one behind your island's recent string of murders."

I frown. He knows that I'm no watchman, no prosecutor. He really has no reason to posture now. "So that was true, then. You really aren't the one responsible."

"Which of us attacked the watchmen? Which stole the necklace?"

"Both of you, to the latter."

He grits his teeth audibly. "All right, but which of us used it to cut a man's face open?"

I'd forgotten the sound and sight of that. I shudder, hugging my arms around my frigid, damp middle. "Let's say I believe you. Why is this man framing you for these murders?"

"I don't know." Nicolai smooths his thumb along his bottom lip, glancing in the direction of those faraway lights and the vibration of music that disrupts the air. "But this much I'm certain of: I wanted proof I'd been framed by one of my own kind, and there it was, in that shop."

"And now he has my necklace."

"Now he has your necklace, and he knows that I know what he's done, that blackguard." He uses my turn of phrase so flippantly, I almost miss that he's mocking me. "Anyone who breaks the Accord deserves the according punishment. But I'm certainly not going to take it for him."

"What are you going to do, then?"

"Find him, of course," Nicolai finally shrugs back into his shirt, "and toss him back through the Rift. The way I see it, you ought to come with me."

The notion is so absurd, I sputter with laughter. "Go *with* you?"

"I've saved your life tonight. I don't know why it seems so shocking that you might be safer with me than alone on these wild shores."

He has a decent point, though I don't want to concede it. No proper Barrow Island girl goes running off on the heels of a stranger she's only just met, armed with nothing but her sodden clothes, pen, and notepad, no less.

But, this murderer..."He has my necklace."

Nicolai pinches his brow. "Yes, Miss LaRoche, we've established that."

"If you find him, I could get it back."

He drops his hand as suddenly as he lifted it and looks hard at me.

There's a glint of something I can't define in his eyes, not that this is anything new for me. "Yes, that's very true. It does seem we want the same thing, doesn't it?"

It does. But if I go along with this, it will give Nicolai precisely his desire—my companionship. And I'm reminded of Nan's stories about the very clever ways the Deathless of the Mirror Lands lure smitten women and dazzled men through the Rifts and into this beautiful but deadly world. The very air is charged with power.

"Perhaps...perhaps I should just go back through the Rift..."

And face Missus Fiona and Mister Metters, and trade in these dull clothes for the ivory smock of the Splendor House. By dawn, I will be back in my old room.

Nicolai doesn't offer to lead me to a Rift. Nor does he try to lure me away. He simply watches, one sleek brow lifted, as if he already knows what I'll decide.

Damn him.

"After I have my necklace."

"Partners, then." He offers his arm gallantly, like a debutant's suitor at a ball. "Shall we?"

I forgo the arm. Standing this close to him, and with my spurt of panic fading now that I've decided I won't face the Splendor House quite yet, I'm becoming aware that the hum of power is not just on the air. It's all over him, a dim and constant throbbing as if from a mending sprain or a bruise pressed too many times. I can almost hear it like a second heartbeat. I have never wanted to touch anyone less in my life.

We pick our way up the dark shore toward distant wharfs growing out of the smooth, flat rock that made such an uncomfortable bed. Soon I'm breathing hard, puffing in a most unladylike fashion, and Nicolai almost looks ready to laugh. Almost.

"Why did you save me those two times?" I ask to distract him. "With the bullet, and here, pulling me from the water when we toppled through."

"I'm already wanted for murder in the Mortal Lands. Best not to convict myself for your death while in the process of clearing my name, no?"

I can hardly fathom my lack of intrinsic value to this immortal scoundrel. We clamber onto the wharfs, which is all that saves him from a stern word right then. What that word would be, I don't know, because the moment we stand he catches my chin in one hand and looks so deeply into my eyes I'm certain he can see the rattling lockbox where I keep my madness tampered down.

"If I'm going to take you, Miss LaRoche, it will be the way that all Deathless do." He tilts his head without looking away from me. "In the Chaos Circus."

CHAPTER THREE

S o. That's where he's brought me.

The Chaos Circus is a figment of Nan's stories, something I've managed to retain despite the fog that blurs so much else before the Splendor House. The Mirror Lands are said to be braided together with a power beyond mortal comprehension, and the Chaos Circus is the hub of that power. No, it *is* power itself, a great and splendid nest of it at the heart of the Mirror Lands. What began as a small carnival in ancient times has grown out to engulf the surrounding streets and homes, and now it's a whole city that is nothing but attraction after ride after booth, where even its hostels and pubs are themed or enchanted, and we are standing on the edge of it. After these wharfs, and a narrow sliver of stone cliffs, and a rickety fence twice my height with only one entrance, we will be inside the Chaos Circus.

My boot heels skid on the moldering wooden planks. Nan's warnings all come rushing back at once, a black current that jerks me off-balance worse than the lake slime slobbering all over the wharf.

This place is not safe. This is the lure that has drawn so many mortals away from our safe, proper world, into theirs: the promise of holding magic and power in one's hands, of touching something fantastic and awestriking and immortal—this is the bait they've used over the centuries, coaxing us to relinquish the Accord's protection and willingly risk our lives on these silly carnival games. The Circus feeds the Deathless with power, and they feed the Circus with years and stamina and debts owed by their mortal victims. In this vicious symbiosis, we mortals benefit in things like small doses of charmed curatives and weapons that always strike fatally and enchanted pens that write the perfect words. But Nan always warned me that what we receive from the Circus is never as valuable as what we give up.

My strong, nurturing, hypocritical Nan.

I start to shake my head. "This is…"

"I'm Deathless, if you recall," Nicolai says. "I'll make certain nothing happens to you here."

Never trust the word of the Deathless, Nan warned me when I was very small. *Their only concern is to tempt you into the Circus so that they can feed on your life force. Parasites, they are. All of them. Never let one lead you. If you see one in the street, turn and walk the other way. If they speak to you, do not reply. And never, ever follow one into the Circus, or you will be lost forever.*

Nan has been the clearest of all the things I remember since my treatment in the Splendor House. I have rarely felt anything but gratitude for her, but tonight I am emboldened by a strangely defiant streak, as if being threatened and chased and shot at has made me reckless. And that recklessness feels familiar and sound, like I ought to trust it.

I must make my own choices tonight, and though Nan's words resonate in my head, they seem so hollow this time. Nan did not understand that one day her only granddaughter would face the precipice of insanity, and that one of her few tethers would lie beyond that wooden fence at the edge of the Circus.

Besides, the very last lesson Nan ever taught me was that all her tokens of wisdom have exceptions. So this could easily be one.

I square my shoulders and march up to the fence gap where a woman, just on the other side, plays a lonely calliope. She might as well be sculpted from marble, she's so smooth and pale. I'm not quite as dark as Nan was, but next to her, I seem clothed in night. She wears a brocade tailcoat and long candy-striped leggings, a sort of irrespective dress that no woman on Barrow Island would so much as be buried in. And yet as soon as I come upon her, I'm almost certain I've seen her attire before.

It's a niggling little thought, hardly more substantial than the flitting of a dayfly about my head. I brush it off and lean to the left, catching a surreptitious glance of the calliope's lacquered body. It's monogrammed with a pair of letter *C*s wrapped up together like canoodling cats, and on either side, tigers rear up and elephants balance precariously on large rubber balls. It all looks very whimsical, quite mainland, where these animals roam free in the mortal world. I wonder if they exist here as well, or if this is merely a slice of normalcy stolen from the Mortal Lands to tempt us into the Circus.

My own thought surprises me. I have so little right to accuse others of deception when I hide my madness daily. I clear my throat and edge around the calliope toward the fence gap.

"Wait."

The music stops, replaced by the soft stir of the wind along the dark water behind us. The silence is so profound, it sends me turning back. The woman looks up with vacant eyes, top and lower lids flecked with small black nibs. A single teardrop is painted halfway down one alabaster cheek.

"You know what will happen if you enter."

This must be a speech for every mortal who approaches, yet I feel that she is speaking it only to me. "Yes, I do. I will apprehend the scoundrel who entered just before us, with my necklace in hand."

Her eyes dart to Nicolai. Then she shrugs, the fine threads of her vest and coat whispering, and the calliope music begins again, a livelier tune than before. "In that case, the Chaos Circus welcomes you. Do enjoy your time indulging in the pleasures of this Land."

Nicolai doesn't touch me, but there's something protective in his sharp strides and curved posture as he escorts me through the gap in the fence.

And then we are inside the Chaos Circus.

It is a daydream in the dead of night, a spun-sugar globe of wonder plucked from a child's shelf. Taffy-thick silk garlands curl around what might have once been plain wooden posts, transforming them into pergolas that drip honeyed shadows over the paths. The cobblestones glitter with a fine skin of lavender dust. To our left there are clusters of buildings that all remind me of *The Alibi Shop*, as though Nicolai and I were fated to meet in a place that was so like this one. But that seems to be the only respectable part of the city, and everything else is booths and rides: a great rainbow wheel of balloon-shaped carriages turning and twinkling, a mushroom stand of twirling chairs fitted on long chains, a severe line of mismatched structures strung together to create a House of Mirrors. As I squint upward I see an array of colorful basketed balloons, just like my necklace, bobbing on enormous tethers like stars leashed to the world.

Perhaps the Deathless are even capable of such feats as roping the stars.

I can hear squeals and screams of delight, the calliope's siren call opposing the hum of attractions in motion and the chatter of hundreds, if not thousands, of circusgoers perusing booths all around us.

I stand agape beneath the tresses of light winking down from within fat glass bulbs and the twinkling booth faces, and I forgive every mortal who ever walked away from their precious responsibilities to fritter off the years of their lives in this place. I can't even remember why I came, but I think I will stay.

A sudden touch jolts me from my reverie. Nicolai has taken my hand, not in any intimate way, but to press the middle of my palm so hard I yelp. There is old scar tissue there from an injury I don't remember, and the pain peels me away from the captivating sight before me. My hand flies to my empty collar, and I remember why I am here.

"We ought to find a hostel." Nicolai's tone is stiff. "Somewhere to rest for the night. On the morrow, we begin our search."

He starts a long-limbed march toward the more respectable portion of the Circus, and I trot after him. "And just how will we find him, pray tell?"

It's only now, confronted with these many city boulevards and pastel visions of circus and carnival fare, that I've realized how ghastly a search it will be. I know that each attraction belongs to one of the Deathless, and any one of them might have been the thief. They could blend into this place like one limpid twist of silk in a whole sheaf of them. I don't have Nicolai's eternal life to spend searching for clues...I must find my necklace and return as quickly as possible before tales of my madness spread from Barrow Island all the way to the mainland.

"I have a thread or two I can pluck," Nicolai says. "Keep your eyes and ears open, you seem good at that."

He's referring to my status as a reporter—my former status, I presume. I try to stuff away the memory of Mister Metters toppling into that booth as I look all around and listen. I can still hear the calliope music bouncing off the many attractions, always to find us again. I peer into booths as we pass by and see paintings here and there, grinning faces forever frozen in their greatest moment of triumph.

"Past winners," Nicolai intones when he catches me staring, and I try not to look at them after that. A few strike me as oddly familiar, but then, some people just have those sorts of faces. Not that I'm really one to judge such things anyway, disoriented and addled as I am by everything. The vendors and owners of these booths shout all over one another at the people ambling by:

"Pretty Pastels, eat these and the men will find you irresistible!"

"Try a Bloated Toffee, just one will feed a grown man for five days at the cost of just one—that's right, one day of your life for five days full! Who's hungry?"

"Have an ailment? Trade it away with one of Lord Mull's Lozenges— now flavored in peach, cherry, and grape!"

"Who is Lord Mull?" I ask as we press into the steadily-growing throng.

"The Circus Confectioner." Nicolai's tone is mildly scathing. "Whatever you do, don't ingest any of his creations. Some have a clear cost, like the Bloated Toffees. Others demand quite a bit more."

I shudder to think what the cost is for curing any ailment or making someone pretty. Perhaps the face sags off after the effect is complete, or the sickness is cured but replaced by something twice as debilitating. My tongue tastes sour just thinking about it, and I tuck myself into Nicolai's tall shadow as we slither through the crowd. I can feel at once that most of these are mortals, lacking the perpetual hum of power that shimmers in the air around the Deathless. It must be that at the late hour, they're all seeking board for the night.

So many like me, all here seeking one satisfaction or another. Most are mainlanders judging by their attire, the bedazzled and bored wealthy who sail for a full week across the sea just to leap through the Rifts and experience for themselves if the stories of this powerful stuff of dreams are all true. Of course, most of them go home in the end—despoiled of their long lives and heavy-hung with strange prizes.

They're all fools, and I'm a fool for being here.

But I *need* that necklace.

The strands of light dim above us, and suddenly the music quiets, and I hear a voice shouting:

"That's right! Your heart's deepest desire granted, no question, you heard me, there are absolutely *no* exceptions! Bring a loved one back from the dead! Turn yourself from man to woman or the other way around! Take a rival's riches, make that handsome vision from the Mortal Lands fall in love with you—step right up, The Wish Granter can make it happen!"

My whole body turns, guided by the lure of those words. I hear a curse as someone knocks into me, but for once I hardly care if I draw attention. My eyes seek the owner of that voice, and my heart punches ruthlessly against my ribs, lunging toward the tantalizing offer.

The speaker stands on a plain rostrum among the vending booths. A homely banner shapes the front of it, bearing the image of a man in a tailcoat and circus hat, a showman's cane in his hand. He is rendered with his head turned, peering over his shoulder, and I have the eerie sense that he is looking right at me.

He is the ringmaster. I don't know how I know it, but the certainty is as clear as my own name. The man announcing him is fair and tall and looks very much like a lion who wished himself into a man. His mane of hair shivers as he laughs, a beguiling chuckle that tempts me closer and closer. He sounds like a brother or a dear friend, someone you would trust absolutely.

"A wish! Five games, five simple games for a wish...five trials to change your future," he says now. "Step right up!"

Five simple games.

It will never be that easy.

I am almost to the edge of the throng when fingers wrap my elbow, towing me to a halt. I hear my name, and swivel to look at Nicolai. He's caught me and watches me now with the unmistakable concern that I'll slip away to the rostrum if he so much as blinks. "Come away, Miss LaRoche. It's not worth it."

"But—the wish—"

"It's not worth it!" he's shouting now, and I'm not certain if it's because of the clamor around us or because he can feel me straining against his grip.

What does he care if I go? Or does he not want to lose the many, many long years I have left to squander to this leonine fellow? So possessive, these Deathless.

But I go with him. Not because I feel any loyalty to Nicolai, not as if my years belong to him, but because I am suddenly thinking very hard about something, and I know Nicolai can find us somewhere private and safe enough to think.

And he does. He chooses a hostel called *Red & Gold's*, which is appropriately paneled in those very shades. If it's in any way uncommon for one of the Deathless to take up at an inn, the keeper is too clever to remark on it. I stand in the broad foyer with its plush velveteen chaises and upstanding mainlanders, all sipping champagne from fluted glasses and chattering gamely. One man seems to mistake me for an indenture and hands me his glass.

"Don't drink it," Nicolai warns as he returns. He's stuffed his hands into his pockets, and a faint scowl frames his high cheeks. He almost looks pained.

I set the glass on a nearby table. "Where are we going?"

He gives a room number, and I almost laugh—the same silly, hysterical giggle that's been hovering in my throat ever since Nicolai saluted the watchman tonight. The room number is my birthdate, according to my records in the Splendor House. I've had no one to celebrate it with in so long, I haven't bothered to really remember it until now. Maybe that ought to frighten me, but it simply makes me feel even more like I'm dancing inside a dream.

As we climb three flights of stairs, things grow quieter until they are almost muted. In fact, I hear not a whisper from any of the rooms. I wonder if they're enchanted to contain the sounds within.

Nicolai halts before our door and takes his hand from his pocket, and now I see a trace of blood along his fingertips. He dashes them to the door, which has neither lock nor lever, and it opens before him.

"Just a bit of Deathless power," he says at my wide-eyed stare. "We have our share of proficient mortal lockpickers streaming through the

Circus. Best to ensure the proper doors can only be opened by those to whom they belong."

"Then…you can be harmed?"

His chuckle swirls like ink in water. "We are immortal, not invincible, Miss LaRoche."

I suppose I ought to be relieved no one can break in, though what do I have to lose if they do? Would anyone here want to steal my clothes? And that's all I have, now that I've lost the silver necklace.

I follow Nicolai into a two-bedded room with each headboard woven in delicate iron rosebuds. As we enter, a handful of them bloom open. I cannot bear their strangeness, and look instead through the triangular window that peers down over a small swath of the Circus. This room faces back the way we came, and I can see the woman at the calliope playing away, and the harbor beyond her. What I cannot see is the man lauding The Wish Granter, and I am pierced with the sharp suspicion that Nicolai has done this on purpose.

I turn to face him. "Why did you pull me away from that rostrum?"

"I told you why." He sits on one bed. "It's not worth it."

"And why not? What is the price?"

Nicolai watches the blood swirl on his fingerpads. "Too high. Far, far too high."

I sit as well, because I think I will be able to reason with him better this way. "Five trials, he said. Suppose that was five games one must play, or five attractions to visit…but that wish. With that wish, we could find the name of the murderer. We could exonerate you and have my necklace back and be done with the whole affair!"

His hand cannot be as fascinating as the attention he's giving it, which suggests he's trying to think of an excuse. But his silence is working against him, because the more I think of it, the more plausible a notion it seems. There is no angle of this where we do not have to dirty our fingers some to find that Deathless murderer. He would not have fled into the Circus if it would divulge his identity easily. And if we must find him, then why not by a means that is certain not to fail?

"I'm not willing to take the trials," Nicolai finally says.

"Well, I am." My cool boldness startles even me. Where are my shaking hands, where is the uncertainty I know I feel? For all my qualms, one thing I have always been assured of is that I wouldn't fall into the trap of the Chaos Circus. And yet, here we are. And it seems that like Nan's rules, my own promises to myself have their every exception.

Nicolai is looking at me differently now, a conflict of emotion on his face. At one moment, he appears devastatingly unsure. The next, his hungry stare devours me with the rapture of a man to whom a great secret had just been revealed.

But I am assuming these things. I hardly know him, after all—perhaps he's having indigestion from whatever he drank in *The Alibi Shop.*

"Tessa," he begins.

"Miss LaRoche."

"Miss LaRoche." He grimaces as if I've forced him to swear. "The Wish Granter's trials are not something to be leaped into. I'm unconvinced that our straits are so dire yet as to require his...*services.*"

"Well, I think differently," I snap. "Because I can assure you I am *quite* desperate. You don't know what awaits me when I return to Barrow Island, but I do, and I am not prepared to go back without my necklace."

"And what is it to you? A charm of good fortune? A gift from a lover?"

My ears grow hot. How dare he speak so condescendingly? "It's all I have that's mine. It's all they let me keep in the Splendor House, and it...it means more than words can frame, so I'll thank you to shut your mouth about it now, Mister Nicolai."

He blinks at me, but with none of the rage I expect on the heels of my outburst. If anything, those dark eyes hold a touch of pity. "What is this Splendor House you keep mentioning? It doesn't sound so awful a place, with a name like that."

I have never discussed it with anyone—I've never had anyone to discuss it with. I pull my feet onto the bed and grip my knees to my chest, leaning back against the iron rosebuds. One of them blooms wider, rubbing a kink in my back. "It's where they send mad people like me. But enough of that. I want my necklace. I will have it."

Nicolai rubs his face with both hands. I have never heard of Deathless seeming weary, but I think that's the word for him now. "Will you sleep on this, at least?"

I consider the ramifications. Perhaps I'm being a bit silly, a bit rash. And perhaps I've taken my disregard of Nan's warnings too far. It's true that I have no proper measure of the sane and insanity, after all. "Until morning, then."

Nicolai shifts his jaw and settles in. I expect the same lazy sprawl as in *The Alibi Shop*, but he is stiff now, sitting up like I am and facing toward the door. He loosens a few buttons and tugs at his collar with a sigh.

I look away from the flash of his throat. It doesn't feel like something I ought to see.

"If not this, we will need another plan, and quickly," I say.

"You're awfully determined not to spend a moment longer than necessary in the Mirror Lands." Nicolai kicks off his shoes and yawns.

There is the arrogance from the speakeasy. "It's not so wonderful here. Not for mortals."

"I'm aware." His tone has a sudden hard edge. "I was mortal once."

I nearly drop my arms from around my knees, he startles me so. "Were you?"

"Most Deathless were," he says as calmly as if this is common knowledge. "We completed the trials. We wished for immortality. But this bound us to the Circus, and now our duty is to it. We are only free to roam if it's into the Mortal Lands to lure in more of your kind."

"And is this all some great scheme to lure *me*?"

"Do you think you're worth so much trouble?"

I consider it. "Perhaps not. How long have you been Deathless?"

"Less than the others. Only a century or so."

Only a century. I nearly choke. He looks hardly older than I am!

"Not long enough that I've been won to their methods," he adds. "Which is why I can only assure you once again that the trials are not worth your trouble."

I gather my knees closer at the grim certainty in his words, reminded that I am sharing quarters with one of the Deathless. Nan would have heart failure if she was alive to see this. "What do they call you?"

Every Deathless has a name, I know. Lord Mull, Mistress Luck, Lady Lore—they're spilling back through me now, memories of stories Nan told me. Deathless with names to match the action they perform for the Circus, everything from confection to guessing games to mazes. I don't know what Nicolai's power is, or what part he plays in the Circus. But I'd be safer if I knew.

"They call me Nicolai," he says with that infuriating, crooked smile. "I prefer no other name. It was the one I was born with. Whatever they call me is only a portion of my true self."

And he considers his mortal name the other portion. Curious.

When I don't reply, his eyes flutter shut. He folds his hands over his middle, and after a while I think he must be sleeping.

I wish I could do the same. But as the bowels of night encroach, broken only by the undying glow of the Circus, I am still watching its fanciful colors dance through the water-facing window. I find myself with a hand to my chest, feeling for that comforting silvery weight, seeking to thread the chain between my fingers.

It is gone. And I am gone. I feel both more and less mortal than I ever have, in this place and with the choices that brought me here. I swore to myself, swore to Nan, I think, that I would never come. And yet here I am, and the power of the Circus robes me with the feeling that this has all happened before, as if I belong here somehow.

My madness within this mad world. Perhaps that's true.

I get up and start to pace, silent in my wool socks. They're still damp from our unexpected swim, but I'm reluctant to remove them even if they'll shrink. They muffle my steps across the room and back again, across and back. I tap my fingers over my heart so many times I make myself want to scream. The lack of that weight around my neck...I never thought I would miss it so much. I never imagined being parted from it.

Nicolai wakes suddenly, with a shift in breathing that brings me to a halt, poised to flee. "What in the world are you doing?"

"Pacing."

He hasn't opened his eyes, and a faint crease appears between his brows. "Go to sleep."

"You go to sleep."

"Believe me, I will," he mumbles. "Darting through Rifts is costly...nevermind keeping the rest of the Deathless from noticing you tonight."

Before I can ask him what he means by that, he's asleep again. For the first time, it strikes me that this might not be a wholly natural slumber. Perhaps the power these Deathless possess is not given freely by the Circus, but drawn from it like a sore tooth, and requires some effort to extract.

Perhaps Nicolai can do much more than whatever power his Circus title would suggest, yet each act costs him something a bit more, begs another tearing from the power of the city itself.

What an oddly particular thought.

I study him in the blend of Circus flare and moonlight. He says we are partners now, and I believe that he's being honest. Or perhaps he's a very, very good actor, and this is all part of his strategy. Perhaps he really doesn't want to share me with the man at the rostrum, or with The Wish Granter. Perhaps he's really not been framed at all, but tempting me here all this time, with the hangings, and the talk of another culprit.

I don't know which is sillier: that I consider the notion for several moments, or that in the end I dismiss it on nothing more than a blind certainty that he is telling the truth.

If I'm really that gullible, I belong in the Splendor House. But if I'm going there anyway upon my return, best not to go empty-necked.

The artist Dawn paints the horizon in rich tones of amber and cerise at long last, and I still haven't slept. I've gathered myself into the windowsill by this time and hold my focus to the calliope player with what Missus Fiona would call the Skull's Stare. It's a trance where I'm fully aware I'm entranced but do nothing to stop it. The world seems to slow around me. It blurs. I blur. In these moments, I can almost grasp the memories that the House's methods bottled up, shook out, and scattered like disturbed waters to the farthest corners of my mind. But it's only possible to do this when I'm very tired, and tonight all it's profited me is the knowledge that the calliope player does not stop her music, ever.

I haven't slept, not for a single moment, and I barely slept the night before, in my apartment where I was also pacing. This is a dangerous combination for a certifiably crazy person, but I hardly care.

I've waited until dawn. That's all I promised to do.

Restless and reckless, I slide off the sill and look at Nicolai again. He sleeps on, even when I tiptoe past. Even when I pick up my winter coat and hustle from the room, down the steps, through the hostel parlor, and back into the street.

The crowd is as thin as the haze of morning fog, and I stuff my hands into my pockets and fold between the few pedestrians, making my way back to that plain rostrum.

The ringmaster's outline watches me with sharp paper eyes as I march up to his lionlike announcer and use up all that's left of my boldness at once:

"I'll do it. I'll take your trials."

CHAPTER FOUR

*T*here is a slight convergence on the rostrum, a handful of curious prospects who cease their chatter the moment the words leave my mouth. The Lion folds his arms and studies me. I notice that his eyes, too, are catlike, the black centers enormous as if he can see more in the waning dark than most people can in the light.

"Well, well," he purrs. "How interesting. Are you sure you want to do this?"

I want to ask him tartly what harm it could possibly do, but some part of me, either wise or frightened, warns me not to say anything. I simply nod.

The Lion straightens, all hints of sly interest gone, and he spans his arm toward me in a gesture I recoil from. "Well, ladies and gentlemen, here she is—a girl twice as bold as the rest of you put together! Step right up, no need to be shy…what's your name?"

"Tessa," I croak as the crowd flattens on either side. My heart makes its home in my throat and suddenly I want to turn and run. Oh, this feels like a mistake, the largest of my life, but I fear to flee now. The eyes of these people are fixed on me. I'm certain if I turn, they'll snatch me, and the Lion will transform into his former self and spring down to tear me apart with his bare jaws.

That's what the Chaos Circus does, after all. How could I have been so foolish?

I step up to him on unwilling feet, knees chattering, bowels tied in a bow, and he offers a hand to draw me up onto the rostrum. There's little I can see of the Circus facing this way, but the heat of revelry at my back is like an open furnace. Sweat rolls down the dip of my spine and the backs of my arms as the Lion lifts our entwined hands high.

"Behold, your new wisher-to-be! A daring madame who will undergo five, yes, *five* trials portioned by the Circus itself, all for the chance to earn a single wish. What will it be, Madame Tessa? Your well-wishers are dying to know."

I may be mad, but not quite enough to put these people on their guard with my words. For all I know, the Lion himself is the thief and murderer, and he's toying with me as with a mouse. The only Deathless I'm certain is *not* the thief is Nicolai. Anyone else may indeed be an enemy.

"It's a secret," I say through lips that tingle as if I've bitten a nettle-wrapped fig.

The Lion's predatory eyes gleam. He lowers our joined hands. "A woman of mystery. How they'll love you."

He flips our hands suddenly, his fingers circling my wrist, and the strength of that grip is so like one of the Splendor House manacles that I yank backward and nearly topple from the rostrum. But the Lion holds me fast, keeps me from falling or fleeing as he whips out a knife from his belt and dashes the blade straight against the scar tissue on my hand, which somehow makes it hurt much, much worse than any normal cut. I thrash in his grip, but he cinches tighter, his fingers like marble, his eyes hunting my face eagerly.

"With this wound, the Circus sees." His voice vibrates like a strummed sitar, a dark song that drifts into my bones. "Listen well, Madame Mystery. Five tests you must face. Five keys you must find. Five games you must win, or else lose your mind. Five doors you must open to have your desire. If five you obtain, you must pass through the fire."

He twirls me on the rostrum to face the Circus, and the sheer unnavigable expanse of it makes me lightheaded. "May I choose *any* game?"

His laughter is condescending. "The Circus will choose for you. Keep open an eye and an ear. The clues for the tests will not always be clear."

"And if I fail one?"

His hand moves to the back of my neck and squeezes. "I think you know."

My mouth dries like a fish in the sun. This was a *horrible* idea.

Now he turns me back to face the small crowd, and when I tear my focus away from my blood as it drips down my unpared fingernails and nourishes the dry wood, my eyes jump straight to a head of dark hair weaving among the people, as if he's called out to me in my mind.

Nicolai is disheveled from sleep, his mouth a stern line but his eyes half-wild. The look on his face is breathtaking. It's as if I've betrayed him.

But that's foolish. He saved my life, but he has no claim over it. And somehow that thought steels my resolve. I fist my hand, press my nails into the cut, and raise my knuckles high. The people clap, and the Lion chuckles as if I'm a Circus animal that's just performed the greatest act of its life.

"If you find yourself turned around," he murmurs against my ear, "seek Lord Libertine. He will grant you a new way, for a small price."

And just like that, he's gone, though I don't hear or see him slip away. The banner on the rostrum rolls up of its own accord, and the people start to disperse. I gather my breath and the frayed cords of my courage and step down.

Nicolai meets me on the ground. "Every tailor, vendor, and booth keeper will clamor for the chance to outfit you for your trials. Unless you're prepared to face that onslaught on an empty stomach, I suggest we return to the hostel at once."

I wonder if he wants to hurry me away from the crowd so that he can yell at me in private. Well, I am too tired and too shaken by my own brashness for that nonsense. I try my best to put authority into my stride as I march ahead of him, but every step sends a stab of pain through my hand and a thought into my head: that if Missus Fiona was here, she would be clutching her pearl necklace in one hand and jotting words like *straightjacket* and *solitary room* and *induced coma for the resetting of mental faculties* with the other.

Drip, drip goes my blood, and *droop, droop* go my shoulders. I'm sagged over like an ancient person by the time we reach our room. But my spine snaps back straight with shock when I see what's waiting outside for us.

A plain, crème envelope leans against the door, embossed with fat currant script: *Madame Tessa*.

My scalp prickles at the notion that the Circus has marked me, that it knows already where I sleep and how to find me, perhaps by that cut on my hand. I glance at Nicolai, and his eyes burn against the envelope as if he would like to make it turn to ash and float away before I can touch it. But I do touch it, and it feels heavy and lovely, like the kind of invitation a Barrow Island debutant would send for her coming-of-age party.

Nicolai swipes open the door. We enter, he takes my shoulder and pushes me onto my bed. Then he says, "Hand."

I surrender it in confusion and wait for the shouting to start as he crouches before me and wraps my injured palm with a corner torn from the fine sheets. His jaw is so tense, I can trace the sunlight and shadows that pool behind the hinge of it. Absurdly, my fingers want to press that square edge and see if it feels as stony as it looks, as all of him looks. But thankfully they are already occupied with clutching the envelope.

"Thank you," I say when Nicolai is finished.

He steps back and collapses on the edge of his own bed, rubbing his brow. "Open it."

I tear the envelope with my teeth, sparing the good work he's done on my palm. The cardstock that tumbles out is heavier than it has any right to be, practically stinking of affluence. I pry open its trifold and read aloud:

Madame Tessa,

Your presence is requested this evening!
Don your finest, come inside
Seek the one who tries to hide
The key is found below the tide

But choose you wrong, you'll be outside.

Regards,

Madame Rouge

I look up at Nicolai. He's taken the edge of a longish curl just below his right ear and begun to circle it between his thumb and forefinger, an absent gesture of deep thought. His silence is heavier than the card.

"It's the first clue," I say, for lack of anything better.

His scowl intensifies. "The Circus wastes no time."

"Where do I go, then? What do I do?" Pleading bubbles in my tone, there's no helping it. Nicolai has faced these trials before, and triumphed. He may be my greatest and only help.

Nicolai goes to the door. He smooths his hands over the posts and lintel as if searching for something buried in the wood grain. He doesn't look at me when he says, "I can't. If they suspect I've helped you, it will be the end of us both. Two people...two cannot complete the trials together, or one will die."

I swallow that thorny, heavy *something* that's wedged in my throat. "Well, I've risked the end of something to help us both, too. So perhaps you can spare a word of advice, at the very least!"

He pushes his brow against the door with a strangled groan. Then he turns to face me. "Every set of tests begins with a Masquerade. This is where the Circus will learn about you, where the Deathless will start to vie for the chance to hold your tests. They will watch your every movement. Any weakness they discover, they won't hesitate to exploit."

There is no hope of swallowing now. I can hardly breathe. The thought of so many eyes on me, seeking weakness, seeking a hint of oddness...it's every day on Barrow Island, in the Morrow Daily, magnified manifold. I snatch for my necklace and hiss when I encounter, once again, a void. "Where do I go?"

"Madame Rouge's Menagerie, by the sound of it." Nicolai jerks his chin at the note in my lap. "The first of the five keys will be hidden at the Masquerade. It always is."

"And these keys, what do they open?"

"The doors to the inner sanctum of The Wish Granter's Big Top pavilion. Without them, you will never see his face."

I sputter. I, who can hardly be trusted to remember five different drinks for the five people in my department of the Morrow Daily, now forced to solve riddles and clues, or return home without my necklace— or *perish*.

Yet, as terrifying as the notion is…somehow, I think there may be a way around it. I must think of it simply as one trial after another. A Masquerade doesn't seem so terrible. Yes, they will be watching me, but haven't I endured stares for over a year now? Haven't I learned to live with the whispers of the crowds and those who know my past? If I can endure Missus Fiona's watchful eyes from a distance, and Mister Metters haunting my every step, perhaps I can learn to focus at this Masquerade, too.

I reread the clue again and again. By the third time, I can feel Nicolai growing restless, fidgety.

"You'll need a dress," he says.

I look up swiftly. "I have no money."

"It's included in the cost of admission." His eyes dart to my bandaged palm, and I resist the urge to make a fist again.

"I suppose I should go looking for clothes, then." I stand, then shift in place. "Are you…will you escort me?"

He slides a hand around the back of his neck. "To the dress shop, yes, otherwise you're liable to pulled in by one of those ravenous tailors I mentioned. Not to the Masquerade, though."

And just like that, another token of security is stripped away. But I should have expected that. He's already made it clear he disapproves of this course of action, nevermind what it will mean to us both if someone suspects him of helping me. Come to think of it…"Why *are* you helping me, if you're so opposed to this entire notion?"

Nicolai turns his head as if listening to sounds on the other side of the door. Then he squints at me from the corner of his eye. "Because you are doing this for your necklace, but also for me. I'm not without some principles, Miss LaRoche. I have a stake in this, whether you succeed or fail. So I'd prefer to offer my assistance when I can, as it profits us both. Better than the alternative."

I join him at the door. "What will happen if we can't exonerate you?"

"One of two things. Either word of the murders will spread, and my fellow Deathless will turn me over to the Mortal Lands for retribution...or the Circus itself will destroy me to strike a balance."

Death on top of death. I offer him my hand. "Then I suppose we understand one another, don't we?"

His eyes brighten somewhat. He takes my bandaged hand gingerly and gives it a shake. "I suppose we do, Miss LaRoche. Now let's go and get you out of those miserable mortal clothes."

CHAPTER FIVE

*M*y stomach has begun an irreverent symphony of gurgles and low roars by the time Nicolai leads me to his tailor of choice. There are so many to choose from: seamstresses, haberdashers and hatters, dressmakers, laceworkers, silksmiths and even a secondhand shop of mortal wear. I can only assume the items there—gently used, boasts the sign in the window— once belonged to mortals who traded all from shirts to undergarments for a better prize at the booths.

Nicolai leads me past them all, and finally stops before an imperial building reminiscent of the enormous bank in the richest district of Barrow Island. The façade of stern angles perches atop and between closely-knit columns of piebald marble, and over the gilt doors an engraving reads *Madame Modiste's Modest Attire*.

Somehow, I doubt the modesty of this place already, and we've barely begun to ascend the steps.

When we enter the shop, my mouth drops open.

I doubt if I've ever seen so much crushed velvet in one place. It flocks the walls, stains all the seats, and even girdles the potted plants. The walls are striped lavender and a gentle deep-sea blue, and the sofas and armchairs are amber wood and cherry grain. Chandeliers sparkle above, their curved golden arms glazed with crystal beads. Even the portraits on the walls are fletched in lurid silver, dripping diamonds.

My gaze halts at the second of the six paintings, and I tilt my head. I could swear I know that face: an elegant woman garbed in a lovely heather dress. But my scattered thoughts and empty belly tug me two ways and I can't place her familiarity, not for the life of me. I only know that her stare makes me think of cold blackness and blood, and that I don't want to be caught in it anymore.

Before I can insist we go elsewhere—that no cut on my palm could possibly make this place affordable or endurable—a voice trills, "Wait right there, I'm coming!"

And then she arrives, the woman I can only assume is Madame Modiste. She hurries toward us across the wide parlor in a copper dress, also crushed velvet, that gathers high on one shoulder and sways low around the opposite elbow. I hardly know how she can move in it, but she is so fluid she might as well be naked and unencumbered. Her scarlet hair matches her painted lips and the fiery artwork around her eyelids, on which are drawn the image of glossy birds taking flight.

"Nicolai, I hardly expected you to bring me another client!" she chortles—then stops. It's strange how still her stillness is after such gliding motion. I resist the urge to shrink from her, as I wished to with the Lion, when her smoky hazel eyes dart to Nicolai's face. "What is this all about?"

"This is Tessa," Nicolai says, "our newest wisher. Tessa, this is Moe, the greatest tailor in the Chaos Circus."

His tone is inflectionless, but I feel him watching Madame Modiste over my head and I feel as if I'm a rock popping out of a river of unspoken conversation. Madame Modiste purses her cherry-stained lips like she wants to say something brutal. Then she flashes forward suddenly to clasp my hands. "Pleased to meet you, Tessa! Call me Moe. I've heard so much about you, I feel as if we're already friends!"

"Oh. Have you?" Next to her effusive voice, mine clinks like fragile crystal.

Moe tosses her hair and laughs. "The newest wisher, of course! What an honor to be chosen as your personal tailor for the trials! Darling, I'll make certain you're outfitted for everything, don't you worry. I may even have some clothes in your size already, you look about the height and shape of one of my former clients..."

Nicolai has the countenance of a man who just swallowed glass. "We could use a platter of tea and scones while you're at it, Moe."

"You'll have them, of course. Corriene, fetch tea!" She seems to be shouting at thin air, but before I can question it, Moe twirls me by the shoulders. "Don't you look like a pretty daydream? If you fail the trials, maybe they'll let me use you as a mannequin."

Nicolai looks as though he's moved along the buffet of emotions from swallowing glass to choking down knives. "Just dress her."

Moe pouts, which somehow manages not to look at all undignified on her. Then she beckons us to follow her through the parlor and into a grand nave lined on both sides with racks of dresses. They're organized by shade, every color I have ever seen, from brightest summer-squash yellow to a black so deep it gulps up what little light exists in this room. The windows here are high on both walls and toss the daylight back and forth between them like a child's ball, keeping the glare from staining the gowns.

I find myself drawn at once to a charcoal gown that resembles my coat—something to keep me hidden—but Moe clasps my arm. Like the Lion, she has a grip of secret iron. "No, not that one, darling! Not unless you want to be called Madame Cinders. With that skin tone, I'm considering something more of a wine-red."

She can't possibly know that red is my favorite color. I keep that small truth to myself, refusing to give the Circus another victory over me. I feel as if the scab on my palm is gazing smugly through the bandage, watching my every reaction.

It's then that Corriene arrives, and the sight of her startles me so badly I let out a rude gasp.

She is what I imagine it would be like if a hummingbird became a human. Her pale face holds all the features of a woman, but with eyes unnaturally large, shiny black, like obsidian chips, and a very small beaklike nose. From her jaw backward, glossy feathers in shades of lime, lapis, and watermelon-pink rustle where hair and flesh ought to be. She wears nothing but a sheer silk shift, and I can see that the feathers cover everything, even her legs.

She catches me staring, and her face reddens. She plops the tray of tea and scones down on a velvet settee and steps back, eyes downcast.

"I'm so sorry," I stammer, "I just...I've never seen..."

"Corriene is a different kind of Mirror Folk." Nicolai mercifully delivers me from my tactlessness. "Her kind inhabit the Fey Woods. They come to play in the Circus occasionally."

"And sometimes they lose," Moe says with neither malice nor mercy. "Thank you, Corriene. Be a dear and fetch me every dress we have in wine-red."

Corriene bows, flashes me an inscrutable look, and hurries off. I feel terrible about eating the food she brought after I insulted her, but my appetite is ignorant of shame. My stomach growls so loudly Nicolai smirks, and then covers it by popping a scone into his mouth.

"Excuse me," he says with his mouth full, "I must see to something."

I lunge for a scone to hide my own anxiety at being alone in Moe's presence. If I'm a crumbling scrap of newsprint burning away, she is the wind that will blow me in pieces.

Unfortunately, she is irreverent and implacable, tossing herself onto the edge of the settee and pouring steaming cups of tea. "So, how do you and Nicolai know one another?"

"He...brought me here." Simple enough, and not a lie, either. Deathless tempt mortals through the Rifts every day, after all. I simply leave off that our partnership is of a more mutually-beneficial nature.

"Of course he did." Moe's sugary tone doesn't change, but I detect a hint of scorn in her eyes that halts the next scone on its way to my mouth. Suddenly, I wonder if they're lovers. I wonder if I've offended her, if Nicolai is using me against her, somehow...and if I should fear a dress made by her hands, some garment whose boning might curl tighter and tighter, piercing my ribs and suffocating me. Or if perhaps there will be hemlock or belladonna woven into the seams, slowly breaking down my body over time.

Horrified, I think I shouldn't even be eating this scone. I set it carefully back on the tray. "How do *you* know Nicolai?"

Moe titters. "I was one of the Deathless he won a key from in his trials. He was remarkable, truly skilled at finding ways around rules. There wasn't a law the Circus created that Nicolai didn't test. When he became one of us, I took him under my wing a bit. Any friend of Nicolai's has been a friend of mine."

The way she is looking at me seems too earnest for this casual talk, as if she's trying to convey a secret. But then Corriene returns under a mound of dresses, and from there it's a series of motions in which I am more puppet than person. Moe stuffs me into dresses that are not only my preferred color, but also eerily close to my exact size. They're a bit tight in the belly, but with a snap of her fingers Moe lets them out to a comfortable width. My restless hands soon discover that each dress has a unique asset: one holds hidden knives under every tier of taffeta; another changes color based on my mood, goldenrod when Moe makes me laugh, then back to blush-red when she praises my physique; the third is more rose than wine and that one, Moe claims, is tough as armor.

I slide a strip of the fabric between my fingers. "Are there coats made of this material?"

"You mean, did I tailor Nicolai's?" Moe chuckles. "Yes. They're quite impervious to mortal weaponry. Here, have another scone, you look so pitifully worn-out."

After a half-hour of this, I am utterly exhausted. Shopping for clothes has never been my pastime of choice, and with two sleepless nights behind me, I'm worse off than usual. Sweat runs into the jagged slice on my palm, and a stitch of distress is thumping at my ribs when Moe tugs the last dress over my head, adjusts it to my breasts, steps back and breathes, "Magnificent. Corriene, the mirror!"

Corriene tiredly turns the body-length glass toward us, and I shoot her an apologetic smile which quickly falls away as I catch sight of myself.

The gown is lovely indeed—strapless, the cleavage forged of a tough white weave that looks like lace but feels strong as metal. I'm certain it's no mortal fabric. Real pearl buttons glint all down the navel to the waist, where the rich magenta fabric flares out into a many-layered skirt of ruffles and silk with an embroidered black brocade covering.

Moe clasps my bare shoulders, her lacquered nails gleaming like spots of blood on my skin. "You look absolutely marvelous."

I suppose I do, but it's only a look. Really, I am a candied apple in this thing, a glossy, beguiling shell cast over something hard enough to break teeth. I smile, and my reflection looks silly and false as it grins back at me.

A brush of feet on crushed velvet. Nicolai has returned at long last, and he holds something in his hands which he must have found elsewhere in the shop: a headband in a riot of colors, splashes of mulberry, mint, scarlet and chartreuse, with a flat bottom stripe and a thin braid across the top. It will absolutely clash with this formal gown.

Moe perches her hands on her hips. "Why *that* one?"

"They call her Madame Mystery," Nicolai says, "and this will add to the sensation: a headband that will make you appear as the perfect personal vision of beauty to anyone whose path you cross."

I almost laugh, it's so absurd. I can't remember ever being anyone's vision of anything. But there's some guile to the notion of a disguise, something to make me blend in and disappear. Anyone who stares at me, it will not be because of my perpetual impression of madness, but because I will seem lovely to them. And if Nicolai believes it will help me win the trials…

I snatch it from his unresisting fingers and loop it around my throat, then tug it back to tame my ringlets. The moment it settles into place, I feel a warm *something* spill down me, from the top of my head to the bottoms of my feet. I shiver violently, gooseflesh rearing across my bare shoulders and wriggling down below the folds of the dress. It must be the power of the Circus, and yet when it settles into place, I no longer feel as if I am being watched. The vigilant presence below my bandage grows dim.

"Pity," Moe sighs. "You were more interesting other way. My idea of beauty is quite boring compared to that. Nicolai?"

He is looking at me with the oddest face, screwed up as if to beat back a frown. "It will do."

Of course it will. I dare not look at myself again, afraid to see what my own vision of beauty is and how much my honest form deviates from that. I order Nicolai out, strip from the dress and tell Moe I'll take it—more out of resignation than anything. I'm too tired to care if I wear this or a chimneysweep's attire. I just want to go back to *Red & Gold's.*

Moe continues to chatter as Corriene boxes the dress, assuring me she will happily outfit me for every trial, I need only come to her, and *only* her. I think perhaps she tells me something more about the dress and what it can do, but I'm slowly picking apart a scone and not paying attention.

It's a relief when we finally leave, and Nicolai takes the dress box from me and tucks it under his arm. "Dare I ask what you discussed in my absence?"

"I have the feeling one doesn't discuss things with Moe so much as they have things told to them."

Nicolai smirks. "She does have that way about her. But as Deathless go, she's less problematic than the rest of them. The power to change fabric with a snap of the fingers isn't as grim as it could be."

"Are you two...well, you know..."

Nicolai casts a funny look down at me. Then he raises his eyes to the overcast sky. "No, Miss LaRoche. I have no desire to put down deeper roots in the Circus by becoming involved with a fellow Deathless."

Neither of us speaks again until we're sequestered safely in our room, where I sit on the bed, pick up the cardstock again and reread it until my tired eyes itch. "Will you tell me where to go tonight?"

"Certainly. It would be a waste to have you miss the Masquerade wandering around in the dark all night." He scratches his cheek. "The gala begins at midnight. You'll have from then until dawn to find the key, or you'll fail the test. Do you think you can stay awake that long?"

We both know I can't. And I'm almost too tired to care that I don't have my necklace with me. I lay down on the thin pillow and tuck my head onto my arm. Nicolai moves around the room, tidying up. There can't possibly be so much to keep him entertained in this small space, but he sounds busy anyway.

"You could go and drink," I mumble. "I assure you I'm not as amusing asleep as I am awake."

"I don't know. You may snore, or drool. That would be amusing."

I imagine myself picking up the spare pillow and slinging it at his head. I imagine him laughing, a dark, rich, warm chuckle with a cool edge, like opening the door of a warm house to the blast of winter's bite.

The next thing I know, I'm dreaming of that very thing.

CHAPTER SIX

*W*ake up, Miss LaRoche." Nicolai shakes me by the shoulder. "It's half past ten."

I sit up swiftly, heart pounding, certain at first I've returned to the Splendor House. But it isn't that. We are still in the Mirror Lands, and Nicolai is no orderly as he was in my dream. He's one of the Deathless, and I'm keenly aware of it as I feel the grit of his power sliding along the backs of my teeth when he steps away. I almost ask him again what his power is, but I'm suddenly sure I just dreamed the answer, and if I could only remember the dream, then I would know.

But there's no time. Half-past, and I still must prepare myself for the Masquerade, and study the clue! I tumble out of bed and straight to the card as Nicolai shifts gracefully out of my way. I'm startled that I've slept so deeply in the Chaos Circus of all places, that I'm so disoriented it takes several tries for me to bring the lines of Madame Rouge's note into focus.

"Did you put me into some sort of funny trance?" I demand.

Nicolai seems about to laugh, then catches himself with a cough and a detestably smug smirk. "Slept that well, did you? Perhaps my presence just has that effect."

I consider hurling the cardstock at him, cutting him with its heavy edge, but it's absurd to think I'd ever manage such a thing. Tossing the card down, I snatch up the dress box and retreat into the adjacent bathroom.

A quick soak in the copper tub wakes me fully, though the water is warmer than anything I can remember bathing in since I lived with Nan. My apartment in Barrow Downs lacked the luxury of hot running water. I'm almost tempted to linger, drifting with my ears clogged and the world whispering around me, but then my palm starts to sizzle at the water's touch.

Patted dry, with grapeseed oil from one of the many cosmetic jars on the tubside table tossed gently through my ringlets, I hurriedly slip into the dress and join Nicolai again. He hardly seems to have moved in my absence, but now a platter of jam tarts sits on my bed, along with a cup of coffee. Not usual carnival fare, but I'm so grateful I almost trip over my gown as I rush to eat.

"Not too much," Nicolai cautions. "You'll be expected to eat whatever Madame Rouge provides, and a lack of appetite can easily translate as a rebuke to her hospitality."

I freeze. "Will the food be safe?"

"It always is for the ball. It wouldn't be entertaining if you ate treacle fudge and went into a stupor for days, after all."

Comforting. I nibble the tart and sit on my bed as Nicolai turns the card over his fingers like a mortal street magician casually busking for his next meal. I almost call him a showoff, but that seems impolite and far too informal. "Have you solved the clue, then?"

Nicolai shakes his head. "But it's not for me to solve. You can do this, Miss LaRoche."

I swallow a particularly rich bite of tart. "You hardly know me. I may in fact be the least-qualified person for these trials."

"I doubt that. I have a sense of these things."

I study him in the deep tawny tones of circus light pouring through the window. "Is that your power? That you sense how people are?"

He smiles, infuriatingly enigmatic, and stands. "Come, we don't want you to arrive unfashionably late."

There is a different atmosphere when we step down into the parlor tonight. The air positively drips with honeyed anticipation, and every man and woman milling at the drinks counter and in the smoking lounges all suddenly turn our way. Their focus is uncanny, their eyes biting at us like bear traps. The muscles in the small of my back gather, squeezing my hips tighter than a lover's hands, and sweat pricks the nape of my neck.

"Do they know who I am? What I've done?" I hiss at Nicolai. Right then, even I don't know what I mean—the madness of my coming here, or the trials.

Nicolai's throat bobs as he keeps his gaze fixed on the door to the street. "I suspect their stares have rather more to do with the headband you're wearing."

I clap a hand to my head, where I slid the bright, braided thing back into place as soon as I fluffed out my curls. Of course, they aren't really seeing me at all, and somehow the notion makes me feel calmer—as if I'm surrounded by an army of Tessas in every shade, every stature, and they're all protecting the real me from eyes that might judge me or think me strange or mad.

I lift my head and bring my shoulderblades together, stepping out into a night that is humid with excitement. A different side of the Circus is awakening tonight, something that wasn't conscious yesterday, marking my footsteps down the veins of its streets, toward the heart of it.

Nicolai leads me down a broad road beneath the vast, inky splotches cast by moonlight breaking against the floating balloons. Sideshow attractions dominate this street, tents of pearl-white and cherry-red promising wonderous things: talking animals, wolfmen, bearded female dwarves, and a host of Fey creatures. I squint at the apexed signs beside the booths, ears blurring as the shouts of the hypemen overlap. "Are these Mirror Folk?"

Nicolai maintains that resolute forward focus, as if to deliver me to Madame Rouge is his entire purpose in life and he will fulfill it without delay. "Most are. Some are mortals who have been changed by the Circus's power."

I don't ask if they work willingly. I know from Nan's stories that consent to the Circus is a funny thing, a braiding of trickery and self-selling that often looks to the seller like they're gaining a great advantage. But that is only if they win, and most do not. At least, not in any tangible way.

I squeeze into the scab on my palm and hiss when I feel it may break open. *I* am a seller now. I sold myself for my necklace. I have no place for contempt.

"You're trembling," Nicolai observes, and I almost snap at him that he's quite astute, isn't he, which doesn't sound like me at all. "I can assure you that this test is the least dangerous. Consider it a mercy. If you fail, you really will only be thrown out."

I grasp for that hope with the desperation of a truly insane person, even going so far as to clasp his elbow. "Really? How do you know?"

"I've seen it happen. I've attended many a Masquerade in my hundred years, you know, hoping to lure someone new to my booth. So I've watched a handful of hopefuls tossed out into the cold. And that's all it is."

I gulp the damp air and almost thank him. But the notion of Nicolai among a hungry crowd of prospective Deathless reminds me what he truly is, so I let go of his arm.

We pass through pockets of the Circus that I'm determined to observe in daylight: ringtoss games, fish bowl dunking, knife throwing, and archery. Once again, the sharp fingers of a fleeting recognition overtake me as I observe a handful of winners' portraits, and I'm very certain I know some of them, but we pass by too quickly for me to sort out the familiarity. Vendors try to waylay us as they peddle sugar floss to make the consumer feel they're flying, candied Fey insects that will give one the ability to climb walls, fluffy powdered pastries made of actual clouds gathered by the floating balloons and sprinkled with stardust, mugs of spiced cocoa dashed with a cure-all, and even one selling cigarettes that can make one see the future for a short time.

"Collusion between Lord Harlequin and Lord Mull." Nicolai shoots a scowl at that vendor.

Lord Harlequin. The name sends a pang of recognition through me, and another old memory distills into clarity: Nan urging me to choose a Deathless doll to sit on my bedside table, and the feeling of her threadbare rugs smooshing between my bare toes as I ran down the hall to choose one. I came back and she laughed, shaking her head because I'd once again chosen the doll of Lord Harlequin.

"He was my favorite," I hear myself say, and Nicolai's brows rise. "When…when I was a child, and Deathless were no more than figments of my nan's stories, his was the doll I always chose."

"Understandable," Nicolai says gravely. "Apparently he dresses quite dapper."

I kick his shin. "You're very rude."

"And you have poor taste." There is bitterness in his tone now. "Lord Harlequin is the worst of all that the Deathless have to offer."

I'm chilled by a thought: if that's true, could he be the thief?

Nicolai halts. "We're here."

Madame Rouge's Menagerie is nothing like I expected. It must have been one of the city's estates before the Circus grew across everything like creeping kudzu. It stands first in a whole row of fine homes, across from a park which spans quite some distance on our right. Between the trees that gather like my own tiered skirt on the park's manicured grass, flashes of light whirl about, and I hear screams. I can't say if they're delighted or terrified, or a mixture of both. Unwilling to solve that riddle, I turn to the task at hand.

The Menagerie is gated, as are most of the estates beyond it. The doors must be open often for spectators, but tonight they're held guard by brutish men whose arms are quite literally swords. Cold sweat dapples my brow as the Circus light gleams on their steel.

"Nicolai, I can't do this."

I have no necklace, no courage. I have no chance.

He secures my shoulders with more familiarity than anyone since Nan ever has and turns me to face him. "Yes, you can."

His voice is low, throbbing with sincerity, and his eyes are bitten with gold light. For the first time, I notice there is a paler ring around his irises.

That I must shake my head to look away makes me laugh, and the sound is hysterical. "I *can't*. Mad people don't have exciting adventures, at least none that aren't made up, and this one…it's too much. It will be the death of me."

"Only if you fail. And you won't."

I hang my hands on my hips so that I won't grab my cheeks instead, or something equally dramatic. "And how can you be so certain?"

"Because we both know you can't afford to. We need that name. And you have every means of claiming it for us. Don't think of madness tonight. Just…*think*."

He releases me, but the sense of his fingers remains on my bare shoulders as if his power had branded me. A small thrill of bravery, perhaps artificial, sings through me. As I turn back to the estate, I feel he's just done something…given me a glimpse of the impossible, like a stone cracked open showing gold ore within. He's shown me what honest courage feels like, and I grasp it, however real or false it may be. I remember how I survived my first weeks at the Morrow Daily, subject to the whispers and stares, the rumors of my interment at the Splendor House better known than my name. Back then, I promised myself just one step, and then one day, and then one week after another.

I take a deep breath and look over my shoulder to find the street deserted but for the array of multicolored lights from streamers and bulbs that hem the booths and vendors together. Like smoke, like the Lion at the rostrum, Nicolai has vanished.

I take the card in my fist and march up to the gate. "I'm expected."

The men spare only a passing glance at the invitation, and then they open the gates. I enter the walled Menagerie.

I know I ought to feel panic at once. The skirting of trees along the gravel drive that collars the front of the mansion itself, the speckling of fountains and privacy hedges artfully placed so that little is actually hidden here, not to mention the swooping shapes of the curved windows, the fencing along the gables and roof edges, and the pristine nature of the home as a whole—why, it's quite the twin to the Splendor House. Almost its mirrored image.

But then, no mirror shows my reflection now as it truly is. So perhaps this image is a distortion, too.

I cling to that possibility as I gather my skirts and start the long walk up the drive. But I don't go inside. When I'm certain no one is following me or watching too closely, I veer off the gravel road and onto the lawn, which is styled like a rich woman's hair, perfectly coiffed and very soft. I kick off my flats and go barefoot so that I will make no sound, prowling around hydrangea and rhododendron bushes and peering through the hedges. There are stone seats I find, and trees that peer watchfully over them, weeping willows and wisteria bunches shedding a gentle fragrance all across the lawn.

But it's the fountains I'm making my way toward. When I reach one and find it vacant, I lean on the edge and read the card again:

Don your finest, come inside

Seek the one who tries to hide

The key is found below the tide

But choose you wrong, you'll be outside.

I'm no good at riddles and I've never liked them, but I think perhaps this one is a trick. What if I'm not meant to go indoors at all, and being outside *is* the answer? What if the key is out here somewhere? Below the tide suggests water, of course...and there are fountains aplenty. It didn't take us quite an hour to walk this far, so there's some time before the Masquerade begins. Perhaps I will find the key before the ball ever starts, and I can simply snatch it and run at the stroke of midnight.

I check surreptitiously for onlookers. If they think me mad already for taking these trials, how much worse when they see a mostly-grown girl splashing and prodding around a fountain? But I am deeply, absolutely alone, so I hike up my skirts and climb into the ankles-deep water for a better look.

This fountain proves itself unremarkable aside from a very expensive bust of a half-naked mermaid spilling a decanter of water into the basin. I poke at her lovely cyan-and-marmalade scales, but none reveal so much as a secret compartment. Nor is there any key swimming among the mortal coins that line the fountain's scalloped bottom, licking at my toes as I slink past.

I wonder what these casual wishes cost the people who made them. Didn't they know that all wishes come at a price? Except, perhaps, the ones from The Wish Granter himself, when the price is already paid by these ridiculous tests.

I climb out, scrubbing my feet dry on the grass as I make my way to the next fountain. I pass lovers gathered on benches along the way, whispering and giggling, and I try not to taste the sweet glee that perfumes the air. I can't remember if I've ever been held by a man, desired by one.

No one desires a broken thing after all, a woman whose mind is not quite right, and anyway Missus Fiona warned me I'm too fragile for such things yet. Wandering hands and coy looks might damage my progress, make me forgetful and too full of whimsy to be useful to Barrow Island.

I rub the nip of cold air from my shoulders and scurry through a patch of garden devoted entirely to love in all its forms, past heart-shaped hedges and strands of soft salmon light that bud in the impressive oak trees. Finally, I come to another fountain, and I see I'm alone. In I go.

Three fountains later, I climb out with nothing to show but wrinkled toes and misery, and lean against the basin, holding my head in my hands. What self-respecting woman climbs into fountains instead of socializing at a ball? Perhaps I'm really just avoiding having to go through those enormous doors that remind me so much of the Splendor House.

"If you're searching for the key, it isn't out here, I'm afraid."

I startle, dropping my hands, and look swiftly down in the direction from which the voice came. Now I know that I *have* gone mad, the maddest I will ever become, because I'm convinced the one who spoke to me is a small mouse perched on the rim of the fountain in a very, very fine dress. Perhaps finer than my own.

I blink several times, and she doesn't disappear. "I'm sorry?"

"So am I. It was a good guess. But the key is truly inside." She cleans fastidiously behind her ear. "And you're interrupting midnight tea with all your stomping and sighing."

I look even further down and nearly take faint, because there is indeed a long table full of mice in the shelter of the fountain, all in very beautiful mouse attire, even some wearing hats with holes for their large ears. I want to laugh, but then it's rather rude to laugh at someone for existing.

"I'm sorry for interrupting." I sidestep from their table. "I didn't realize mice took tea so late."

"We aren't mice, we're Mirror Folk," she says. "I'm Mistress Mirabelle, head of the craftsmiths guild that designs all the Circus amenities. And you're the newest wisher, aren't you?"

"So they say."

She waddles closer and places a very small hand on mine as I grip the fountain's side. "Don't sound so deprecating! If it's any comfort, you're the first to ever think of searching the grounds for the key. Most can't wait to go inside."

"I don't think that makes me clever. It makes me odd."

"Well, and what is wrong with being odd? Plenty of Mirror Folk are odd. It's how the Circus had its start. The odd and unlikely banded together to make use of the Land's power, and here we are now, gainfully employed and well fed."

"I suppose so..." I find myself desperately wanting her words to be true.

"Anyway, better to be odd than boring." She pats my hand again. "Now, hurry inside. At midnight, those doors shut, and they won't open until dawn unless you guess wrong. Be clever, you!"

She takes a flying leap from the fountain and her skirts poof around her, sending her floating down among her kin, who welcome her with open arms. Heat gathers in my eyes as I imagine anyone ever welcoming *me* so happily. With my parents dead and Nan gone, there was not even anyone to greet me when I left the Splendor House...only a necklace in my fist and a bag of clothes under my arm, and a long, empty road ahead that I've been walking on my own ever since.

I suck in a breath and turn toward the mansion. I must go. I know it. There's no time left to waste.

A greeter awaits me, thankfully with fleshly hands this time. He carries a shining silver tray full of masques in a full palette of colors from garnet to boysenberry. Some are on sticks and others draped in silk ties. A few are crafted in the likeness of animals, but most taper gently at the corners and eyeholes, fitted perfectly to the face. I dither over them, delaying on purpose, and finally force my shaky fingers to select a golden taper masque that I think compliments my dress. It feels like an added layer of protection beneath all the other Tessas I am as I fit it into place and bind it beneath the edge of my headband. I dip my chin to the greeter, step into the foyer in splashes of silver chandelier light, and almost collide with the Lion.

Appropriately, he is wearing a lion's masque, and I hear Mister Metters in my head, a bitter snort of "*Trite*" before the Lion seizes my hand and rather forcibly kisses my knuckles. His lips burn like sandpaper, like being licked by a housecat. I plaster on a smile which I hope is less horrified than I feel.

"Welcome, Madame Mystery," he says smoothly, "to your first test. I assume you received the note?"

"Yes, it's how I knew to come here." I cast my eyes around the foyer, hoping that someone among the crowd of well-dressed loiterers will rescue me from this man's singular attention. Unfortunately, they're all snatching wineglasses and hurrying through another pair of doors into the belly of the Menagerie, from which a familiar waltz wafts out. When I try to peek through that doorway, the Lion blocks my view.

"Have you brought the note with you?"

"Yes?" My tone tilts in confusion.

"May I see it? I've been instructed to make a slight addendum."

I surrender the card, and he turns it over in his fingers like Nicolai did. For no good reason, the similarity in that gesture makes my hair prickle. When he gives it back, the cardstock feels sunbaked, but its fletching is as cold as his predatory smile.

"Read it carefully," he warns, "and do enjoy this ball. I don't suppose you see many of those."

The comment smarts, but I can't think of a clever retort before he slips into the crowd. I flip the card over to reread the clue:

Don your finest, come inside

Seek the one who tries to hide

The key is found below the tide

But choose you wrong and you will die.

My comprehension of the last line is punctuated by the snap of a latch as the mansion doors whip shut at my back, trapping me inside my own tomb.

CHAPTER SEVEN

*T*hink, think! my mind cries.

Breathe, breathe, my lungs beg.

I blunder through several useless gasps of incense-spiced air and grab for a flute of champagne when it's offered, because my nerves demand steel. The ground feels as if it corkscrews toward the doorway, and I am toppling headlong down a flight of steep steps.

This was meant to be the safe challenge, the chance to fail softly. Why have they changed it? Who changed it? The Wish Granter? The Lion? What have I done so wrong as to draw their ire? Or has it always been like this, and did Nicolai trick me into thinking I was safe so that I wouldn't run from the estate?

I fist up my hands until the bandage on my palm frays, and I draw on the imagining of his face full of smug austerity, and his silly dark hair that so badly needs cutting. Then I grip the champagne glass tightly and step into the Menagerie.

My first impression: it's splendid.

My second: it's a horror house.

Oh, it certainly wears a fine skin, bejeweled with ballgowns and suits. Trapeze artists twirl among silk streamers and float across the air in great metal hoops spaced along the ceiling, changing the light with their raiment from deep blush tones to brassy golds and then to mellow blues. The waltzes are every bit as good as mortal ones, I think.

But the servants...oh, the servants.

I see now that Corriene was not the only one of her kind indentured to the Circus. There are more of those silken birdlike Mirror Folk dashing here and there with serving platters, and other fey creatures with peeping ears and elongated faces and silky, full-bodied fur offer refreshments to the Deathless. These are the fortunate ones, panting to the point of near-collapse as they attend the Masquerade, because the rest of their kind are in cages, yes, *cages* that line the walls. The Deathless go up and down the rows, peering and pointing and exclaiming. They select the occasional Mirror Folk from confinement who are then escorted to enormous wooden wheels lined up on a half-moon riser in the apse of the ballroom. To my horror, these pitiful Folk are strapped on by their wrists and ankles and sent twirling while Circus performers hurl knives at their bodies. Their aim is precise, but the terrified screams are still real. And because of that, I think the knives are real, too.

The crème steps glisten before my eyes, and I must grip the silky mahogany railing to keep from tumbling down to the ballroom floor. I am garnering enough looks without that, it seems. Though I appear different to each of these people, the bandage on my hand barks out precisely who I am.

Nan would have told me to imagine them all naked, to let amusement be my defense, but the Deathless seem just as dangerous nude as clothed. I hurry straight to the buffet on one side of the floor as soon as my feet unstick from the steps, and I select a jam-slathered, sugar-dusted tart. Nicolai was right that it tastes harmless, so I go for another, then another, while I look around the room and try desperately to think past what sounds just like the crashing surf of my heartbeat.

Crashing surf, tide...I must look below the tide! But I see no water here, unless the tears of the Mirror Folk count, and those are plenty. Or perhaps one of the servers with their sloshing goblets is carrying the key. But how much champagne will I have to ingest to visit with every single one of them?

This is an utter and embarrassing disaster after all, but I don't want to die. I don't even want to come near it. So I make my way to the nearest server and ask for one of the glasses while I look all across his body for the key. Then I drink half the champagne and move on to the next server. Then the next. By the time I reach the fourth, the Deathless start to take notice of my strategy. To my undying humiliation, they begin to call out advice:

"It's only a *tide* if you're lush, darling…you'll have to drink more than that!"

"Can you trust those mortal eyes? Go on, use your hands!"

"Yes, feel all over their clothes, they don't mind."

I peer up at the Mirror Folk I'm currently taking champagne from, a male of Corriene's kind, and the embarrassment throbbing in my breast is matched only by the shame in his face. But he balances the tray in one hand and bares his vest and trousers as if he expects me to do it. As if that's what the Menagerie is all about.

"I'm not going to do it," I tell him, and for once I don't care if that makes me odd. I hand him the untouched champagne flute and start to turn away.

Around the stem of the glass, his fingers close over mine. "It's not us."

As my gaze shoots back to him, he tucks his head, takes the flute, and hurries away. I stand there staring after him. The Deathless, bored now that I haven't given them a show, scatter back to dancing and knife-throwing, and to some fire-jugglers and sword-swallowers who have made their way inside. I stand in the sea of them, my body absolutely aching with frustration. I've wasted more than an hour working up the courage for this attempt. What do I do now?

Bathrooms, I suddenly think. They have water, do they not?

A server points me in the direction of the facilities on the second level, which is mercifully much quieter, but I feel at once that I'm being followed. The eyes of the portraits on the cheery-cherry hallway walls seem to watch me, and I pause to observe them. Perhaps it's just an artist's trick that makes their gazes seem to slide after me…but then it strikes me, just as it did in Moe's shop and in the gaming booths, that I know one of these faces.

But from *where?* Frustration makes me want to scream as I gather my skirts and hurry along. I try to dismiss the recognition and the sense I'm being followed as paranoia, one of the generous diagnoses Missus Fiona insisted on reading at each of our sessions…but by the time I reach the washroom I know it's not that. A cluster of women follows me inside, and they stand so alarmingly close in the small space that to surveil the pedestal sink will mean holding up everyone.

So I flatten myself to the wall and let them go first, though I feel the drag of time ticking past. They ignore me and chatter on, yet I'm pricked with the suspicion that they're purposely taking all the time in the world powdering their noses and discussing the newest attractions so they can watch me in the mirror.

I shut my eyes and curl my fist, plumping up my rage in great heaves until they finally, finally see themselves out—no doubt disappointed that the wisher didn't perform some madness for them to report back to the ball. In their absence I check the sink and the chamber pot more thoroughly than I really care to, but I find no key anywhere. I am running out of damp places to search.

Back to the ballroom. I saw off part of a garlic-dusted hog flank and swirl it with apple sauce as I watch the dancers spin across the floor. There are some dresses here that far outshine Moe's handiwork. One gown mimics a flock of crows when the woman twirls, and I swear I can hear the seams croaking. Another glitters like living fire, leaving a taint of scorch on the air as the wearer pirouettes past me. I see lightning crackle in the distance and watch skirts shed autumn leaves and rose petals to the floor, creating a floral carpet that wreaths the air with comforting natural notes.

Nature.

Seized with a thought, I set down my platter and blurt out to the nearest server, "Is there an indoor garden?"

* *

The Menagerie garden is insulated by ribs of power that I can feel as soon as I step out of the hall and into the walled-off, unroofed inner chamber. I wonder if that's meant to keep me from climbing those tall walls and escaping the death that waits for me if I fail. But for the moment, I don't care about their cunning, I'm so relieved to be mostly alone. The garden is pleasant, if one forgets where it is. Not so different from outdoors, it's stuffed with the same wisteria trees, ivy-covered trellises, and rosebushes. I've stepped out onto a terrace painted butterscotch by threads of globe lights, a whole canopy of them enshrouding the patio cobbles. In the distance, I hear a stream running, and I spy a blackwood bridge crossing over it. A few distant murmurs tell me others have escaped here as well, but at least they don't rush to bother me.

I fold my arms on the terrace railing and gather my wits. It will be a long search through that stream, and I do hope no one comes peering around to see what I'm doing out here, or why I'm taking so long. But I feel calm, almost safe.

And then it strikes me, a feeling of déja-vu so sharp and deranging that I press a hand to my brow like an actress and tip forward. Cold sweat swims in all the creases of my body and steals the feeling from the back of my neck downward. I'm suddenly certain I've been somewhere like this before, on a color-bathed terrace at night. But when, and where? I've never been invited to a party this lavish.

Shaken, I tilt back my head and frown. It must just be my imagination how far the moon seems to have traveled already. Paranoia is a close friend in this sweltering place. I need to finish my test and escape before any other uninvited feelings decide to join the ball.

So into the stream I go. I wade along bare-toed, feeling for anything that isn't a river rock, but it all feels very predictable, and anyway my toes begin to freeze so quickly that I couldn't tell a key from a carp if it swam under my soles. I crouch behind a bush and a tree here and there when I see tophats and bustles bobbing by, and once I feel a crackle of Deathless power sizzle across the air just before someone strolls out of a hedge and goes inside. I don't let myself wonder what *that* was about.

Eventually, I give up the fruitless hunt. I rub my toes on the grass to warm them and read the card yet again. This time I'm hung up on a different line: not the tide, but the one who tries to hide. It's a Masquerade, so that hint seems silly and predictable. On the other hand, perhaps I've paid too much attention to water and not enough to who is avoiding me this evening.

Sliding back into the flats, I hurry inside, feeling clumsy and unbalanced with my cold toes. I go straight for the food table again, this time to cover my active watching.

The macabre scene has continued in my absence and perhaps

worsened somewhat. The firebreathers are now spewing their heated breath toward the cages, sending the Mirror Folk cringing in terror. Blood spots the floor by the wheels and the Deathless hang off one another in laughter, wagging their heads. I wonder if they are so bored by so many years of the same attractions that they can only find amusement in the profoundly disturbing.

But that is no concern for tonight. I try to see the crowd as a whole rather than the individuals, searching for a gap of sorts, a definitive turning away. But now it feels as if *everyone* is ignoring me just to confuse my latest aim. Frustrated, I go for the treacle fudge—then think better of it as I remember Nicolai's mention of it at the hostel, and select a slice of lemon chiffon pie instead with a candied twirl of peel and a mound of whipped cream on top.

"I hope you like the pie. One of our newest cooks made it. Please let me know if you have any criticisms of the fare. It's just for you, after all."

I stop chewing, cheeks bulging with airy chiffon as I turn toward the speaker, who is one of the loveliest women I've ever seen. She perches one hand on the table and spoons custard straight from a ramekin with the other, the dark waves of her hair marrying well with her dark skin. Definitive rosy slashes on her cheeks, along with her greeting statement, leave me with no doubt of who has just addressed me.

More than ever, I want to disappear, and at once I'm determined that even if the food all tasted like chalk, I wouldn't breathe an ill word about it for fear of what would become of this woman's servants.

"I'm honored to have been chosen to host your emergent ball," Madame Rouge spans an arm as if all of this, even the torture wheels and caged Mirror Folk, is for my benefit. I feel ill to my guts as she hovers before me expectantly.

"This is a…colorful Menagerie you have." Even to my ears, the words sound stiff.

Madame Rouge laughs. There is nothing amused in the sound. "How kind. Though I'm afraid that in intrigue, you quite outshine anything I have to offer in my meager little zoo." She pops a cherry cordial into her mouth, and a small streak of juice travels along her chin like blood. "I can see why they call you Madame Mystery. No one ever accepts the trials and then vanishes to privately select a tailor! Such an enigma. We're all simply dying to know what you covet so greatly as to put yourself through this…madness."

I fight not to wince at her choice of word. Oh, if only she knew I was doing this for a necklace! But it doesn't have to make sense to her, only to me. And to me, that prize is the only precious thing I have.

"But that's the fun, I suppose," she adds. "You can have *anything*. Why, you could even wish all of this away if you chose."

My eyes catch hers. They glint a strange silver in the light, tempting me with a thought I had not considered until just now. Something I don't *want* to consider. I push aside notions of any-wishes and force a creaky smile onto my lips. "That's true."

She sips from a goblet of plumb wine. "Oh, if it isn't Lord Mull."

I stifle a gasp as a meaty hand spins me, and I almost sink from nose to earlobes into the impressive girth of a Deathless man in a pinstripe suit. It hardly covers his plump waist, and the marmalade-and-ivory stripes are difficult to look at for any length of time. I peel myself back from Lord Mull so that I can observe his round, red face with its thick mustache and bald top, looking not at all unlike the confections he's known for. In fact, he so resembles a lollipop with a bit of lint stuck to it that I almost burst into laughter and must hold my face shut with both hands.

Madame Rouge mistakes my social blunder for nausea, and pounces. "The pie?"

"No, no, nothing," I gasp. "Just a bit of hiccups."

"I know the right cure for that!" Lord Mull exclaims.

"A lozenge?" Madame Rouge says tartly.

Lord Mull's look suggests a bitter nightshade berry lurks under that sweet outer shell as he drags me toward the dance floor. Too late, I realize what he's doing, and I start to sweat so profusely I'm amazed his thick hand doesn't slide from my wrist. "Oh, no, I-I can't dance…"

And I never have, but that doesn't stop him. Suddenly I'm tucked into the ends of his hands and am being spun like a top among the dancers, my feet on his. It's the only thing that keeps them from battering into me like an unmasted ship, I'm sure.

"So, Madame Modiste is your tailor?" Lord Mull has the sort of booming voice that is more meant to gather an audience than convey thought. He reminds me of Mister Metters that way. "That's really a shame, she's been a bit of a disgrace ever since her last wisher lost. Hardly anyone buys her wares anymore, and I do mean human or Deathless…I would have directed you toward Lady Lovelace, she tailors all my suits, quite a gem of a woman. Now tell me, Madame Mystery, what is your history with sweets?"

Before I can think my way around the barrage of subjects, someone bumps into us, and we switch partners. A tall, tawny-skinned woman twirls me until I'm so dizzy the chiffon pie threatens an untimely reappearance, and I barely catch that her name is Lady Lore, and that she's *quite* interested in my mortal schooling. Then I'm tossed to someone else, and I hear a deep, throaty chuckle that makes me want to leap to the other side of the room in a single bound.

"Enjoying the party?" The Lion smiles toothily. "They're all desperate to devour you. I wonder which ones the Circus will choose in the end?"

"Not you, I hope!" Shrill with discomfort, I tug against the cage of his arms, but like the others before us we continue to spin. Now I wonder if perhaps they're doing this on purpose, distracting me, because I certainly can't see a thing, much less search for the clue as we go around and around. And the time is ticking by.

The Lion tows me closer. "It could be me. It could be any of us. It's always such an honor to test a wisher. But the Circus will choose those that challenge you the most. Judging by that frightened look on your face, it seems it already has."

And with that, he unwinds from me and slinks back into the dancers. I'm in the middle of them all, trapped between whirling pairs, knocked left and right. No amount of polite pushing shows me the shore of the buffet table, and my breathing quickens. I need to escape, to gain perspective over the room again, to search for someone who is ignoring me in a room that seems increasingly intent on paying me so much attention that I'll surely die of it.

Arms close around me from behind. I smell exotic spices and a crackling singe of power, and even before he turns me around by my elbows, I know who I'll come to face—though it doesn't look like him. He wears a beaked masque that hides all but the slyest edge of his jaw. I can't even see those untrimmed ends of hair.

"Will you dance with me, Madame Mystery?"

I don't dare say his name. I toss up my hands in a silent, dumbfounded question, and he grabs one and slides his around my waist so that we are pretending to dance. When I don't beat him off in rage, he guides one of my arms around the back of his neck. The other, by some instinct, falls on his jutting elbow. I step up onto his glossy dark shoes and we start to dance. I'm still staring at his mask, trying to sort out whether I'm truly angry with him for sending me here or not, and why I'm relieved when by all his professions he's endangering us both.

"I thought you weren't coming!" I finally hiss.

"To the untrained eye, I never did." His tone is unruffled as ever. "That's the point of the masque, after all."

"This is madness! You're mad!" It's the worst thing I can think to call him, the dirtiest slur anyone's ever called *me*. "Did you know they would change the card?"

"Never. I heard the whispers as soon as you went inside. The guards knew that this Masquerade was not like the others, that you wouldn't be thrown out, but killed if you failed." Nicolai's hands tighten, an oddly reassuring squeeze. "I'd never felt like such a blackguard, Miss LaRoche. I sent you inside under false pretenses, and I couldn't let you face the outcome alone."

Well, now I want to thank him as much as I want to slap him across the face. "I see you do have a heart after all."

Why did I say *that*? Embarrassment dampens my armpits, but he's smirking beneath the masque as he spins me out with one hand and taps a finger to his chest with the other. "Buried somewhere deep in there."

He pirouettes me back in to him, and absurdly I find myself relaxing. "Well, we have a few hours left. With two of us, it ought to be easy."

The visible muscle in his jaw jumps in a way I do not like. "Unfortunately not. Whatever power they've placed over the mansion is speeding things up a bit. Time moves differently here. I know it seems it's only been an hour, two at most, but it's in fact thirty minutes or so until dawn."

I stare at that beaked countenance as we go around the floor again. I try to find a trace of humor in the line of his face, but there is none. My upper lip begins to tingle, then my cheeks. Pain darts down my back from the meeting of my shoulders, where it seems a nerve has fainted. The rest of my body is wholly jealous of it.

"That can't be," I say, as if that will make it so. "That can't be, they will *kill* me if I fail, the Lion told me so, and I...I can't only have thirty minutes left!"

Nicolai changes direction suddenly. He spins me through the throng of dancers and to the edge of the apse, where the bustles of its dark curtains are gathered off to the side. With a flick of his arm, he parts the folds and hides us inside.

"Tessa, Tessa." He cups my face urgently. "Listen to me. You are capable. You will do this, and they will not kill you. I won't let them."

A parlor trick, his words—no more trustworthy than the rest of this ball. But I let them dull the sharpness of my panic until I remember the things Missus Fiona taught me about how to breathe properly so that I don't faint, and how to bring my mind back into control.

How many minutes do I waste on that? I finally blink Nicolai's face back into focus. "Couldn't you have come inside a little *sooner*, then?"

Now I've no doubt he's smirking under that masque. "There's the sass I so admire. Quickly, read the clue aloud."

I do, though it's difficult to see in the snuffing folds of the drapes. Nicolai traces his bottom lip with his thumb—he's wearing gloves and I wonder where he got them for his costume tonight—and then he says, "Did you check the washroom?"

"And the stream, and the servers. Everywhere below what might be construed as a tide in some form."

"Then that isn't the right hint. It must be something else—one of the dancers who ignores you, who tries to blend into the crowd."

"I've already thought of that. What help are you?"

He flicks the edge of my masque. "I can tell you it isn't one of the Deathless. They're all paying you the closest mind tonight."

Well. That does narrow the possibilities considerably.

A spurt of laughter sounds from the riser. Many feet shuffle about all at once. To my horror, it sounds as if the festivities are dwindling. And if they dwindle entirely before I take hold of that key...

I pop my head out of the curtain, making a wild sweep of the ballroom, and to my relief no one is leaving—yet. The Deathless are changing partners during an interlude in waltzes.

And that's when I see her, and I know at once why I haven't noticed her before: she was most definitely not here before Nicolai dragged me into the drapes. She comes slinking down the steps now, clearly not seeing me at all, and slips in among the dancers while she presumes I'm gone.

She's no doubt been hiding all this time—except perhaps when I was in the garden, or in the bathroom. Had those been her friends who'd followed me there, to make certain I was gone and then to report to her before I returned?

A hard finger jabs the small of my back and I squirm. "What do you see?"

"The person I've been searching for." I shift the seam so that Nicolai can see her, too: a fair-haired, sunkissed Mirror Folk with diamond studs where her brows ought to be. One half of her head is shaved, and an intricate whorl of henna blooms along her hairline and down the side of her face. Her complexion and the dye appear darker next to the bright seafoam green and gentle pastel blue of her dress, with its lace and silk banners resembling a crashing ocean surf. A gull necklace bobs in the dip of her throat.

Nicolai's fingers close over the fringe of the drape just above mine. "The key is found below the tide."

"It must be hidden in her skirts," I say. "But how in the world will I take it from her?"

"As quickly as mortally possible." Nicolai produces a pocketwatch from his fine vest. I can't remember if he carried it before or if he stole it from wherever he acquired his masque and gloves. "Less than a quarter hour left."

My heart drums. Oh, I know what I will have to do, but I despise the very idea. It will be the maddest thing I've done yet. It will certainly draw the eyes of the entire ballroom. If I had more time, I would implore Nicolai to flirt her into a side room away from prying eyes, and then I would creep in after them and demand the key. But we have no time. This will be messy and ridiculous and unflattering, and they will all think I'm odd as an inside-out crab.

But if I don't do it, they really *will* turn me inside-out.

Mustering what little threads of a plan I've just concocted, I seize Nicolai's fingers over the edge of the drape. "Whatever happens to me, don't interfere. Even if this fails."

I don't know why I say it, but it seems the brave and noble thing to do. I start to step out, and Nicolai holds me fast by my fingers. "Meet me at the gates the moment those doors open for you. Don't wait."

I let him leave first. Then I barrel out from behind the curtain and straight toward the girl.

I know she sees me and I know she truly thought I was gone when her eyes go wide, and her mouth forms a perfect *O* of shock. That is right before I crash into her, taking her down to the stairs in a tussle of taffeta and tulle. She slaps and rakes like an angry turtle, buried in her skirts, but to my amazement Moe's armored gown is much, much easier to navigate than the drowning rip-current of those stunning blue silk waves. Swimming through the sea of the girl's dress, I cast around for the feeling of something hard and key-shaped, but I don't encounter it until I drag my sharp nails against her leg to stop her kicking me, and I find a garter and a finger-length strip of metal dangling from it.

The poor silk-and-lace contraption is no match for my sheer desperation to be out of this maddening ocean of pinching, shouting, angry girl. I rip it free in one hard yank, stroke to the edge of her massive skirts, and clamber to my feet. I put the key in my other hand, as far from the girl's reach as possible, and when it touches my bandage a shock seems to sweep the room. What few Deathless prattled on despite our small fight go silent. The dreaded attention of the entire room settles on me, and I feel the shift from fleeting intrigue to atavistic intensity all at once. It's almost worse than when they touched me without permission, when they forced me to dance.

I know that this means I have passed their first test.

No one claps. No one cheers. No one does anything at all as I lunge up the steps, through the foyer, and to the door. The greeter opens it, and a cool rush of night—no, of *dawn* air strikes my face. I feel the same as I did leaving the Splendor House, fearing I will look back and find the whole mansion sliding after me as I sprint down the drive toward the gates.

To my relief, the sword-armed guards are gone. And there Nicolai waits for me, on this side of the fence, casually propped with his shoulder to the black iron. I gasp his name as if it's waited inside me ever since I recognized him under that beaked masque. He straightens, puts out his hand, and I take it as we run across the threshold of the estate, just as the sun breaks the horizon.

Nicolai halts our headlong dash just inside the park. A touch to my bare shoulder turns me toward him, and he tears off his masque, revealing the glitter of distress in his eyes. I hold the key up for inspection. It's a tiny, ornate thing, silver with a budding rose and clock parts for the bow.

Nicolai smiles. "Well done, Tessa."

Pride bursts in me, brighter than any dawn. I'm not certain I've heard those words spoken with any sincerity since Nan left. But he's right—it *was* well done, if clumsily, even if I created a scene.

Tonight, I showed the Deathless what I am capable of.

CHAPTER EIGHT

espite the harrowing night and breathtaking dawn, I find I'm not tired at all. My body practically sings with joy when we return to the hostel, a brief stopover on our way back to Moe's shop, and not even the sight of a blue-scripted snow-white note waiting outside can dampen my spirits. I tuck it into my skirts as Nicolai sheds his stolen gloves and masque, and then we're off again.

Moe greets us with a scrumptious platter of party sandwiches, crunchy pickles, and glittering pink lemonade when Corriene ushers us into the parlor, and at the sight of my tailor, I'm dumbstruck. Instead of the rich lovers-red hair she sported at my last dressing, she's bedecked in merlot locks and lips, her eyelids painted with flourishing grapevines.

"Oh, good, you survived!" she beams. "Come, have a celebratory sandwich. Then I'll show you the dayclothes I've made for you."

Apparently, she has taken her task as my personal tailor quite seriously, as if she seeks to redeem herself from her past disgrace through betting on a wisher she believes will win. I'm almost in agreement with her on that, so bright is my satisfaction as I lounge on a velvet chaise and put away my fifth sandwich, waiting for Corriene to assemble the new attire.

"How do you do that?" Nicolai asks. "After my Masquerade, I couldn't eat for a day."

"Food is comforting," I say, "and I'm starving."

Moe laughs her glistering crystal laugh. "Near-death terror will do that to you. Not that you would know, Nicolai. Fear is too frightened to come over you."

He preens a bit, reclining with arms spread on the wingbacked sofa. But I notice he hasn't touched a sandwich, not even the chicken ones, which I know are his favorite.

The thought pauses me with my last bite halfway to my mouth.

"So, Tessa," Moe says, missing my confusion entirely. "You clearly have an affinity for carnival games. Have you ever been to one in the Mortal Lands? I hear they're nowhere near as exciting as ours."

"I wouldn't know." I set down the last bite of sandwich. "I don't recall if I've ever gone to one."

Moe cocks her head, birdlike in her intrigue. "You mean that possibly you went as a small child?"

"Or as an equally-small adolescent?" I try to match her smile, but it's the same false grin I wore in the Menagerie. "I don't know. There are many things I don't know."

"And you don't have to say." Nicolai still sprawls, but a hardness has come across his shoulders like slipping into one of Moe's armored coats. "It's not relevant to the tasks at hand."

But I find that I want to explain some of my strangeness. I want them to know I'm not altogether my own sort of crazy. "Your Circus is…is interesting. But where I come from there's not too much allowance for oddity. I did something, though what I can't recall, and they brought me to the Splendor House because of it. Which is where all the mad people go."

I can tell by the crease in Moe's brow that this concept is befuddling to her. Nicolai on the other hand is looking up through the round parlor windows above and twisting that curl between his fingers again in sharp, agitated circles.

I pick up my lemonade and swirl a small vortex in it, listening to the ice clink on the glass. "Whatever they did to me to treat my oddness, I was cured. Somewhat. But it also devastated my memories. I have some from when I was very small, of my Nan and...my parents. But besides that, I find I'm very lost when it comes to who I am and what my life was like before. So if I've gone to a carnival, I suppose it would have been during that time."

Now Moe's mouth hangs open, and I realize how barbaric the Mortal Lands must sound—how cruel. After all, here in the Chaos Circus they seem to thrive on a healthy diet of the insane. How could I make these strange Mirror Folk understand that the foundation of mortal society depends on lucid, tame people making rational decisions for the good of all? And I was not like that, back then. I did not fit their box. Something had knocked me slantways, and I'd become a liability to Barrow Island. Until Missus Fiona had set me right, and removed whatever it was that made me so...so...

"Interesting," Moe says. "I think I understand now why you're facing the trials."

Her glance is all-knowing, and her tone reminds me of Madame Rouge, so convinced of how I will use my wish. It reminds me that I could wish for anything, and that these people don't know I will wish for just a name.

Won't I?

Moe licks juice from a cranberry-chicken sandwich off her painted nails and extends a hand to me. "Let's see the next clue, then."

I surrender it just as Corriene returns, weighed down with a stack of boxes. Something more than sympathy bounces me up from the chaise to help her—it's as if my cautious thoughts and notions have forged a swarm around my face, and Nicolai and Moe will see what I'm plotting. I find refuge in unburdening Corriene, who offers a grateful smile as we lay out the boxes and I begin to crack the lids.

Moe has certainly been hard at work this past day. The first box contains striped leggings of sheer silver material and deep scarlet in rows, a short skirt overlay, and a button-down blouse with an overcoat the same red shade that will hang to the backs of my knees. The second is another dress—this one with a shorter plume of a skirt in serrated red and black, a straight neckline, and small, lacy sleeves to hug the upper arms. The third box contains what I must call a prism dress: ethereal silver-white fabric inlaid with tiny crystals that reflect the pools of daylight cascading through the parlor dome, sending rainbows bouncing all about the room. Nicolai looks up at the glow, a lock of hair cascading across his eye, and our gazes meet. Hasty with a sudden rush of shame, as if he knows what I was thinking before the distraction of the clothes, I shut the lid.

The last box is more dayclothes: a wine and goldthread blouse, black and white leggings, an asymmetrical sash of crushed velvet, and a black high-necked jacket that will hang no lower than my breasts.

"I'm particularly proud of that one." Moe hasn't looked up from the card. "The strongest armor I've made yet. It can withstand most anything, or so I suspect. You won't know for certain until you take a nasty tumble with something very sharp. Well, what do you think of the clue?"

"I haven't read it yet." I shut the last box and smile at Corriene. "Thank you for bringing these."

She brightens slightly and bends at the waist. "My pleasure, Madame."

"Tessa, come sit here." Moe pats the sofa, and I sidle over next to her. It's rather like crouching beside a friendly tiger. The atmosphere of her power is different from Nicolai's, a rich royal-blue hum that clings low to her curves. I think that, unlike Nicolai, her power is bound into the threads she weaves. Whatever Nicolai does, it's a static that hangs in the air around us. "You as well, Nicolai, come see. We'll solve it together."

Nicolai slides into the seat on my other side, surrounding me with a cocoon of Deathless might, and I fight not to squirm. Moe hands me the note, and I blink several times before I read it. There is no formal salutation this time, only four lines:

> *Here you choose the way to go*
> *Peach, persimmon, black or gold*
> *Only one will move ahead*
> *The others leave you ill or dead.*

I can feel Nicolai watching me from the corners of his eyes. Moe peels an apple with a butter knife as if this is all very boring. My elation from the Menagerie deflates like a pricked balloon, leaving me sagging over the card. "All is well, it's just that something else wants to kill me."

"You'll find you're not unique that way in the Circus." Nicolai gives the card a tug, and I let it slide out of my fingers. "Let's consider this rationally. Four colors, but they're very specific. Not always found together."

"I suppose," I grumble, "if it was red, orange, yellow, green..."

He smiles. "Then it could be anything in the shades of a rainbow. But not this. This is specific."

Moe taps the blunt of the knife against her chin, peeking through the curtain into her hall of dresses. "A respectable tailor's shop contains all those colors."

"It can't always be about dresses!" I say.

Now Nicolai chuckles, a sound as dark as his spirited eyes. "I don't believe it's dresses. *The way* suggests a road."

"The maze?" Moe lifts her glitter-dusted brows.

"I hope not!" I cry. "I'm terrible with directions. Mister Metters would say I couldn't find my way out of a single-roomed shack."

Moe scoffs, but this time Nicolai doesn't show any amusement at all. He slides the card against his lips and stares absently at the door. "I can't think of any attraction that sports these specific colors."

"Perhaps the hint is in the ill or dead, then," Moe offers. "Master Serpentine has many snakes that could leave you one or the other. Perhaps she's to cast her arm into one of his jars. Or Mister Mite, with his beehives and spider boxes..."

I can't manage more than a horrified whimper now. The room tilts, and I go with it. Nicolai pushes me upright with a glare at Moe. "Not that."

"Well, it would certainly challenge *her*, I think." Moe seems to be enjoying my discomfort, but the notion of thrusting my hand into anything containing a crawling, shimmying thing is just so repulsive I instantly lose whatever appetite I had left. I jump up and start to pace.

"Serpentine's snakes don't wear these colors." Nicolai seems to be trying to reassure me, which I suppose he must—it would be terrible for him if I was cowed by the second clue. Finding the first key undoubtedly gave him the same taste of success that it gave me, and a glimpse of his own survival no less!

I stop just short of touching my bare collar. I don't want to think about my necklace, or Nicolai's survival, or the rest of it. My head feels tossed and tangled after Madame Rouge and Moe's comments about the wish. I'm suddenly exhausted, as if my mind is running to escape itself. "Perhaps I should sleep on it."

Nicolai stands with a long-limbed stretch. The hem of his white shirt has come untucked, baring a strip of his olive-gold midriff. When he settles, I busy myself gathering the boxes and wonder why I feel flustered by the slip of a man's flesh.

"We appreciate a meal we can trust, Moe." Stranger than that Nicolai speaks for both of us is that I don't mind. He seems to know when it's the right thing to do. "No doubt we'll see you again."

"Yes, and enjoy those!" Moe leaps up to steady me as I lift the boxes, and Nicolai relieves me of the top two. "Look after yourself, Tessa."

I nod, and heat pricks my eyes. She's been so generous, really, they both have, even if one is using me to clear his name and the other to restore her reputation. I submit to a peck on the cheek from Moe, and then we go.

*   *

Iron buds unfurl like nightflowers above me as I collapse into bed. I've slipped back into my mortal clothes, comforted by the musty scent of my apartment that still wreathes the fabric. Tucking the key beneath my pillow, I burrow down tightly and draw the covers up to my chin.

Nicolai sits and splays his fingers in the air. He flips his hands over and back, examining his knuckles and palms as if the answer to the clue lies in the lines of them. "Your necklace. Did you have it before the Splendor House, or did you find it after?"

"Before." I'm too exhausted to feel tense at the subject. "I don't know why, but I've always felt it gives me courage. It…it's the most precious thing I have."

A trace of a smile turns Nicolai's lips. "Go to sleep, Miss LaRoche. There are mysteries to solve when you wake." He stands, stretches again, and picks up his coat. "I'm going to take care of a few things. I'll be back by sundown. Don't leave this room. Just sleep."

I want to, but as soon as he's gone, I'm thinking of wishes again. A dark, bitter seed takes root in my mind, and errant thoughts water it into a nettling bloom. Suddenly, my peace is gone and I'm wide awake again. I flip onto my back and stare at the dark apex of the ceiling. Without Nicolai here, I feel safer to prune through those weedy buds of thought.

What if I could wish for more than just that thief's name? What if I could wish my mind backward to a time I don't remember, before the therapies that numbed every memory from Nan's disappearance until I woke up in the recovery ward clutching that balloon pendant in my fist?

What if I wished to be well again? What would that mean for me? And where would it leave Nicolai?

My mind offers no solution as the sad buds shrink shut again.

CHAPTER NINE

J wake to late-afternoon shadows. I know this is what they are because when my depression was at its worst in the Splendor House, I would often sleep this late. I've become good friends with these shivering dark lines, though I suppose Mirror Lands shadows are not *my* shadows.

Groggy, I sit up and tow my hair from my cheeks, squinting about and licking my lips. I was just dreaming of mice inviting me to tea in a house so small I couldn't wedge inside, and now I'm waking to an empty room that also feels too small, because I can't leave it.

Because Nicolai hasn't returned.

I tell myself it's no cause for alarm, but my still-exhausted body doesn't believe me. *Whap-whap-whap* goes the pulse in my wrists, kicking at my bones, and I stand and circle the room. I could leave and find food, but if I do, I won't be allowed back in—not until Nicolai returns. *If* he returns. What if he's been caught and dragged before the powers of the Circus, and they've executed him or tossed him back through a Rift for the watchmen to deal with?

I feel as if I'm going to be ill, imagining Nicolai with a bloody face, held by the bribe-taking watch…and me, trapped in this small room that is shrinking like the one in my dream, shrinking to the size of a mousehole…

I dart into the washroom and turn on both faucets of the sink just for the noise, splashing my clammy face. I feel as if all the pigment is draining from my skin, leaving me corpse-gray. I shake as I grip the pedestal and bend over it, struggling to breathe. I am a too-large girl in a mouse house, and soon I'll be crushed. My ribs already collapse around my heart. I want to scream, but if I do, someone will come running and think I'm mad, a girl bent over a sink and screaming into its basin.

I know now that it's worse to be thought mad than to actually go there.

And suddenly, true to my oddness as I watch my deformed countenance warping away in the particulars of the copper surface, it strikes me why I've been dreaming and thinking of mice.

When Nicolai returns at last, I'm sitting in the washroom, unkempt and sweat-mottled from my small fit of terror. I lean against the wall with my pressed hands trapped between my knees, my eyes plucking the tiny threads of my leggings apart from one another. I hear him come inside, hear him say my name. Then the door all but crashes open, and my eyes yank upward to his face. His haggard, panicked face.

He stares at me. "I thought you'd left."

"I thought you'd been taken."

Drip, drip, drip goes the faucet. Except the faucet is my eyes.

Nicolai edges into the room. He's carrying a package under his arm that smells strongly of pastry, and my heart leaps. Somehow, I know it's powdered sugar donuts, their sweet seductive call lifting me a bit out of my misery. It's not something I'm proud of, but for as long as I can remember—which admittedly is very little—I could put away whole platters of sugary treats without pause. The Circus is indeed a dangerous place for me.

"I had my own attraction to attend," he says. "I'm remiss to draw attention to our clandestine partnership by making myself completely scarce. So during the day, I must go. At night, I'll become your escort. Is that fair?"

He opens the donut box—a peace offering. I trust him that these won't poison me or make time speed up again. I take one and let its soothing sugar notes fool me into believing all is well.

"That's fair," I say around a mouthful, "just as long as you're honest with me about where you've gone next time."

"You have my word." He leans back against the edge of the tub.

"There's no time for this!" A spike of daring races through me as the sugar goes to work on my nerves. I hop up, buttoning the long coat that Moe tailored for me.

"No time for donuts?" Nicolai arches a brow as if I've blasphemed.

"No time for anything." I stretch out my hand. "Come, Nicolai. I know where we need to go next. I know who can tell us where to find those colors."

*   *

Mistress Mirabelle's Crafting Guild: Home of the Finest Circus Paraphernalia in the Mirror Lands, boasts the sideways sign above the door. Mirabelle's shop is in a very remote corner of the Circus, a relic from a time when it was just a modest city, a sliver of the Mirror Lands like any other, I assume. Though decorated as lavishly as any attraction, this shop and those around it show signs of neglect by Circus patrons. Most people don't come to a Circus just to see how it's made, after all.

Only me. Only mad Tessa.

I ring the pulley bell, and Nicolai breaths into his hands. It's unseasonably cold tonight, more like the Mortal Lands, and I'm glad of my jacket. What felt like summertime in my strapless dress the night before now flirts with an autumnal chill.

The plain wooden door opens, and we find ourselves assessed by an ox of a man sporting long, shaggy tan hair all down his back and sides. His bull's face scrunches and his broad, pink nose twitches. His tongue, human except for its blueberry color, swipes his lipless muzzle. "This is a surprise. Need something for your attraction?"

Nicolai clears his throat. "I'm only an observer. It's Madame Mystery you ought to speak to."

The ox looks at me with two very different eyes: one sharp and human, one gentle and beastlike. I fight not to quail at that suspicious stare.

"I've come to see Mistress Mirabelle," I say.

With a grunt, he swings the door wide.

Mirabelle's shop is a confectionary of a different sort. The walls are white, and the machines are painted in the cheeriest colors—cherry, lime, lavender, lemon and marmalade. Printing presses whir, carpenters saw, lacquered boards are slapped into box shapes. I see a calliope in one corner, painted with a woman in white robes and a glinting mask, arms spread wide while the world tornadoes around her. I hear shouts that vary from tinny and meek to houndlike baying and bull bellows.

Oh, if I ever told Missus Fiona about this place, I'd be not only straightjacketed, but muzzled as well so I could never speak of such wonders again.

"Is everyone here Mirror Folk?" I ask as we sidle around a great machine spewing out playbills for an acrobat's show.

Nicolai nods. "We Deathless are occupied with running the attractions, not with their design or maintenance. Some of these workers are indentured to the Circus, like Corriene. Others are paid a wage of food and board for their services. Since a great number of Deathless come from the Mortal Lands, they would never be skilled enough to work with Mirror materials, anyway."

I'm about to ask him what sort of materials he means, when one of the playbills shivers and the lion's head on the top lets out a thin, high roar, startling me so badly I leap and knock Nicolai sideways. He catches us both against the nearest wall with a smirk.

The shop all seems to be in one room of three tiers, the upper levels supported on iron stilts. But there is a tiny office, thankfully not mouse-sized, tucked into a corner.

Mistress Mirabelle's desk is far larger than she, but she commands it like Mister Metters rules the Morrow Daily. Stacks of invoices and charts lay before her, and she marches up and down the line with the authority of a seasoned veteran. Without a glance up, she says, "You know not to bother me in here, Reg."

"Madame Mystery to see you," Reg the Ox says.

Mirabelle looks up with bright eyes. They soften just a bit when she recognizes me. "Hello, odd girl." She bounds to the nearest edge of the desk and props up on her haunches, studying me. "We wondered if you'd survived. Reginald bet not, but I see he owes me a whole box of peanut butter truffles."

"Those are my favorite," I smile. "Perhaps we should split them, since

I did the work of staying alive that won you the bet."

"Half the work," Nicolai intones. I kick his shin, and Reg guffaws.

"I take it you didn't come to lay claim to my sweets," Mirabelle says. I'm reminded I'm wasting her time as much as my own with this banter, and while she might've been kind to me in the Menagerie yard, she is a businesswoman after all.

So. To business. I produce the clue and lay it on the desk beside her. "I'm wondering if your guild has crafted anything fitting these colors for a specific attraction. Anything at all, even a booth's palette."

Mirabelle looks at me, her small dark nose tweaking. "You know, candies come in all different colors, too."

Until now, I hadn't even thought of food. Poisoned candies that could leave me ill or dead…I risk a glance at Nicolai and see by the faint crease in his brow that the notion hadn't occurred to him, either.

"Let me worry about Lord Mull." My voice just barely wobbles. "Can you help us?"

"Should I?"

"Yes."

Mirabelle looks unimpressed, in a mousy fashion. "I'm very busy. Why should I waste my time with you?"

My lips pucker indignantly. "Why, because…because…" I hunt around, mouth opening and shutting like a goldfish won in a tossing game. I can't think of a single reason she would want to help me. "Because, I don't know. Someone in this Circus took something from me. I want it back, so I need that wish. And I think you bet on me because all of you want to see a human win again. For the first time in a century."

Mirabelle regards me with beady, intelligent eyes. I wait and wait and try to look worthy of her help, somehow.

"The Circus takes from everyone. But it's true the Deathless are becoming quite plump on smugness when the humans fail the tests, and it's rather obnoxious." Mirabelle leans both paws on the card. She studies it for a while, and Reg reclines with brawny, manlike arms folded over his barreled ox chest. I glance at Nicolai to see if he's offended by Mirabelle's accusations of obnoxious smugness, but then again, I think the term was invented for him.

I can feel the sugar rush slowly fading, leaving me nervous and fidgeting again. It seems a whole season passes, the air turning colder than ever, before Mirabelle darts suddenly across the desk to a heap of files. She paws rapidly through them, then drags out a large invoice that she drops before me.

"It was the wording that confused me," she says. "These Deathless are so specific. If they ask for goldenrod and you give them simple gold, they'll have you remake it without payment. So we're trained here to think in very specific shades. But, if you exchange the *black* in the clue for *sable*, and *gold* for *saffron,* I think you'll find all four colors together here."

I tear unabashedly through the invoice, searching for the colors. Warm spice notes tickle my nose as Nicolai comes to the desk and leans a casual hand on the edge, right next to mine. Absentmindedly it seems, his smallest finger grazes the bony knob on my wrist. A funny shiver dances in my stomach, and I jerk my eyes back to the page. And that's when I see it.

"There!" I stab a triumphant finger at the words, relieved to move my hand away from his. Yet somehow I'm also disappointed. "Small, lidded boxes in peach, persimmon, sable and saffron."

"Mistress Luck." Nicolai taps the name on the invoice. "She runs one of the many guessing booths on the main strip."

"*Here you choose the way to go.* That sounds like guessing to me." I look up at him, and he stares down at me. The worried frown has not left his face, but he shrugs.

"It's worth a visit."

CHAPTER TEN

*J*he atmosphere of the Circus has shifted from chilly to downright cold as we make our way across it. My legs are beginning to tire from so much walking, certainly more than I've had to do since I started work at the Morrow Daily, even when rushing around to deliver drinks. Nicolai sets a swaggering stride down the winding brick roads that skirt the park, and I'm startled that the trees, which wore crowns of healthy jade and emerald the night before, are now dripping in flaxen, rust, and bright carmine.

A shiver runs through me. How long have I been here already? Has it truly been only two days, or is time turning to taffy, stretching and shrinking around us? Is this a seasonal change, or the power of the Deathless dashing across the veins of the Circus, transforming summer to fall overnight? Do they even know how long proper seasons last, or is this just Mirror Lands weather?

I hurry to match strides with Nicolai. "Are there any Deathless who remember what things were like before the Circus took over the city?"

"Some. They claim it was dull. Apparently, Mirror Folk were incapable of making their own fun without mortals to bat around like balls of string." He glances down, to make certain I perceive his humor, I'm sure. "In truth, I doubt if they want to remember. This land had no name before mortals laid eyes on it, and everything was simpler…plainer before the Rifts. Now it wears the name your kind gave it, and proudly. It boasts the merit of what it can do, but it owes a great deal of that power to what it steals from mortals. It's forgotten its simple roots on purpose, and that…that's a shame, really."

"Is it?" I mean that *I* think it is, but I'm fascinated to hear him say it. Of all Mirror Folk, the Deathless seem the most unlikely to take shame with their conduct.

Nicolai shrugs. "If more of us remembered what it was like to be weak, I think we wouldn't abuse the strength we've been given. It takes a very special person to deserve the power of the Circus. Someone who knows what it is to go without, perhaps."

A tiny, gentle finger of thought grazes my mind as we reach the end of the park and slip back into the Circus proper. Then it's gone.

No one else seems bothered by the sharp dip in temperature. Shrieking laughter drifts from the chained swings and the great wheel. We pass axe-shaped posts that swing lazily higher and higher, finally crossing at the top, tipping the riders upside-down. I think my life feels quite a bit like that nowadays—swaying back and forth until all of a sudden, I'm looking at everything upside-down with the blood curdling my brain.

A few people pause to stare at me, and I touch my headband. I think I prefer their stares because of the mirage of beauty over the attention I would receive if they recognized the girl from the rostrum, but it's still unsettling. It reminds me of dreams I've had where everyone on the street was a disguised orderly from the Splendor House, and as soon as I spoke a word, they pounced to secure me for admittance.

I shift slightly closer to Nicolai as we pass under the shadow of the lazy upright wheel, turning a slow revolution that lifts its riders up toward the stars. I press the pad of my pointer finger to the empty dip of my throat, and like activating a lever, back come the thoughts that kept me awake at the hostel. Oh, finding a refuge for my frayed mind tonight is like searching for shelter in a storm.

I'm almost relieved when Nicolai slows, then suddenly tugs me off the main path. We shelter in the darkness between booths, on a narrow verge of grass. Here, it's all one wooden stand after another, and a graveyard of limp balloons, discarded streamers, and sad confetti litters the landscape.

But we are hidden from prying eyes.

"Mistress Luck." Nicolai points over my shoulder, and I glance at the booth. Its bright pearl siding sports an image of a woman's turban-wrapped head, her bright cherry mouth spread in a smile that is both welcoming and threatening at once. Her teeth form the words *Mistress Luck's Box Game: Win the Prize of Your Life!*

I shudder, raking my nail against the cardstock in my pocket. "Is this trial also timed?"

"I don't know. I'm afraid that here, my insight is of little use, and this is as far as I can go with you."

Sweat gathers at my hairline. "Do you really mean that this time, or will you come dashing in at the first whiff of danger?"

He chucks my chin with his knuckles. "You won't even know I'm around. But I will be."

That shouldn't comfort me quite as much as it does.

Nicolai vanishes into the pressed shadows between the booths. I straighten my rumpled coat, draw my shoulders back, and finger the weight of the first key in my pocket.

I can do this. I have done it once already.

There is a lazy curve of path that crisscrosses the grassy median between stalls, vendors, and the rides, creating angular shapes in the grass. Mistress Luck's Guessing Booth is in the middle of a long row of games, and it is the only one still open. Garish silver-blue light spills down from twin lanterns on its posts, shedding an unhealthy brightness across the booth's wooden counter. Mistress Luck herself leans an elbow on the edge of the counter and drums her fingers on the wood. She looks very like the painting, except really her teeth are not words.

"Welcome, Madame Mystery," she says. "I see you solved the second clue. Are you ready to play a guessing game?"

I wonder if she sees how my legs wobble as I walk up to the booth. It feels so eerie, so solitary, so very dangerous—like approaching a gathering of bawdy drunks under a lonely streetlight in the worst neighborhood of Barrow Downs. Not that I have ever done something so reckless.

But I am doing this now. I am here, my hands gripping the counter. "I'm ready."

I feel the Circus take a breath behind me. I feel its eyes watching me, from bulbs that have gone to sleep, from booths with their screens rolled down. From the palm of my own hand.

Mistress Luck snaps her fingers, and a plume of gray dust fans across the counter. It distills down to four numbered boxes: peach, persimmon, black, and gold.

"Two of these boxes contain a sedative dust that will put you to sleep for a year. One contains a poisonous fume that will kill you before you realize what you've done. The fourth contains the key." She spans a hand. "Choose."

I stare at her. "That's all? No hints, no...no showing me and then switching the boxes?"

She raises a very finely-groomed brow. "You've already been given a clue."

Her tone strikes like a slap. Never have I felt more condescended to, even by Missus Fiona. It's as if she thinks me slow, or simple, or...

Or mad.

I'm shocked by the bubbling red fissure that cracks open in my belly, the heat that fans my cheeks. This is not humiliation. It is *anger* boiling through my blood. Such an unexpected response, but I'll gladly take it over the feeling of shrinking down to two inches tall that comes whenever my oddness is implied.

"May I *touch* them?" I must bite the words out, my jaw rattles so.

The second brow joins the first, and Mistress Luck slowly nods. "The choice becomes final only when you open the lid." She settles backward on heel, mouth stretching into the same leer frozen forever on the back of her booth. My nails bite into the glossy wood as I bend over her boxes and play her little game.

Four boxes, four different colors, each lovely one etched in fine threads of silver. I wonder if perhaps that is the riddle to solve. I pick them up and examine the intricate curlicues, but all the patterns look the same. Mirabelle does fine, consistent work, indeed. There is no salvation there.

I rearrange the boxes in numerical order. First is persimmon, then peach, then gold, then black. I would assume the darkest box to contain the deadliest poison—so it must not be. It's too simple. I consider my aversion to light and darkness, and perhaps the solution lies in the darkness after all.

I pick up that box and shake it. Then I do the same to the others. Although one must contain a key of considerably greater dimension than vapors, they all weigh the same, and none rattle.

I walk my gaze from box to box as if observing a night watch patrol. They are all splendid, except that one will kill me and two will see me in a coma. And when I last woke from one of those, the pall had been cast over my memories. I'd rather not lose the few I have left from before, or the new ones I've spent two years creating, unpleasant though they are. They are mine, and my life is mine, and I don't intend to lose either tonight.

I pick up the black box again, because in a strange way it seems to sing to me. This time, when my fingers touch it, I know precisely why.

My necklace came in a box just like this.

I remember it so suddenly and certainly that I gasp. I can see it in my mind now: the same silver volutes, the same well-crafted body and lid, even the same sable shade. My thumb grazes the edge of the lid as if to lift it, and uncertainty washes over me.

Is my necklace a Mirror charm? Is that why the thief in *The Alibi Shop* looked twice, why I thought he seemed to recognize it? Why he stole it at all?

Mistress Luck tucks her hands behind her back. "Stuck?"

I drop the box, and the impact booms through the otherwise-silent path. "Concentrating, actually. And I would appreciate silence."

Her smile is only as enchanting as a brew of snake-venom tea. I can tell she enjoys seeing me rattled. How they all must. I'm such an interesting little plaything, with my oddness and my mortal tendencies. I'm not certain at that moment if I'm more furious with myself for allowing my flaws to show, or at the Deathless for being entertained by the poor display. I focus on the boxes again and consider chucking them at Mistress Luck's head.

Well, if she has such a low opinion of me already, it can't possibly stoop much lower. So I produce the clue card from my pocket and deliberate over it, ignoring Mistress Luck's quiet snort.

I have already chosen the way to go. I have the boxes before me, in the proper colors. But I can't fathom which one will move me ahead. I check the boxes again, weighing and turning. Mistress Luck yawns and sighs and lounges on her stool, tapping her fingers against her jawline.

Long fingernails of sweat slide down the sides of my neck. I can feel more eyes than the Circus on me now. Nicolai is somewhere close by, his will pressing against me like a wall of summer heat. He wants this just as badly as I do, and now I don't feel so alone in this isolated place. I feel almost reassured.

I settle on my heels, flip the card over, and search it once more. And suddenly I feel as if I'm reading it with new eyes.

Only one will move ahead.

What if it isn't one, as in a single box...but *one* as in *Box One?*

Shivers traipse down my back as I rest my hand on the persimmon lid. This is risky, and I can hardly trust my own problem-solving skills. But it's the closest to a real hint I've seen in the card. It seems like a Chaos Circus sort of solution to such a riddle. And anyway, I must choose eventually. The booth's name implies that half the win is luck. I suppose I've met luck halfway with critical thinking, and now I must throw caution to the wind.

I slide the box closer, and Mistress Luck sits tall. The lights gutter as if they suck in their breath. This is the moment, and right or wrong, they are all intrigued. The luminous eyes of the Circus bulbs stare unblinking as I fit my fingers to the edge of the box, and Mistress Luck's brow creases triumphantly. "Are you *certain?*"

I freeze, her tone replaying in my mind. And then I find a bold smile dragging my mouth up at one side. "I wasn't, until you said that."

I open the lid.

A puff of white mist curls up into my face, and I forget to hold my breath. I choke on the taste of crushed ice and shaved helixes of power that decorate the wind. My eyes water. I swat the puff of fog away, and stare at my prize: a sheer porcelain key arrayed in decorations of blue-flowered vines, nestled in a haystack of cotton that kept it from rattling against the edges of the box.

* *

I can feel Mistress Luck's piercing eyes on my back as I stagger away. Lightheaded with relief, I gulp clean air and lose myself in the candy-colored twists of the streets until suddenly there are hands on my shoulders, spinning me around.

"Which box did you open?" Nicolai demands. "Was it the sleeping dust?"

I shake my head mutely, but still he skims his hands along my arms, maintaining delicate contact, as if he thinks I'll collapse in the throes of an enchanted sleep and he'll have to catch me. He only stops his mother-henning when I open my palm and show him the key.

Nicolai laughs and shakes his head. "You are a marvel."

"And you fret like an unbroken carthorse. I am *fine*."

"I can see that. Meanwhile my nerves are ravaged." He threads his fingers unsteadily through his hair.

"Peanut butter is good for ravaged nerves," I blurt out, and immediately wish I hadn't. How silly that sounded!

Nicolai looks at me with genuine surprise. "Is it?"

I ponder, then shrug. "Well. It can't hurt to find out, can it?"

And that is how I find myself sitting on a curb of the Chaos Circus in the foolish hours of the night, sharing a whole paper flute of peanut butter truffles with a Deathless whose title I don't know, in a land that isn't mine, with a pair of keys tucked in my pocket from tests that *I* completed with—mostly—my own wits.

And for the first time since leaving the Splendor House, I feel slightly less hopeless about my whole life.

CHAPTER ELEVEN

O nce again, I sleep like the dead, even without my necklace. The Circus leaves me too spent to pace and panic. I wake to the aroma of fine coffee and pancakes, and my blurry eyes find Nicolai, who has already returned from his own attraction. He's perched on his bed, shirt fully unbuttoned, a mug in one hand and a silver square of black-scripted cardstock in the other.

He's reading my latest clue without me.

"Pardon *me!*" I launch from the bed like a human cannonball and crash forward with grasping fingers, but Nicolai drops the card and catches me gently by the jaw and chin and holds me easily at bay. Power thumps in the pulse that meets my skin, and I'm reminded yet again that whatever Nicolai really *is*, I don't yet know what he can do to me.

"There was no other reading material," he sighs. "I was nearly crying with boredom waiting for you to wake."

"I will give you something to cry about if you don't hand that over to me, now!"

"Tessa, Tessa. I've already shed so many tears on your account." With a smirk, he releases me, and my momentum sends me face-first into his bare chest, practically kissing the muscular planes of his pectorals. I can't push away fast enough, but of course now it's worse, because I'm kneeling between the sprawl of his legs and gripping the bare definition of his hipbones.

"You. Are. Despicable," I grate out.

"And yet, you're still clinging to me. Perhaps you like despicable, hm?"

I let go of his hips and thrust myself off his bed, and he surrenders the clue with no further contention. I want to ask him if that was really so hard, but after touching the alarmingly-chiseled contours of his body, I don't want to discuss it. He's managed to take the serenity of the previous evening's shared truffles and chatter about nonsense things and turn it into the embarrassment of a lifetime.

I flip the clue over and hide my hot face behind it as I read:

Here you sit with death itself

And raise a glass to your good health

Beneath the great clock's second arm

Those who flinch would do you harm

"Oh, look!" I infuse false cheer into my voice. "More death! No wonder you have such a jolly look on your face all the time, living in this place."

I send the card flying in a sharp, deliberate cut toward his head. Nicolai catches it easily and doesn't remark on my good fortune to have thrown so deft and straight. "You're quite sassy when you're upset."

"What's worse, I think I'm growing rather numb to having my head threatened." I sink onto my bed and rub my face. "Well, now where do we start searching?"

"So eager to leave this place, as usual." I hear a rustle and then the merciful whisper of buttons in their sheaths as Nicolai makes himself proper again. "We have several clocks here, not that their accuracy can be trusted. There's the watchmaker, the great clock that tells a different sort of time altogether..."

"Let's start there." I bounce back to my feet, and Nicolai chucks a plate of pancakes toward me. Just before it hits my chest, it suspends, hovering at level with my breasts.

"Eat," he offers with a sinister and sensuous grin. Or perhaps I'm imagining the latter bit. I shouldn't be having these thoughts about my partner.

"How did you do that?" I ask as I slather my pancakes in a fountain of thick, dark amber syrup. "Make it float that way, I mean."

"Deathless are capable of much within the Circus, less when we're without it." Nicolai picks up the card and rereads the clue. I have the distinct impression he wishes not to meet my eyes. "In the Mortal Lands, I am only able to use my particular gift. But here, I can do all the things you mortals tell stories of. Rearrange the stars. Suspend or hover things. I can do even more than that, but I prefer to save my strength for if we truly need it."

"Because it tires you." I haven't forgotten how his deep sleep the first night of our stay enabled me to sneak out to the rostrum.

"Precisely."

"Then that," I gesture to the plate with my fork, "was just for showing off."

Now his eyes do alight on me over the card's feathered edge. "What can I say but that your show of talent in these games inspires my own?"

I laugh the strangest laugh that's ever come out of me—rolling and slightly biting and full of a mirth that I don't know I've actually ever felt. "Feeling one-upped, Nic?"

We both freeze—me in mortification that I laughed at him, that I teased him so. And him, staring at me as if I've slapped him across the face like in all my fantasies since we met.

"Miss LaRoche," he says with the breathlessness of a man who's taken a punch to the tendermeats, "it would be an honor to be outshined by you for an eternity."

Now I'm sure I'm the one who looks punched. I hardly know what to do with a simple compliment to my clothes, nevermind a thing like that.

I chew through four bites of pancake before I manage a clever response: "Shall we go?"

I try to think of some other distraction as Nicolai helps me into my coat and we step outside. The air is not quite as chilly as last night, but it does still feel of autumn. The wide straps and corsets on the ladies around the Circus have been traded for light coats all depicting images of exciting carnival sights—tigers bounding through flaming hoops, men juggling swords, women breathing fire. All the men we pass have rolled their sleeves back down.

So it wasn't just us: the seasons changed in a blink, and everyone is taking it in stride.

We pass Mistress Luck's booth, where a child is playing a guessing game. I find myself slowing and holding my breath as I watch her pull the lid from a box, but it only emits a spray of glass-blue butterflies. One alights on her hand, and Mistress Luck's smile is all teeth and crinkled eyes as she waves the girl, her new pet, and her mother away.

"What did that cost her?" I cannot help but ask.

"A day of her life," Nicolai says. "Or perhaps a tooth that Luck can sell as a trophy. The games change in the day, Miss LaRoche—the stakes are different for these people than they are for you. The other boxes might've contained a rotten egg, or a rabbit's foot, newly bloodied."

"But not death or poisoned powder?"

"Never that." Nicolai pockets his hands as he walks. "If danger here wore a face people recognized, none would ever come to it. Believe me, we have become very good at baiting the line with all the best lures: cures and longevity and pleasure. Few mortals ever notice that death is the fisherman who's reeling them in."

I chew on that thought like a tough piece of licorice as we weave in and out of colored pockets: more vendors, a few rides for children. I feel as if I'm seeing the Circus for the first time, truly noticing how much of it appeals to youth. I've never taken stock of how many whole families came to Barrow Island from the mainland. I've never thought of how the Circus must draw them in. "Even the children, Nicolai?"

I don't mean for my tone to sound accusing, but I fear it does. Nicolai surveys a small train that circles a track in our path. Four small boys and a little girl inside munch happily on fritters and tarts and hang their free hands out the windows. "We demand less from them. But we wouldn't have to demand anything if they didn't come at all."

"They don't know better! They're children!"

"You don't give them enough credit, I'm afraid. They come because they're desperate. They hear tales of endless platters of food, and games that don't cost money. They come from all over because they want a better life, and the Circus props up the notion until they're entangled in it enough to dare the trials." He veers suddenly from the grassy verge where the train runs, and we walk through a twisting avenue of ride after ride, game after game. "The Circus preys on any weakness. It preys on desperation. And then it offers a fistful of gold that soon reveals itself to be lead, fatally painted."

His tone is strange, sad and frustrated, and so very tired. All at once, I think I've just realized something about Nicolai. But before I can pursue the notion any further, he stops us. We've reached the watchmaker.

* *

Much to my chagrin, our first foray into the world of timepieces is fruitless. The wizened old watchmaker makes a living selling false or funny watches. Some of his clocks tell not only time, but the place of a person whose name is scratched onto the back. Others tell time in both Lands at once. I even see one that's rigged to tell mainland time as well as time on Barrow Island. I find it all very superfluous, and not a bit of help.

"There's still that great clock, isn't there?" I ask as we emerge from the back of the shop onto the edge of another small park, this one laced in winsome jacaranda and cherry blossom trees. Despite the season, they bloom as if it's always just the right temperature. More Deathless power, I suspect.

"There is." Nicolai scowls. "I despise that clock."

He offers no explanation, and leads me on a jaunt through the perfume of crushed blossoms under our feet, down a very narrow alley where a handful of unpopular vendors sell charmed bracelets that are claimed to bring good luck in the games, and then we emerge back onto the main strip with the great wheel, the multifarious vendors, and the swings. We go even further—crossing a bridge over water that must empty eventually into that lake we tumbled through from the Rift—and reach a street that is much different. Darker.

There is very little to see here, just a few covered wagons with sides rolled up. These vendors sell even stranger things—potions to replicate love, to slow time, to hide one from any pursuer; bandages to adhere to any wound, no matter how grisly; alcohol that can wipe away any ill feelings for a full day. These sellers wear many imitation-gold bracelets and a great deal of cosmetics, both the men and the women. There's a strange, pungent leafy odor in the air.

"What is this place?" I find myself sidling closer to Nicolai than I ever have as they watch us go by.

"This is where people come when the Circus takes too much." Nicolai lifts his chin at several sprawled mortals in top hats and disheveled clothes nursing thick bottles of that forgetful sauce. "When they realize the steep price they've paid for their fun and false fortune, they often need to forget...or to have their ails soothed. Everything you see here is rumored to take the edge off the Circus's cruelty."

"Does it?"

Nicolai's lips twist into a humorless and not-at-all-Nicolai smile. "One could say. Although it also begs a price of its own. They're not truly finding relief, only paying for a different poison."

I shudder as we pass a woman without eyes who drinks and drinks, curses, and drinks some more. It seems whatever brew they gave her was not strong enough to cleave apart the grief of self-inflicted blindness. My heart aches on her behalf.

Finally, where the road forgets it's a road and becomes a weed-infested dirt track instead, we find it: the great clock. And it truly is great, twice as high as even Nicolai's head. I make toward it, and he touches my shoulder. "Carefully, Miss LaRoche. Many who go mad here, it isn't from strong drink. This clock is rumored to tell the time of one's death."

I keep my hands very close to myself. I have no desire whatsoever to engage in such nonsense. For all I know, seeing the time of one's death is the very thing that brings it about. I consume myself instead with searching the grass underneath where the second arm points. But all I find are a few mortal trinkets left like offerings to time itself, begging for more of it, and a whole buffet of nothing else besides. Just tall grass and weeds.

I look again, and again, just to be certain. Then I stand back, arms akimbo. "Odd."

The world lurches suddenly, as if we're in a box that's just been shaken by a child. My vision shimmers, going black and red like the walls of *The Alibi Shop*. I hear a wretched, choked gag from behind, and in my state of wobbly shock it's a moment before I realize that sound, unbelievably, came from Nicolai.

I spin toward him and stifle a scream with both hands.

He's touching the clock. No—*clinging* to it, one arm wrapped around its black iron post. His eyes are white, and above him the clock face spins and spins, settling, settling....

I lunge, tackling him backward against a sickly-looking aspen so that his arm separates from the iron clock. I grab his shoulders and then his face and shake him, shouting his name, but it's all unnecessarily dramatic. He's already come back around, breathing hard, and he grasps my arms right back and sways as if he'll pitch against me and drive us both to the ground.

"What did you see?" I shake him again. "What did it show you?"

"Nothing, nothing." His tone fights with every syllable to return to its usual calm. "I thought perhaps if I touched it, it would show us the way."

"Then *I* should have touched it!" Though I know I could never have brought myself to do it. But perhaps that's what the Circus wants of me— to drive me back over the precipice of madness to complete these tests. Perhaps it's sanity I must pay to have my necklace back. To have that name we need.

Nicolai peers at me, his hair already drenched with sweat from the short moment he touched the clock. And I realize that he knows all of it, everything I just thought. He already suspects what the Circus will ask of me. That was why he did it, after all.

I'm suddenly quite aware that he's let go of my shoulder, one hand cupping the back of my neck instead. Power pinions over the surface of my skin, setting patches of hair on end as it travels along my scalp. I slide my own hands from Nicolai's shoulders, but they don't seem quite ready to return to my sides yet. I grip the open front of his jacket instead.

"What did you see?" I ask again.

He says nothing, which I think is the only way he can keep from lying to me. His eyes float upward, and I look over my shoulder.

The clock face has settled back to its normal time. But I know. Had I looked at it just a moment ago, I would have seen what Nicolai saw: the time of his death.

"Is it soon?" I don't know why it matters to me. But it does. I can't lose my guide, not when I have three trials left to complete.

Nicolai lets go suddenly and swings a casual arm around my shoulders, steering me away from the clock. "Have no fear, I won't be leaving you before the five tests are over. And I just remembered there's a booth where one guesses time on four separate pocket watches…"

He rambles a bit about that as we leave the desolate corner of the Circus, which I think shows the true heart of this fantastic and fetid place. I can't help looking once more over my shoulder at the clock, but it ticks, ticks, ticks innocently away. It will not disclose its secrets.

It will not tell me how much time Nicolai has left.

CHAPTER TWELVE

We spend all day searching, and when I ask Nicolai if he ought to return to his own attraction, he simply shakes his head. It's dusk again by the time we exhaust everything remotely related to clocks in the Chaos Circus, and even a few hopeful guesses that prove equally fruitless. Nicolai sulks and I fret as we make our way through the familiar threads of darkness and splashes of merry light toward *Red & Gold's*. "What if I never solve this clue?"

"Then it's over." Nicolai doesn't sound as cavalier about the notion as in the past. I think the clock truly rattled him, and all on my account. I might have wondered more why he did it, if not for our conversation on the way to the watchmaker. I think I understand him a bit better now.

I tuck a conciliatory hand into the crook of his elbow, like I've seen women do for their fussing men on Barrow Island. "That won't do. We'll solve it, Nicolai. Somehow."

His crooked smile is as charming as always, but this time it falls shy of his eyes.

We order up a tray of food from the hostel kitchen, and when a server delivers it and demands payment, I have a sudden thought. I flash the scar on my palm, and he leaves at once.

"How did you think to do that?" Nicolai asks as I set the platter on the center of my bed.

"I don't know. I just did." I absently survey tonight's banquet: lavender pudding, tiramisu, cheese-and-bacon stuffed mushroom caps, steak medallions in a red wine and rosemary reduction, and julienned vegetables with a honey glaze. The plates are pure gold and the napkins bloodred. It's all very magnificent.

"Is all of that for you?" Nicolai props himself against the foot of my bed. "Because you seem to be hoarding it over there."

I fold up my legs and draw the platter closer. "You should join me."

He does. We pick quietly over the portions, but despite the delectable sight of every piece, neither of us is very hungry. It isn't long before I set aside my fork and knife and tell him what I'm thinking. "The Lion…"

"The who?"

"The fellow on the rostrum. The one who gave me this." Again, I show my wound, and Nicolai frowns. "He said that if I got turned around, I could ask for help from a Lord…Lord Liberty." I think I've said it right.

"Libertine." Nicolai dabs steak juice from the corner of his mouth and tosses the wadded napkin onto his plate. "A visit to him would not be wise."

I almost remind him that he said the same thing about the trials. But now I'm beginning to think he was right about that, so I keep my mouth sewed shut.

"It's your choice, of course," Nicolai adds. "But the price will also be yours to pay, Tessa. I won't be able to accompany you. Or to take that cost for you as I did at the clock."

I still doubt that was entirely about me, but I let him have it as I lean back into the headboard. It blooms against me, rubbing knots from my shoulders. I circle my temples and try to think around the problem. "Would he be guaranteed to give me a hint?"

"That's what he does." Nicolai twirls his steak knife over his knuckles. "I'm not saying he wouldn't, only that the hint will come at a cost. And that could be anything."

I slip my hand under my pillow and butt the tips of the two keys against one another. I hate to admit it, but I'm eager for the third. I'm beginning to feel for the first time since the Splendor House, if not the first time in my whole life, that I'm truly succeeding at something. And perhaps that is the lure of the Circus—that it makes you feel powerful, clever, and in control, when really you're being strung along like a beast on a leash.

But see how the Circus will laugh when it has no choice but to give me my wish. The Lion said it could be anything I wanted.

Tessa LaRoche will not be denied.

A sizzle of determination shoots through me like the golden tines of Nicolai's power. I suck in a sharp breath. The knife stops moving. He looks up at me.

"I'm going to do it." I slide to my feet and stuff the keys in my pocket. "Tell me where to find Lord Libertine."

* *

Of course, Nicolai does more than tell me. He takes me there, to a portion of the Circus that's devoted to tents. It's a wide plaza ringed in potted trees, and all the tents are awake in the dusk, their thick magenta-white striping and gold pennant crowns licked in rising moonlight that cuts through a gentle incensed fog. The tents are staked between the wide stones, and their flags declare their attraction: conjoined twin acrobats, the one-legged unicyclist, the twelve-foot giant. I notice there is no one collecting cost at the tent flaps, but hypemen shout at wandering mortals, inviting them to see the spectacles for themselves.

"Is there no entrance fee?" I ask.

"For the spectacles, no." Nicolai's voice is gravelly as we slip around the edge of the plaza, between the trees—keeping out of sight. "But for Libertine, for Harlequin, you pay within."

My heels catch on the stones. Lord Harlequin...his tent is just there. But it's dark, oddly dismal. I know at once there is no one inside. "Where is he?"

"Likely in the Mortal Lands, snatching up his next quarry."

"Is it true what they say, that Lord Harlequin can see the future?" I'm practically jogging to keep stride with Nicolai now. "That he can show that future to anyone?"

"Yes."

"I wonder if he could tell us if we'll succeed," I muse. "Is the clock also his invention, another collaboration as with Lord Mull?"

"He had a hand in it, yes." Nicolai slows. "There it is."

We're behind Libertine's tent. I tug the hem of my embroidered vest, adjust the long train that touches my knees, and herd all my courage together. "Well, then. Be ready to go to the next test as soon as I emerge."

"Miss LaRoche." Nicolai secures my shoulder, which is all right. I had no intention of leaving just yet. "Remember that until you make an agreement, nothing is settled. You can leave that tent any time before you strike a price with him. If he asks for too much, you can still walk away."

Even as I nod, I feel like a liar. I will not walk away. I need that hint. But for his sake, I nod until I'm quite sure my head will bob clean off. Then I step into the heart of the plaza.

I know a few eyes graze over me, perhaps even in recognition, as I walk around to the front of the tent. From the corner of my vision, I see Nicolai slip away into the smoke. No doubt he will appear from nothing once I emerge again.

I steel my wits. I tell myself I'm prepared for whatever awaits. And then I step into the tent.

And fortune and fate laugh at all my plans, as I find myself face to face with the Lion.

CHAPTER THIRTEEN

*M*adame Mystery, what a surprise," the Lion chuckles. "I expected to see you sooner. Take off that mask when I'm talking to you."

He means my headband. Of course, illusion is no good with him—he knows my true face. With shaking fingers, I remove that braided headpiece and feel just as naked without it as without my necklace.

The Lion sprawls on a floor of cushions. He's clad in very little, just a cloth that hangs to the midthigh and a sheer robe of vibrant mauve open over the plains of his bare, bronze chest. He's a different sort of dark from me, and even from Nicolai. He doesn't look suntouched so much as suncursed, as if he paid a price for his complexion and now something sinister lurks under his flesh.

"Speechless?" he preens.

I twist the headband around my fists. "You're...Lord Libertine?"

"The only." Oh, how clever he must think himself, tempting me straight into his den with that offer at the rostrum. A mouse beckoned by the Lion. "Come for a hint, have you?"

I remember Nicolai's warning—I could flee now. Nothing has been demanded, nothing given. But even as my toes wiggle toward the tent flap, my heels hold fast. I fear I'll chase myself in circles forever without a clue.

This card has thoroughly stumped me. "What would be the price?"

Libertine sits up with a languorous stretch and grabs a platter of candied plums and dates from behind the cushions. He offers them to me. "Eat, please."

"Oh, no, I couldn't possibly…"

"I insist." His eyes flash, and I know I'm about to be told to leave.

I select an innocent-looking plum. I make sure to sniff it, but it doesn't smell like one of Lord Mull's confections. I chew slowly and swallow. It goes down like lead, despite my love of sweets. "Was that the price?"

His lips twitch, fighting off that feline smile and failing. "You're a bold one, aren't you?" He sets the plate aside. "No. That was just to loosen your poor nerves. I'll admit, none of us expected you to survive the first test, not to mention the second. The Deathless are all agog. But some are nervous, too. Some don't like your murky intentions."

I fight back a giggle. As if I'm so dangerous, so threatening!

Libertine must see the amusement in my face. His smile grows. "Do you know what my place in the Circus is? I trade in information, Madame Mystery. You will find no better help than me. Would you like a hint now?"

Tension pricks its mighty claws into the small of my back, stopping my laughter. What weakness could he possibly want that the world can't already see? Small and crumbling, lost and lonely and *mad*.

But I didn't feel so small after the Menagerie. I didn't feel as if I was crumbling this morning. And whenever I'm with Nicolai…

Oh, Nicolai. He would likely tell me to leave now, to get out quickly. But if I can just move past this confounding clue, the greater portion of our adventure will be behind me. I'll be another broad step closer to going home.

"Yes," I say, "I would like a hint."

I'm feeling light and my tongue very loose. My head is slowly spinning from my shoulders. It's the plum, the sugar, something in it makes me suggestible…he wasn't lying about that. But now there's no going back.

He grins. "I will give you one hint if you'll tell me what you plan to wish for."

So. That's what he wants. The truth that makes the Deathless shift, that makes the Circus creak and cough as it peers over my shoulders here and there. The Circus craves my deepest desire.

Dare I trade it to him for this? Will I ever achieve it if I don't?

I take a step back, back again to the tent flap. I've given nothing, struck no bargains yet...

"My necklace." The words jump from my mouth and flee into Libertine's hands. Curse that plum! "One of the Deathless stole it, and I want to know who, so that I can get it back."

He tips his head, his golden mane cascading across one bare shoulder as the robe slips down. "That's it. You're enduring all of this for a *necklace.*"

I flinch at his tone. There it is, that subtle suggestion that I'm unhinged. After all, what sane girl would risk life and limb, quite literally, all for a chiseled piece of silver? It's not only that, of course—it's also for the name of Nicolai's opponent—but I bite my teeth around that secret so hard my jaw aches.

I will not tell him that. I will *not.*

Libertine studies me for a long, long moment. I wonder, not for the first time, if he's the Deathless we're searching for, and if he won't give me my necklace now to absolve himself, to keep me from treading on his tail. The thought is so delicious my lips curl. I don't know that I've ever tasted the power of making someone else nervous, but in this moment I am thoroughly enjoying the sensation.

Libertine's jaw tightens in response. He stands, and I'm reminded of how tall he is, how he overshadowed me on the rostrum. Yet I find I don't sink quite as much into his shadow this time. He looms, but I lock my spine and tilt my head to gaze up at him. I defy him with my eyes.

"Go for a balloon ride," he says.

I blink, my concentrated strength imploding. "Pardon me?"

"That's your hint." His tone is bored as he turns away "Go for a balloon ride. Out of my tent, now. I have other clients who wish for insight."

I gawk at him as he returns to his cushions and stretches out, the proud cat who's devoured his prey. I don't want to know what he sells to mortals who aren't playing this game. I don't want to know if he's duped anyone else as badly as he just duped me.

"You're *despicable.*" It comes out much more convincing than when I said it to Nicolai this morning.

"So I'm told. Enjoy your flight." He wiggles his fingers, and I'm dismissed. The sharpness of his gaze suggests that if I linger and pout, I will be tossed out on my backside. And that will really give the Circus something to laugh about.

I'm about to turn and leave when I notice something tucked between two cushions, just barely peeping out: a framed painting roughly the size of my palm. It sports a woman's face, stormed by flyaway russet curls. She's rouged to look like a doll, eyes charcoaled and lips scourged black, with a thick trickle of fake blood sliding from the corner of her mouth. And it's all at once, looking at her this way, that I know I've seen her before—and unlike the various portraits I've recognized in this Circus, I know precisely where I've seen her, too.

"That girl," I murmur. "She was from Barrow Island, was she not?"

Libertine follows my gaze, and for just a flicker I see something in his tight jaw and gleaming eyes that might pass itself for regret. Even for heartache.

Then his face closes up coldly. "Get out."

The shroud of incense is thick with spice as I storm through it. I don't place the change in scent until Nicolai is right before me, hands extended but not touching my shoulders. "What happened? What did he demand?"

"It hardly matters." My confusion over the portrait is quickly swallowed up as my rage flashes hot again. "He practically stole from me, the blackguard!"

"What was the clue, Tessa?"

"Nothing!" I slap the cardstock against his chest. "He told me to take a balloon ride, and then he sent me out!"

Nicolai blinks, looking as lost as I feel. We stand embraced in the unnatural fog thinly shredded by the delighted *oohs* and *ahhs* of the spectators in the oddity shows. Perhaps that's where I belong—on display. See the Mad Woman, how she'll believe anything you tell her. Go along then, take advantage! It'll be such great fun.

Nicolai turns abruptly on heel and walks away. I suspect I've disappointed him so thoroughly that he's done with me, but he only goes a half-dozen steps before he calls, "Coming, Miss LaRoche?"

I force my heavy legs to trudge after him. "Where are we going?"

"I don't know about you, but I'm feeling like a balloon ride."

* *

"This is a waste of time," I grumble. We're gathered with other prospective riders on the lawn near the watchmaker's shop, where a broad swath has been cleared for the baskets and balloons to settle. We've already dithered away an hour in line, and it's nearly our turn. But I doubt that the loft of a balloon will raise my spirits.

"If I didn't know better, Miss LaRoche, I might think you were nervous of flying," Nicolai teases. He's wearing a funny masque snatched from a vendor, a plastic imitation of the one he wore in the Menagerie but this time in lurid pink, and I might've laughed if my mood wasn't so sour.

"I'm not nervous." Contrarily, my hands fidget at my sides. "Eager to solve the clue, is all." And eager for a chance to mull over the portraits with all the familiar faces, but I don't tell him that yet. I haven't sorted it all the way out for myself.

"Forget the clue." Nicolai pays it no more respect than a botched dinner party. "If nothing else, you need to relax for a bit. Change your perspective, see the world around you in a different light. We've been searching down the same roads for two days. I'd say a new outlook is welcome."

"Easy enough for you to say." But of course, it's no easier for him than for me. He needs me to solve this riddle, too.

A laughing couple exits the basket ahead of us, and it's our turn. Suddenly, I balk. I shake my head. Until this moment, it hasn't occurred to me that maybe I *am* nervous of flying. It's not something that's done on Barrow Island, where we're all meant to keep our feet firmly planted and our heads *out* of the clouds.

"Don't be afraid." Nicolai offers his hand. "Tessa, I have power beyond your imagination. I won't let you fall."

I consider that outstretched hand, then the line of his jaw. He isn't smirking or laughing at me behind that mask. I take a deep breath, introduce steel to my spine, and take his hand. He escorts me into the carriage like a true gentleman, and as the fire flourishes above us and heat puffs into the enormous balloon, I gulp. "You're absolutely certain this is safe?"

"Absolutely, no," he chuckles, and I glare daggers until he amends, "but what's life without a bit of risk?"

"Oh, risk!" I mutter. "You Deathless and your risk. If I lived as carelessly as you do, I'd be back in the Splendor House already."

His thumb chafes my knuckles. Until now, I hadn't realized he still held my hand, it felt so oddly natural. "And that's what you fear more than anything. Being sent back there."

"I don't want to seem odd to anyone."

Nicolai tugs me down to sit on the hip-high bench that girdles the basket and hangs his masque from his belt. "There are worse things to be than odd. You could be cruel. Vindictive. Loveless."

I'm embarrassed that I've never considered that before. I ponder as the balloon expands and expands and then, all at once, we are weightless. We are beginning to float. I grab onto the edge of the wicker, and Nicolai chuckles and squeezes my hand. Perhaps that's why he's still holding it—he fears I'll make a daring break from the basket and fling myself back to safety. But my legs have puddled and there would be no moving me now, even if the basket caught fire.

Up and up we climb. The wind is both hotter with the flames and colder as we rise. I shiver, then relax, then shiver again. Nicolai removes his jacket and offers it, and I slip into it, too miserable to be stubborn. My stomach feels like a jagged hollow with all the good things scooped out of the middle.

"Nicolai," I say as the treetops fall away, "about the clue…"

He presses a finger swiftly to my lips. "No talk of that. Just float tonight."

I consider licking his finger to disgust him with my mortal slobber, but think better of it. We both grip the bench now, our hands close but not quite touching, and I'm startled to find myself yearning that he'll take mine again.

It was nice. Like the tether that holds this balloon, it made me feel grounded.

We reach the end of the rope and bob gently in place. I peek out and see that we float in a sea of balloons just like ours, speckled, spotted, and striped, some baring the Circus's name in bold script, some depicting the Big Top events. We're like the lanterns that Barrow Island casts off over the water to usher in the tourist season at the start of every summer—a spectacle that's visible from the mainland, a silky stream of pink-and-gold at the horizon that beckons them to us, and to the Rifts.

I fold my arms on the basket and rest my cheek with a sigh. Are we islanders really any different from the Deathless? We profit from the tourism at the Rifts, from those who go into the Circus to fritter away what's most precious. We take their money for trinkets and board just as the Circus takes their lives.

Nicolai stands and stretches, then beckons me. "May I show you something?"

I'm not certain what there is to see with a thick shawl of fog curling around us now, but I follow him to the opposite edge of the basket. At this height, I can barely see the other balloons anymore, their dim forms weaving in the mist like gravestones in a boneyard. It's peaceful, but eerie.

Beside me, Nicolai's uneven smirk is back. With a flick of his hand, the fog disperses, and suddenly I can see *everything*.

Beyond the boundaries of the city that is the Circus, the Mirror Lands lay open around us. Rolling fern-green hills and lapis lakes give way to flint mountains crowned in periwinkle snow. The Fey Woods, bisected by a glittering jade river, twist away into the distance. Wildflower meadows and fish hatcheries dot the terrain, circling around the remote shards of egg-white, ruby, and marigold cities that jut from the fertile landscape.

Tears sting my eyes, and not just from the wind. The height doesn't bother me at all. It isn't fear that fills me, but instead a fathomless melancholy, and a yearning so intense it lifts me to the tips of my toes, fingers wrapped around the thick edge of the basket. I've never climbed so high before, and yet...I feel as if I have. As if I was born of the sky itself, looking out from these lofty heights. As if I could take wing and soar from this basket and out across those wild lands.

"Marvelous, isn't it?" Nicolai's tone is distractingly soft. He is watching me, not the world around us. "It's where Corriene and Mirabelle's folk are from. It's a world I've never seen, since I'm tethered to this Circus. But I think that to explore it would be a great adventure. Don't you agree?"

Adventure. Oh, how that word bursts and clamors through me, like a song I've known all my life but forgotten its tune until just now. "You've never ventured across the Mirror Lands? Not in a century?"

Nicolai's brow folds, the softness extinguished as he leans against the edge of the basket beside me. "Remember, I wasn't Mirror Folk before. I came from your land. From Barrow Island."

Naturally. A century ago, before the riots, before the protests, it wasn't considered so odd for islanders to journey through the Rifts. "Why did you come here?"

"I had siblings," he says, "William, Nathan, George, Alice and Lola. Four were younger than me. William and I saw to their upbringing after one of those old plagues took our parents."

I shudder. I've read of those plagues in the books at the Splendor House. A hundred years ago, they carved the population of Barrow Island down by half.

"William and I worked, but then he fell ill. Again, the plague." Nicolai's eyes are glazed with unhappy memories. "I couldn't support all of us. We were starving. And then one of the Deathless recruited me…he saw how we were suffering, and offered me a game. A cure for my brother in exchange for a year of my life to play. So I went."

Part of me wants to beg him to skip to the end of the story, to know if it will be happy or tragic. But he is here, and he has such a look on his face that I think I already know the answer.

"It should have been one game, and that was the end. But for a vagrant who discovered he had a talent with his hands, one game was all it took," Nicolai says. "I stayed, and I kept earning things to send back to my brothers and sisters, until one day I realized I'd spent a large portion of my years at the booths. Too many. I was desperate, and that was when Libertine trapped me."

Libertine. How I wish I'd had the gall to punch him in his smug face, for both our sakes. "He convinced you to take the trials."

"I was a bit of an easy sell, just like before. My plan was to wish for immortality for all of us. Then we could do what we'd always dreamed: travel and explore both Lands to our hearts' content, never dying, never fearing poverty or sickness or starvation." He shakes his head. "I thought I had the perfect plan. But after I made the wish, they told me that my family was already dead. The plague. The only one who was immortal was me. And they don't tell you that the price for immortality is that only Deathless are immortal, and Deathless always serve the Circus."

So he is trapped, just like the Menagerie folk, only Nicolai's subjugation is a leash rather than a cage. He can travel through the Rifts to recruit humans, just as they recruited him, and he can float so high and see all that he once wished to sink his hands into, the roads his feet wished to tread with his siblings beside him. But he can have none of it.

For the first time, I feel that I truly understand him: his resentment of this place. His dislike of his fellow Deathless. He has not been one of them long enough to forget his mortal dreams, or how they were stripped from him.

How sad he must be. How lonely.

"Where on Barrow Island did you live?" I ask.

"Bleeker Street. In the Downs. It's the one that always smells of fish and hardtack."

"I know it!" Surprise raises my voice. "Nan used to buy fish bones for broth from Mister Cortese there."

Nicolai hangs his head with a dramatic groan. "Cortese! Haggling with him to buy and filet our fish was more dangerous than anything in this Circus. He's still in business?"

I laugh at his morose tone, as if he wished death on that skinflint fish-butcher. "Well, it must be his son who runs it now, after all this time."

"I doubt it. Old Cortese was too vindictive to die. He would easily live past one hundred just to make Bleeker Street a more miserable place."

"It's not so bad. There's still the bakery there."

"The one with the pecan muffins?"

"The same!"

We share a deep sniff and then laugh, as if we can both catch a whiff of those delectable treats, and Nicolai's smile is genuine and broad as he stares into the Mirror Lands again. I feel as if I've given him back something precious that the Circus stole away.

"Do you still miss your family very much?" I ask.

"I do. Sometimes I still dream of them, even." Nicolai casts a glance my way. "And you, Miss LaRoche? What adventures do you dream of?"

"Oh, I don't. Adventuring! I can scarcely hold a job."

Nicolai frowns. "Then the breadth of the world doesn't intrigue you? Haven't you ever longed to go where mortal feet have never trod?"

Wild laughter bursts from my lips. I want him to stop talking, but I'm not certain precisely why. "I have quite enough to manage with the Morrow Daily, and my apartment, and Missus Fiona! Why would I ever want to complicate my already-complicated life even further? Grand aspirations leave you dead, or mad, or Riftless."

Nicolai straightens up slightly. "Riftless? What is that?"

Now I've gone and said it. I fold my arms on the basket's edge and look down at the soft periwinkle and blush of the trees that dot the park. "Riftless are mortals who disagreed with the Accord. They used to hold peaceful protests and demonstrations near the Rifts. It was all very orderly back when my parents joined."

Nicolai shows no surprise at this. "Your parents were Riftless?"

"They felt that we should have no relations to the Mirror Lands at all. They would go to every possible protest, sometimes ones at separate ends of the city on the same night. They were hardly ever home, so Nan raised me most of the time. We would listen to the radio to hear how the protests went. I think I was five, perhaps six, when things started to turn violent."

"Things often do."

I nod. "The Riftless felt their voices weren't being heard, so they shouted louder. Then they threw stones at buildings. Then they burned things." I rest my chin on my arm. Of all my remaining memories, this time is one of the clearest. "Nan tried to talk sense into my parents. She reminded them that they had me to think of, but they insisted that was why they protested: so that I could grow up in a world where Deathless weren't propositioning me for the Circus. In the end, all they gave me was a world where I didn't have parents."

Nicolai shifts closer, our arms nearly touching on the basket's edge. "What became of them?"

"A struggle broke out between the night watch and the Riftless mob, Nan said. They fought when they should have run."

"I'm sorry, Tessa."

"I hardly remember them, and not just because of the Splendor House. It was Nan who raised me. It's Nan I remember the most."

Nicolai is silent, and waits. And perhaps that plum is still working its dark designs on me because I blurt out, "Nan warned me all about you. About how whimsical and vicious Deathless were, and how I must never, ever go through a Rift, or go to the Circus, *ever*. But when I was still just a child, she was the one who went away. She left me to come *here*, to gamble for money so that we wouldn't lose our house. And she never came home."

Nicolai's eyes dart to me. "And what became of you when the house was gone?"

"I don't remember. Something else the Splendor House took away from me. It's all haze and fog until I woke up there, two years ago."

Nicolai rocks back, spreads his hands on the rim of the basket, and leans his weight into them. Somehow, I think he's angry, but not at me. It's flattering to consider he might be furious on my behalf, at all the people who chose something else over me. "Look at us: coinless orphans given the chance for everything. But can we take it—and will we?"

"All I want is my necklace." But even as I say it, I know it isn't true. I've already considered otherwise, the night Nicolai left me alone. And from this height, with the world spread out below me...

What if I could *have* more, and not only dream of it? Adventure seemed silly when he first mentioned it, but there is so much to see, so much more than impoverished streets and dark alleys that seethe with murder and worse. There is magic and power and Lands beyond reckoning, and I feel suddenly as if I've wanted them my whole life. As if I've never wanted anything quite as much as I want *this*.

"If you could travel anywhere," I ask, "where would it be?"

Nicolai's stiff posture loosens like I've given him an answer, not a question. He sinks down again, pushing up his sleeves to the elbows. I have never found a man's forearms particularly worth the attention, but Nicolai has a worker's physique, like the fishers at Barrow Docks. I think I even spy the tiny, telltale pimpled scars where fishhooks found their mark. The thought of dignified and mysterious Nicolai cursing and peeling barbs from his skin while his older brother bellylaughs nearby almost sends me into a fit of giggles myself.

"The Horn Mountains." He gives a nod to the blue-capped peaks. "They're said to hold legendary gem quarries and old treasure hoards from ancient Fey wars."

I slip my arm further up into the sleeve of his jacket so that I can whap him with the empty cuff. "Nicolai, really? Treasure and gems, is that all you're after?"

He tucks sinuously away from the blow, chuckling. "What do you expect from the poor son of plague victims? Notions of prosperity consumed me once, and the hunt for treasure is really just the same, but with a more dashing flare."

I pull a face. "Hardly dashing."

There is real humor in Nicolai's laughter now. "The Deathless ought to fear the whip of your tongue as much as your mind. You're an extraordinary woman, Miss LaRoche."

Heat storms my cheeks. I look away from him. "I assure you, there's nothing beyond ordinary about me at all."

Suddenly his fingers are on my jaw, gentle but insistent, turning my head back toward him. "It's all right to be something other than ordinary, Tessa. It will not condemn you in this place. Everyone's a bit mad who works the Circus. What makes you unique is not that…it's everything else about you."

I'm struck by the nearness of his lips. I can feel his breath on my nose like a secret when he speaks, and for a fleeting instant I wonder what would happen if I conquered those few inches. If I was so bold.

Nicolai drops his hand, and the moment dispels. I withdraw, tongue-tied with shyness, but unable to forget what he's said—or the sincerity of his tone. I prop my elbows back on the basket's edge and peer down at the Circus. "Do you really, truly believe my madness doesn't make me…you know."

"Worthless?" Nicolai says it without force, yet still I shudder. "Miss LaRoche, nothing you are and nothing you have done devalues you. I suggest you don't devalue yourself."

I only half-hear him. My eyes have taken dominance over my ears, filling my brain with a whir of shock as I stare at the Circus. And stare, and stare.

"Nicolai." I grip his arm, tugging him so hard into my corner of the basket that the golden sheen of his power heats the air around us. "Do you see that?"

He braces one hand on each angle of the basket, folding me between the cornered sides and his chest as he follows my wild pointing. And I know he sees it when he catches his breath.

From this height, the Circus is visible from fenced edge to fenced edge—only they aren't edges so much as curves. The sweep of the city is a full circle, and at the center is the carousel, a bright white blot amid the park's thick coat of autumn trees. Directly above it, a glittering moonstone path wends away toward the upper curve of the Circus.

"Like the center of a clock, pointing at twelve." My face practically tingles with excitement.

Nicolai points to the right of the carousel, following a faint thread of pumpkin lights that curl through the trees. "Would you say that resembles the right arm of said clock?"

"I certainly would." I smooth my front and swallow hard. "We should go."

"And you should dress in something warmer," Nicolai's tone is suddenly grim, "for your next test."

CHAPTER FOURTEEN

J choose the silver dress. It seems navigable but refined, a fitting match to the atmosphere of the park as we maneuver between its broad oaks and weeping willows on our way toward the slender radiance of the lights. I've returned Nicolai's jacket and donned my own, the sleek black thing that clenches at my throat and hangs just below my breasts, with long, ruffled sleeves. Perhaps it's mismatched, but I feel safer in its embrace, and it keeps away the chill of full night that's descended across the Circus.

The lights pulse hotter as we approach, and though they're encased in glass bulbs I feel as if I'm walking toward a furnace. Sweat gathers across my clavicles and in my ringlets, and I slow. "Do you know what this will be?"

"I've never seen anything like it." Nicolai takes my arm, the tightness of his grip betraying how much that upsets him. He pulls me suddenly off to the side, behind a colonnade of trees so broad that three men couldn't wrap their arms around one. He backs me into the smooth bark, resting one hand next to my head. "I can't risk any nearer, but I'll be close by. Be careful, Miss LaRoche."

I square my shoulders and tug up my hair, letting my neck breathe. "Yes, of course."

"Tessa," he adds as I slip under his arm. "Remember that you're far braver than you realize. Whatever this is, it's no match for you."

I want to ask him how he can be so confident in me, but I don't think I want to compromise the moment. His faith feeds my own as I button the clasp at my throat and press my skirt flat to my thighs, striding toward the haze of squash and daffodil ambiance.

The voices reach me first—many raised in chatter, sunbursts of radiant laughter tearing through the shawl of uncertainty that hangs above me. I find myself rushing, drawn to that ethereal sound like a drowning sailor to the wink of sunlight on the wavecaps. I surface.

And oh, I know I'm not a sailor, but a moth tricked to the fire.

A long table extends before me, decked in a flawless chiffon-white cloth and heaped to the uttermost with food: whole suckling pig with a candy-coated apple in its mouth; tureens of vegetables dressed in rich balsamic glaze; savory lilac custards that jiggle in their porcelain settings as if sharing in the jokes. Towers of rainbow fruit, decanters of brandy, water, and wine, and scores of potatoes line the table's spine, all the way to the desserts: three-tiered trays of decadent chocolate mousse pies, heart-shaped tarts, and tiny cakes in frilly pink cups dusted with crushed almonds and peppermint stalks.

There must be more—my nose twitches and my mouth weeps with hunger at the smells warring for my attention—but I cannot overlook the guests. Under the crisscrossing ropes of globe lights that drip like overripe apricots and oranges through the leaves, they lean elbows on the table and laugh as if all the world is a great joke. And I suppose to them, it is.

This is a banquet of Deathless, and I fear I may be the main course.

I step back and slam into a soft belly. Spongy, hot fingers clamp my arms, and the succulent sweet smell of Lord Mull chokes me.

"Welcome, Madame Mystery!" His booming voice traps me as surely as his hands. "Welcome to the Feast of Fools."

All talk stops. All eyes turn to me, and I wish to melt into the autumn-cursed grass and trickle away. My cheeks flame and I find it's quite a contrary experience to the moment Nicolai and I shared in the balloon tonight.

I should not be thinking of Nicolai. I tell myself to only think of the test as Lord Mull marches me past seat after seat, toward the head of the table. I catch flickers of familiar faces, including the women who conducted my previous tests. Madame Rouge seems enigmatic as ever, but Mistress Luck wears a scowl suggesting she fully expected to be my downfall—and is sore that she failed.

I ponder for just a moment. Then I offer a slight wiggle of my fingers to prove I've seen her and won't be cowed. Her glare, if possible, sours even further, and I'm truly shocked by the spurt of satisfaction it gives me.

As usual, the Circus is quick to remind me that there is no victory without imminent challenge. Lord Mull pulls out a chair seemingly at random—there are several empty at the table—and seats me across from none other than Libertine. He smiles at me, all sharp teeth. The scoundrel. He could have just told me where to meet him, instead of sending me up in the balloon.

Though I find I don't really regret that small adventure at all. A great weight feels as if it lifted from me when I told someone other than Missus Fiona about my sordid family history. Someone who didn't simply nod and say "Mm-hmm" and take clinical notes as the truths poured out of me.

"Madame Mystery, I see you found your way." Libertine's voice has lost its provocative purr, and there is new metal minting his eyes. It's a strange look he gives me, and I discreetly check that I'm appropriately dressed. But for once my instincts have served me: everyone is decked in their supper finest, very like the richest of Barrow Island in their rooftop restaurants where we of the poorer sect could only spy on them from below. I think if their meals were anything like as sharp and strung with feelings of doubt as this one, I was missing out on very little. But Libertine still gazes at me with that crouched-wildcat-boldness, and I feel the same urge to strike back at him as I did at Luck.

"Yes, I did. Your insight was very astute." I raise my voice slightly to be heard by those nearest. "And you asked for so small a price...one would almost think you gave it away like a lust-struck fool."

I bat my lashes and wonder if I've finally gone completely insane. But it's hard to consider that a terrible thing when the shock on Libertine's face is easily the most sublime morsel at the entire table.

A few of the Deathless have stopped conversing and look at us with new interest. Libertine rallies below their scrutiny with an ease I wish I had. Then he rises and bows. "If you'll excuse me, I have something to attend to."

I'm almost sad when he goes. Much as he terrified me at the beginning, I've given him enough of my headspace, wondering if he was the thief and murderer, that he intimidates me less now than the unfamiliar Deathless around me. Lord Mull sits on my left, a dark-skinned man on my right. They talk around me as if I'm invisible and somehow that's worse than trying to invent table conversation with them.

I'm momentarily relieved when a woman rises from the head chair, but then the look of her sends fear tingling across my body. She is wicked as a serrated blade, dressed in a backless black dress with severe straps across the bodice that complement the deep tan of her skin. Her salt-and-pepper hair is drawn into an equally-stern bun, as if not a thread would *dare* straggle beyond her control. Her slate eyes take in the table and settle on me with the disdain of a head of household observing a dog someone invited to her stately banquet.

If Missus Fiona and Mister Metters melded into one person with all the shared pity and condescension they hold for me, it would be this woman.

She waits for me to look away, and when I finally relent to the cold stab of her stare, she lifts her crystal goblet and clinks it with her fork. Immediate silence wraps the table as all turn expectantly toward her.

"Welcome, all, to Madame Maligna's Feast of Fools." The simmer of her stare suggests I am not counted among the *all* who are welcome at her table. "Here, you are invited to—"

"Wait!"

The sudden cry earns a dour look that could melt metal as Madame Maligna's grand speech is aborted. We all look to the end of the table as the trees and foliage rustle there, and Libertine makes his return.

He is not alone. I don't know how it's possible, but he is leading Nicolai.

CHAPTER FIFTEEN

*D*elightfully unexpected, isn't it?" Libertine's recovered that booming sensationalism that first beckoned me to the rostrum. "I found him wandering about in the park. It seems someone is feeling a bit left out of the fun and good fare! So I thought, why not invite him to the spectacle?"

His pointed look gives me the hair-raising sense that he already knew Nicolai was nearby and sought him out specifically to humiliate me after my sly remark about the hint. Regret rakes pinpricks down my cheeks as Libertine returns to his seat. Hands in pockets, casual as anything, Nicolai follows him. His eyes don't even find mine as he settles into a chair three down and across from me. Meanwhile, I must fight not to stare at him.

"As I was saying before that interruption," Madame Maligna growls, "here you are invited to partake of the offering before you. Eat and drink to your heart's content. The meal is an impartial judge. It will take those of worthless constitution and leave those whose strength is true."

Again, that pointed look. But now I feel a steady stare from the other side—from Nicolai. It's my own hands I look at, not because I can't bear their eyes but because it strikes me suddenly that finding this clandestine banquet was not the test. I still must survive what the clue called *those who would do me harm.*

The air ripples with sudden, unseasonable heat, and the pocket of my dress grows unbearably warm. I pull out the cardstock only to see there is a new engraving on the back, embedded in swirls of thick golden power:

Don't eat. Poison.

I glance swiftly at Nicolai. He appears by all accounts unbothered with my very existence, but he twirls and chafes at that one unruly curl. I turn my attention back to the card as my heart thumps in havoc.

Here you sit with death itself

And raise a toast to your good health

Of course the dishes are poisoned.

"Well, what are all of you waiting for?" Maligna snaps. "Is my food below your impressive tastes? Eat, or leave!"

Cutlery clatters. The chatter rises. Portions are sawed and scooped from wholes, and I decide to wait and see what lies untouched so that I know what I can eat. But to my dismay, in mere moments there is not a single platter that hasn't been plucked over. Either the Deathless are impervious to their own poisons or they are taking poisoned food onto their plates to confuse me.

I sit back and fold my arms. If it's all poisoned, I'll eat none of it, I suppose. But Madame Maligna thwarts that notion when she notices my empty plate.

"You must all eat *something*." Her uncompromising tone leaves no question that this isn't a matter of her pride. It's part of the test.

Twittering numbness clenches the back of my neck and flushes down my arms and sides. I take a bit of this and that and sniff it, but it all smells delicious and my tongue cleaves to my teeth with desire. I look to the least-appetizing offering on the table—a peacock-green gelatin mold—and glance at Nicolai for a hint. But he's discussing something with the Deathless on his left, leaving his own portion untouched.

I hear chewing all around me. They *must* be eating, but in such quick snatches I have no hope of seeing what untainted fare passes their jaws. My stomach grumbles like distant thunder, and Lord Mull laughs and passes me a meat pie. I have the brilliant notion to fritter off pieces of it from my plate onto the grass.

This only serves until I catch Madame Maligna glowering at me, and then my portion piles back up to normal size.

Frustrated, I reach for a decanter of water. Nicolai reaches at the same time, and our fingers touch. The golden flare of his power travels straight down into my bones, and I meet his eyes. They hold mine with an intensity that seems to slow time beneath this second arm of the imagined clock. And in that heartbeat's pause, I think of the rest of the clue.

Those who flinch would do you harm.

I withdraw my hand. Nicolai takes the decanter and pours. I stare and stare as my mind tumbles all over itself.

Why would the Deathless flinch but if the poison could harm them, too? They take a great risk to threaten me. If I must eat, I must learn what food is untainted. And the clue suggests that to do *that*, I must make the Deathless' own fear of poison betray them.

But how? It's not as if I can spoon-feed Lord Mull. Perhaps I could start a food-fight, but there are several problems with that: it would be ridiculous, for one, and I might catch some tainted food to the mouth for another, or Madame Maligna might dive across the table and throttle me for ruining her banquet.

Then again, it's not that I must make them eat. I must only make them flinch. Flinching, as I've often experienced of late, is an involuntary reaction to fear or shame. So I must make them fear, and then whatever they flinch from must be poisoned. Whatever doesn't frighten them, I can eat.

Now, then…how to strike fear into the most terrifying creatures I've ever met, without giving away my plan in such a way as to make them flinch *voluntarily*?

Almost as soon as I wonder, I have a thought. But my own mind rebels from it, and reminds me I mustn't do this ridiculous, mad thing. I can already feel Missus Fiona peering from the undergrowth, pen raised to document my lunacy.

But no. Missus Fiona is not here. There is me, and there is Nicolai, and if I don't carry out this plot, one or both of us may be poisoned and dead before dawn. And it startles me to realize that equally as devastating as the thought of my own death by poisoning is the notion of watching it take him.

There are worse things to be than odd. I could be cruel and wait for the poison to take Nicolai so that I know what not to eat.

I could also be dead. That would certainly be worse.

I take in several wobbly breaths. I seize for my courage as I push back my chair. Every eye jumps to me at once, and the conversation ends so abruptly that I know it was all for show, anyway. Just another part of the ruse to make me believe I'd come to a banquet, not a final supper. Deathless power fumes out and lulls the insects and nightbirds to slumber in a hedge that will keep me from running, as if that's what they expect I will do. Uncanny, absolute silence washes from the shadowed crevices between the trees and gulps at the fringes of my resolve. I waver.

Then I press my fingernails into my scabbed palm. I look at Nicolai and I force myself to remember what he said tonight, about oddness and madness and what he believes I am. What it seems no one else does.

But perhaps…perhaps I'm beginning to.

Then I grip my skirts, step up onto my seat and then the table. And to the evident horror in Madame Maligna's bulging eyes, I begin to dance.

It's the only thing I can think of that won't give my plot away, and it's nothing at all like dancing at the Menagerie. Much more jigging, twirling, and hopping, like the times I would dance on the wooden bench at Nan's table instead of eating. I can feel the whimsical fingers of those daydreaming days covering mine, rucking up my skirts almost to the waist as I plant each foot and spin, spin, spin. I feel so silly at first—there is no music—but somewhere halfway down the table, I notice all the prisms that gather and bounce with me, reflected among the diamonds on my dress. The hedge of power that trapped us when I stood is now a cage of color as if we are living in the very heart of a rainbow.

Unbelievably, I have turned the sickening might of the Deathless into glory.

I still twirl, and now I don't want to stop. I skip and kick my heels toward the dishes, grazing porcelain bowls worth more than my life I'm sure, and their shock-panged gazes in slack-jawed faces slowly morph from intimidating to funny. They've played this game with my life, with all mortals, but I've finally managed to stun *them* for once. All this wonder they offer, all this power and splendor they bathe in and yet it takes a mad girl in a diamond dress dancing on the table to drop their mouths open.

For once, Tessa LaRoche holds all the cards. Such a surge of confidence rolls through me, I even spread my arms as I whip along the tabletop. And that's when Libertine starts to clap—keeping time with my dancing feet—and the rest of them join in.

This is not to my benefit, I know. They're trying to steal back this moment, to make it theirs instead of mine. Fury crests in the wake of my confidence with a natural and stunning vigor, and I slam my heels and the balls of my feet into the wood, punishing it with every strike. I twist away from the beat they want me to keep, away from those grabbing Splendor House hands that want to remind me that this Tessa is useless, odd, and unlovable.

I don't care, I don't care, I don't care! My head sings the only song I need. Now that they're captivated, it's time to turn this dance in my favor again.

I drop my skirts and whirl, sending a bowl of glazed peaches skidding across the wood toward a Deathless on my right, a handsome redheaded man smiling with far too many teeth at this performance of mine. He shoves backward in his chair so hard that it wobbles on its hind feet and he barely catches it in time.

Pity. I would have enjoyed seeing him topple into the grass. But I suppose my victory will be even sweeter than that, because now I know precisely what I'm doing.

My turns become more calculated, my steps sending trays and bowls sailing toward the Deathless at random. I don't choose deliberately, so they can't possibly plan to hide their reactions. Soon the whole table is dotted with shivering winces as the Deathless try and fail to mask their disgust when the poison sails toward them.

I am a wind blowing down their middle, making them sway. My laughter sounds nasty, but I feel strangely free. As if I've already won all the tests. As if, for the first time, I've glimpsed what it will be like if—or *when*—I do.

The suckling pig is in my way, but not for long. I look down its golden back to Madame Maligna, who grips her cutlery like weapons and eyes me as if considering how to stew and serve me at her next vile feast.

I plant my bare foot against the chiseled silver platter and kick it straight down the table. Maligna slams her hands down, shoots to her feet, and catches the pig by its throat.

"Enough!" Her voice cracks with frustration. "This is a banquet, not a ballet!"

The clapping stops. I stop, not because I'm frightened, but because I see the healthy, natural juices seeping down the pig's chest where her nails pierce the crisped flesh.

I climb down from the table, unaided by anyone. I take the platter and slide it out of her reach. "Thank you for your hospitality, Madame Maligna."

Then I take the whole pig to my seat, carve off a slice of its flank, and start to eat.

They all stare at me like ravenous scavengers watching a predator with its kill. Perhaps I'll let them have the carcass when I'm done with it…or perhaps I'll slather what's left in deadly jelly and let them slobber over what could have been. But right now, I am enjoying this untainted pig's meat too much to decide.

Over its delectably-seasoned hide, I catch Nicolai's eye. If there's any hunger in his eyes, I don't think it's for the meal. His elbows are propped on the table, chin resting on his folded hands, and he smiles.

And that's when I know I've won.

* *

I'm the first to leave the table. They let me go, I think, because they really are hungry and now that I've had my way with the untainted food, they want it almost as badly as I did. I take pity at the last instant and leave the jelly off the pig. Being petty would feel nice, but solve nothing in the end.

I leave that fairytale place of hanging lights and the glittering motes of forgotten carnival wishes gathered up beneath the trees, and the sounds of them mongering over the food. The key is warm in my hand from

Maligna's sweaty grip, and with it she handed me a damp square of cardstock. I know she thought she would be the one to undo me, but I should thank her instead. There is a great bounce to my every step as I go out into the park and the darkness closes around me. It leaves me so lightheaded that I must stop, lean on the pillar of a tree, and laugh. And then I cry good tears.

So perhaps I am a terrible reporter. Perhaps I daydream too much, and I don't see through the same lens as Missus Fiona and Mister Metters and everyone else on Barrow Island. But any one of them might've failed these tests because they think the only way to be properly mortal is without a hint of Circus whimsy or a trace of oddity to confound the realism of life.

I've tasted both—madness, and their stuffy way of being—and I realize that Nicolai is right. I would rather be odd than wicked. I would rather be a bit strange than make a girl fear every day of her life to be unordinary. And I wouldn't ever put women in clean white jackets and solitary rooms simply because they dared to see things differently. I know my own mind, and I think it is not something to be feared or reviled or fixed.

I am not broken because of how I perceive the world. And tonight, I think I've proved it.

I'm still reclining and smiling when the shadows part again, ushering Nicolai through. Soft autumn leaves are woven into his hair, and he knocks them away. "Quite the production tonight. That was brilliant…they never saw it coming."

I grin like an absolute goof. "I suppose they're unfamiliar with that particular sort of madness."

He smiles and leans against the tree as well. "Miss LaRoche, if that was madness, it was of the highest form."

"Don't think I'm being morose! In fact, I can't remember ever being this happy," I beam. "You know, on Barrow Island they say that oddness ought to be stamped out. Everyone must perform for the tourists, for the good of the island. So perhaps I don't belong there. But I don't think I belonged in the Splendor House, either."

It's the first time I've ever spoken the words. They are chilled with uncertainty, yet sweet on my lips. I want to believe they're true, so I say them again.

"And what's more, I...I think whatever put me there maybe wasn't a flaw in me," I add. "It was a flaw in how people perceived me. After all, hasn't my silly, strange little mind helped me survive this place?" I spread my hands in a shrug. "So surely it can't be as faulty as they say."

"Well," Nicolai says, "you never seemed mad to me, either. Not in the way that requires reformation, anyhow."

I sigh happily through my nose in a gentle billow of mist. The weather may dance with autumn cold, but I've rarely felt so warm.

"You have the key?" Nicolai asks.

I flash it to him in my palm: a great silver thing with black wings spreading out, and a thick dark silk tie as if to hang it around the neck. "And this, too."

He frowns as I hand him the next clue. "It's always the fourth card that they give to you in person. The last two challenges are the most difficult."

I let him open the envelope, and together we lean into a shaft of moonlight so slender that our shoulders press as we strain to read:

For once look back and not ahead

To face the memory that you dread

If you survive the life you had

You'll go along...or else go mad

A blustery wind stirs fallen leaves around our ankles, and I shiver. The threat of death has taken its leave from this clue, but I'm not comforted. It feels as if the Circus was listening to our conversation just now and poses a subtle threat in this elegant scrawl: if I accept I'm not truly mad, that I never was, then the Circus is determined to make me that way.

Nicolai looks no more consolable than I. The cardstock trembles in his hand as he passes it back to me. "So. That's what they're doing."

"Do you know where this clue leads?"

"Yes." Nicolai's tone is the gravest I've ever heard. "It's the carousel."

CHAPTER SIXTEEN

I can't go to the carousel just yet. Nicolai and I decide that on my own it would have taken considerably longer to decipher the clue, since I'm not meant to know the intricate details of the Circus rides yet. But Nicolai explains that that attraction for mortals to this carousel is that its gentle spin removes bad memories at the cost of an equivalent share of time: one year's memory for one year of the person's vitality.

But this will be different. The tests always are, and this clue seems the plainest of all, a challenge rather than a riddle: I must endure my darkest memories to progress.

I choose to wait two days, but I think it is cowardice more than cleverness that drives that choice. Even in the Mortal Lands, this carousel is a legend—not the truth of it as Nicolai tells it, but the alleyway whispers: the gift of forgetting the worst of life. I chase that thought around in circles while I'm cramped up in our room at *Red & Gold's*, waiting for Nicolai to return from his Deathless duties. I even entertain the fleeting notion that I've ridden that carousel before and that's why I've forgotten everything. But I can't imagine I would have willingly given up a single memory, much less the vast spate of them that I lack now.

By the second day, I'm restless enough to start pacing again. I try to follow other thoughts down other paths, but they all return to that carousel. It's as if the power of the Circus has folded the space between here and there and I can feel its luminous two-tiered presence lurking just outside the windows, letting the eyes of the lacquered animals peer into our room as I walk circle after circle, wearing a track into the rug.

"I suppose it won't be so bad," I mumble as the sun's lazy eye drifts closed on the day. "All of my worst memories are recent, after all, I don't remember anything before the Splendor House...and I've faced those memories plenty in my, in my..."

In my nightmares. But I'm shy to tell that to Nicolai.

He's freshly returned, sprawled on my bed this time, not his. It allows a better view through the window at the triangular slit of the great blue sky. In the days since the Feast of Fools, the cold of autumn has given way abruptly to spring. I wonder if perhaps the Deathless muddled the seasons just for the autumnal appeal of the trees that one night. What vain creatures.

Nicolai sits up. "Let's take a walk, shall we?"

So we do. He wears his mask and I keep my headband as we press our way through sweltering flocks of circusgoers in floral pastels to match spring. I wonder how many of these people were wearing thick brown cardigans and gentle beige vests yesterday, and how many will wear butter yellows and bright magentas when summer pounces suddenly back onto the Circus. We mortals try so hard to blend with the magic here, yet the clash of our different habits feels corrosive.

The crowd thins with the road, until we're walking a well-tended but empty street away from the Circus proper and toward what sounds like the edge of the city closest to the lake beyond the fence. I can hear its windblown surf brushing the shore, I think.

But it isn't that. Sunset strokes a great striped structure ahead of us: not a building, but a tent as broad as a lawn and three times as high as our hostel. It's removed from the rest of the Circus by a deep moat and a rocky shore, and accessed only by a glittering silver bridge with fine curlicue stalks of bejeweled railing growing up above the height of a man. On the tent's peak flaps a lonely standard: *The Chaos Circus*, it reads in gold thread on a bloody backdrop.

It's the Big Top, The Wish Granter's domain. Seeing it for the first time fills me with belly-plunging dread such that I stop cold in my tracks, and stare. Nicolai halts ahead on the path and looks back. I expect impatience, but there is sadness in his eyes.

"Why are we here?" I ask. "I haven't gotten all the keys yet."

"But you will," he says with quiet confidence, "and I thought you should know the way, in the event something happens and you have to come alone."

I tilt my head, effectively distracted. "And where do you suppose *you'll* be in such a scenario?"

Nicolai pockets his hands and shrugs. "Here, there...the Circus may call me away. One must be prepared for all things, Miss LaRoche."

I study him, that lean frame silhouetted by the same peach-and-salmon light as the tent, and my stomach flutters with tension. "Do you doubt me now, Nicolai?"

"Never. But I've lived too long and seen too much to assume things will always go my way."

Of course, with his family's tragic past, this doesn't surprise me. He hardly expected them to be ripped away before he completed the trials. Loss has made him cautious, just as madness has made me.

I link my hand into his arm. "Well, I've seen it, but something tells me we aren't welcome across the bridge. Come away, Nicolai."

We go down to the water. It's a gentle grade to black rock and the black ring of the moat, and we sit on the shore. I kick off my flats and dip my toes into the water. Nicolai circles his knees loosely with his arms and stares up at the Big Top as if his eyes alone will unlock the last two doors and spare me the remaining tests.

The wind ruffles the water, a soothing sound. The echoes of the Circus are muffled here. I sink into the peace like a warm bath and find that outside the confinements of the room—which really felt more like a cage, like the Splendor House—my thoughts take wing and float. I'm doing just as Nicolai told me during our ride in the balloon, which is to not think of the tests. So my mind wanders down a different path, no less dark, where I've vaguely explored while he's been away both days.

"I've never seen such a horrid frown," Nicolai smirks. "Is it possible the indomitable Tessa LaRoche is having doubts of her own?"

I know he means to cheer me, but the Big Top is whispering notions to me, stirring up thoughts I've had to put aside for the sake of the tests. In this lull, they all seep back in, like water lapping gingerly into a tidepool. If I keep these ideas to myself any longer, I fear I'll burst, or run screaming down the shore. I must air them out before I finish the last trials and make my wish.

"Nicolai, I'm going to suggest something," I say. "You may listen, but no matter how impossible it sounds, you mustn't call me mad. All right?"

He half-turns toward me. "Tessa, I would never."

I believe him, perhaps more absolutely and immediately than I should. But then, I've been waiting days to ponder this with him. "I've been thinking about how much the Deathless love the Circus, like we saw at the Feast. And how you'll be in such deep trouble with them if they learn about the murders in the Mortal Lands, because you'll have put their way of life in jeopardy."

"Thank you for the reminder, I was nearly beginning to relax."

I ignore his stone-faced wit. "Well, whoever killed those people also endangered themselves, didn't they? And the Circus. Only, unlike you, they wouldn't have any real reason to do it. You're the only Deathless I've met who isn't fond of this place."

Now he's quiet, watching me closely.

I ramble on: "I've been going over all the murders in my head, and it does seem like a serial affair. But what if it's not—or at least, not the way the watchmen think it is? I've seen some pictures here and there in this Circus, images of past winners from the various games and booths, and…and some of them were murder victims on Barrow Island." I bend forward to fold my arms on my knees. "So, suppose they didn't pay the cost of their victories all at once in years and such. Suppose those weren't murders after all, but suicides. Suppose our thief, our murderer, called in old debts to the Circus and told these people to fulfill them by taking their own lives in a very, very specific way, to make it *look* like serial murder."

Nicolai slowly streaks a hand back through his hair. "Then when I'm dead…" he pauses, swallows. "When I'm dead, that Deathless would come forward with proof, somehow, that they were suicides. No one on Barrow Island would feel remorse for having wrongly put me to death for murder, they would be too proud of themselves still for getting the jump on me. Your Morrow Daily would print the story about the suicides, and the tension over a mass-murderer would evaporate."

"Relations between the Lands would smooth back out once it came to light that there was never a rogue Deathless, only a string of people hanging themselves. Barrow Island would be quick to bury their memory as madness because it looks terrible for our reputation." My voice is barely louder than a whisper. "And life would go on. Without you, and without there ever having been a murderer."

All is quiet but for the steady lap of water on the rocks below.

"That being so," I finally manage, "this is all a great game to remove you from the Circus. That's all it's ever been about. Not those people's deaths, not anything but you. Can you think of any Deathless who would go to such lengths, call in such debts from past visitors, for only that?"

Nicolai peers into the water. "Yes. Yes, I can. The Wish Granter."

My heart lunges and thuds, hitting the hitch in my throat. "The same man I'm to meet? But why?"

"I did something," Nicolai's voice is hoarse, "something that drove a wedge between us. He's not a malicious or a benevolent man, but he's the most powerful of us all, and the most dedicated to the preservation of the Chaos Circus, which is why he's the ringmaster. He could never kill me himself, that would disrupt the balance of the Circus, replace the fun with fear in the hearts of the other Deathless and make them believe he's cruel and capricious and playing with their lives. Possibly it could even turn them against him, to overthrow him and take the Circus as their own. But he *could* have me done away with like this, painted as a murderer and a betrayer of the Accord, and I think...I think he would easily call in those debts to have it done. To make me a Mortal problem, with a Mortal solution."

"What did you *do?*"

"It doesn't matter. What matters is that if you're right, which I suspect you are, then we know who has your necklace." He flashes me that lopsided smirk. "Which means you don't have to wish for a name. You can wish for the necklace back."

I stare at him. The first night he left me alone in the hostel, I might've been ecstatic to know the identity of the thief without having to waste my hard-earned wish on it. But this feels wrong to me. Nicolai is acting utterly offhand, as if the most powerful man in the Circus hasn't forced twenty mortals to kill themselves just to frame *him*. "But what are we going to *do?*

How can I beg a wish from someone who did…*that?*"

Nicolai's brow creases. "I told you, he isn't malicious. He plays by what's fair, and I suppose that for what I did, he thinks my death is the balance. He'll give you what you've won if you pass the tests. Let me deal with the trouble I started between us. I'm already trying in every way I can."

I harbored so many notions, so many whimsical thoughts of what I *might* wish for if I didn't have to have that necklace and the name of the one who stole it. But I could make a different choice now. "I could wish for your name to be cleared and the man behind these things exposed."

Nicolai turns wide eyes on me, sweet coffee depths sprinkled with sugary shock. "You would do that?"

I grip the rock and slide my heels on the smooth stone. "If we know who has my necklace, I think we can get the necklace back without wasting an entire wish. I mean, it seems such a silly thing…all this work for a *necklace.*"

"But it's important to you."

"Not more important than a life. Don't be mad."

What I don't tell him is that ever since our journey by balloon, I haven't felt that I needed my necklace quite as much. Everything it embodied is beginning to make sense without it. I've slept better these last few nights, and I find that I don't need to grip and saw at something to steady my nerves.

Perhaps I'm changing, and for the better. So perhaps I can also consider life without my necklace if it means saving someone from death.

Especially if that someone is the infuriating, charming Deathless sitting beside me.

I stretch out and stir my feet in the water. It's surprisingly warm for the season, and a faint tinge of power rides the currents below. I sigh with pleasure, and Nicolai chuckles. "Are you a swimmer, Miss LaRoche?"

I begin to shake my head, then pause with it just tilted as a memory occurs to me: "Nan took me to Barrow Beach, sometimes. I collected shells, and…I think I swam, yes. Though I don't know if I was any good."

Nicolai drums his fingers on the rock, then rises and removes his masque. "Let's find out."

I gape as he saunters down the slope of the shore. "You aren't serious!"

"Perfectly." He skins from his shirt, and I catch my breath at his toned physique. It's just not done, all this gazing at bare-torsoed men…not where I come from. But I can hardly ask him to stop, can I? He's allowed to swim if he wants to—and clearly, he does. Clad in just his dark pants, he dives straight into the water. A poignant longing brims in my chest as I watch the surf close over him. I want to be just as bold, just as carefree. I want to dive in with him.

And what's stopping me, really? Only the shackles of my own fear. But can't the girl who tackles Mirror Folk, who plays guessing games with luck and dances on tables of poison and rides the wind in a basket strung from a balloon, not have the courage also to leap into dark waters?

Brash as it seems, I'm already on my feet and stripping to the thin shift below my day-dress by the time Nicolai's head breaks the water. I wade instead of leaping, fearing the cold will come, but the flickers of power warm the moat all the way through. I shiver at the delicious, bubbly fizz of that energy, like soaking in a tub of champagne. When my feet leave the shore, I kick out more strongly than I meant to, meeting Nicolai close to the bridge's shadow. It's all darkness slathered across darkness at this time, and I can barely see the whites of his eyes. But I think they're touched by a smile as he says, "Fancy seeing you here, Madame Mystery."

"Fancy seeing *you*."

Perhaps I can hope to win a prize for the least-imaginative rebuttals in the Mirror Lands.

Nicolai treads water in place, sleeking his dark hair flat to his scalp. He's never looked so mortal, and I can imagine him looking this way after a long day at the docks with William—damp, ragged, but at home in the water. The remnants of our morbid conversation about The Wish Granter gather into his eyes, blotting out their gentle depths. I know that despite his cheery attitude, he's afraid of all that power bearing down against him. Afraid that he will have to outwit the ringmaster alone, as he's been alone for a hundred years.

I have the absurd urge to run my thumb along the dark circles below his lashes, to erase the tension that comes from knowing he's hunted. I know a bit of what it's like, after all, to have someone with power over you always watching, always calculating your movements.

"I'd like to show you something, if I may." Nicolai holds out both hands, and I'm doubly glad of the dark. It masks the contours of his body and hides the heat that climbs and climbs from my core to my hairline as I take his hands. He draws me closer, supporting us both. My toes no longer touch the bottom, but I'm not frightened by the abyss below. Not with Nicolai's steady fingers around mine.

If all life's an ocean, I think, then his touch is a harbor. My battered sails tuck in, and I feel safe in this moment, and this place, with him.

He takes my elbows next, and then slips one arm around my waist. Nothing separates our torsos but my soaked silk slip, my hands pressed to his bare chest and the water lapping halfway along my knuckles. I chuckle nervously, and he grins down at me. Mischief cuts through his eyes. "Are you ready?"

There is no hesitation before I nod.

With one strong kick, he swirls us around. With his free arm, he makes a deft cut through the air, and I feel it crystallize. A shell of glistering golden power encapsulates us, a thin web I can only see in flickers like faraway summer lightning. It rapidly shrinks until it hugs my skin.

Nicolai's arm slips even lower. He dips me, and I gasp as my head sinks under the water—and gasp, and gasp again, because the breath remains in me. This thin husk keeps out the choking force of the water.

"Another of your powers?" My voice trembles slightly.

Nicolai flashes a smile that makes me feel as if I'm drowning anyway. Then he releases me and dives. The flirt of his bare toes with the black glass surface seems like a dare. I take one last deep breath before I plunge.

The water is a clear sort of dark, like swimming through the night sky. Flickers of moonlight and dancing bubbles migrate across our path, distant stars by which Nicolai seems to chart a course. I follow him, hands brushing stalks of spiny magenta and sage vegetation that climb the splinters of rock all around us. The further we dive, the deeper the darkness, until it's truly pitch black.

And then, just as my eyes begin to adjust to the gloom, light sears my face again. At first I think it's Nicolai's power, but it doesn't carry that hot metal tang. No, I can see that he's swimming against the backdrop of great domes of stone covered in a beaming silt that awakens to glow at his touch. He spins to tap rock after rock, sending phosphorescent light cascading over the bed of the moat as if we float in the heart of the moon. It is the most enchanted thing I've ever seen, and it comes from nature in the belly of the Mirror Lands.

It's in this place that I finally understand all the horizons Nicolai wanted to explore, and all the reasons why. I never knew these things existed. Barrow Island couldn't dream of a place like this. I can fathom at last why someone would want a whole lifetime of this, would want an adventure through these power-dipped veins of a foreign Land even if it was the strangest thing to desire. I think I'm beginning to desire it, too. And now that I could wish for anything...*anything* at all...

Nicolai swims back, agile body cutting like a blade through the grainy light until he reaches me. He takes my elbows again to steady me as I turn my head wildly, drinking in the beauty on every side of us.

"What do you think of it?" he asks.

"Stunning." But that doesn't do the sight any justice.

"Yes. It is." Nicolai isn't looking at the rocks. "Consider this my apology. I'm sorry you've had to do all of this, to risk so much because of my mistakes. If it wasn't for me, you could have whatever life you wanted."

"What a silly thing to say," I laugh. "You didn't send me to the Splendor House. You didn't choose the path I walked before I came here, and not since I arrived, either. And besides...I'm beginning to want something different than I did when you first led me into this Circus."

"Oh? And what might that be?"

"Adventure. An unordinary life."

"That's two things." He slides his hands up to my biceps now. Our legs start to tangle as we tread. "What about *extraordinary* instead?"

"Are those things not the same?"

"Not in my experience. The Circus is full of unordinary things. Unordinary can become boring. But you, Tessa...you are extraordinary, and that never tires. It never becomes plain again. It is unforgettable."

My legs go still, so that he's all that's keeping me from sinking straight to the bottom.

"I mean that," he adds. "You've taught me much about perseverance, about true strength. It isn't the magic of this Circus that conveys power. Mightiness is in the smallest and weakest becoming strong. Your courage ought to be commended by mortals and immortals alike. And I admire you very much for it."

I don't think anyone has ever admired me or thought me strong. The notion is so absurd, and yet I believe it's true. I am not the crumbling scrap of paper burning to cinders after all. I am the fire itself, and I will consume anything that threatens my future and my right to choose what that will be. Whether that is Fiona or Metters or the Deathless, or anyone else.

They have no right to dictate my life. Nothing Mortal or Mirror does. I do not owe them my normalcy or conformity or complacency. I will take that power back, however I must.

I feel the grin slash across my face, burning as bright gold as the husk of Nicolai's power that keeps us breathing. I bring up my legs, press my toes into his abdomen, and kick away from him, daring with a curl of my fingers for him to chase me. And he does, and off we go, skimming our hands along the rocks and lighting a trail through the darkness at The Wish Granter's feet. We tell him and all the Lands that we are here, and we will not go quietly. And that we are not alone.

* *

It's so late that it's early by the time we climb out of the moat, bedraggled and breathless and deliriously at peace. We sprawl on the black rocks to dry ourselves, and I remove my headband and wrap it around my wrist, letting my ringlets spread on the stone. The shroud of power eases from around my body, and I can *feel* that I look like me again, the real and true Tessa. The thought doesn't frighten me as it once did.

A question occurs to me then, silly and a bit selfish perhaps, but I find it irresistible: "Nicolai, will you describe what you see when I wear this headband?"

"You wouldn't believe the sight if I told you." His tone is oddly flat, his mind clearly elsewhere. I roll toward him, propping my head on my fist, and he turns toward me. "Tessa, will you do me a kindness?"

"That depends on what sort of kindness it is."

"Whatever you see at the carousel tonight," he says, "come to me right after. Don't hesitate, let nothing delay you. I'll wait under the same trees where the Feast took place."

It's such a strange request because of how earnestly he makes it, as if everything hinges on my agreement. So I tell him that I will, and he sinks back down. But the peace is gone, if it was really ever there for him.

I can't fathom his unease as I settle onto the rock and close my eyes. I still feel as if I'm spinning through the water, a star shooting across the night, rocked in the embrace of the dark gaps between constellations.

When I wake, it's only briefly. I'm in my bed at the inn. Nicolai sits on the other, his head cradled in his hands.

I want to ask him why he's so bent, why I can see his shoulders shaking as he weeps. But the darkness has become a current, and before I can do more than slide a hand toward him, I tumble back into my black, dreamless slumber.

CHAPTER SEVENTEEN

*T*he night seems darker than usual as I make my way alone through the park, like swimming in the sky again. The moon hides its face behind clouds the same way Nicolai hid his while he wept. That image haunts me, particularly because he was nothing but his arrogant self, if quieter, when he returned at dusk from manning his attraction today. We shared a meal of poached eggs and roasted bird—I hesitate to call it quail, since nothing in the Mirror Lands is truly how it appears—and then I arrayed myself for the test. I've chosen the serrated black and red dress this time, with dark leggings and ankle-high boots in case I must move quickly.

Something tells me I will.

The park feels oddly deserted tonight. Damp, thick spirals of fog curl between the trees and skitter across the grass as I approach the two-tiered carousel, its iridescent bulk rising like a gravestone from the dense white shroud that blooms at ankle-height. It's freckled with enchanted lights on both levels, its top rim and broad middle shaft sporting great panes of glass, and a thick balloon tips the pennant pole in its middle. It's also very still, lying in wait for me. No one else is aboard.

My heart flutters as I approach the ride. There's a flavor of anticipation on the air, the same as the night when Nicolai brought me to the Circus, as if I stand on the cusp of something remarkable. Sweat dews my palms, and I wipe them hastily clean and change course slightly toward a booth off to one side. A pale woman stands there, blank-faced as a stone wall. When I halt before her, she inclines her head. "I am Madame Memoir. Are you prepared for the test?"

I almost say something witty—*as ready as I'll ever be*, or, *I was born ready*—but humor does no justice to the feeling of this night. It truly is as if I walk among a boneyard of memories, reluctant to stir the dead. For comfort, I remind myself of the peace and freedom of my swim in the moat and all the profundities I realized there. Resolve wraps my bones, and I nod.

"Then go and select a seat. You may rise if you wish once the ride is in motion. However, you may not disembark until the carousel comes to a complete stop. You must endure all of it. And you must endure with sanity intact, or I will not give you the key."

I'm not certain my heart has ever raced so hard. Beginning to feel like one of Nan's dolls with a broken, wobbly neckpiece, I nod yet again and pick my way across the damp grass to the carousel. After a moment's hesitation, I grip one of the poles and step up.

Nothing changes around me, nothing at all, and yet I feel that the carousel takes notice. I could swear all the animals—some Mortal, some Mirror—shift at once, and a murmur and sigh goes up from them. It's silly, and yet I can't shake the feeling that I'm among living things as I walk between the lacquered beasts, skimming my hands across rainbow-scaled fish, great umber bears, amber wildcats and striped antelope, and strange horned horses of shocking violet and currant-red. I'm not certain if I should sit near or far from the column of mirrors that turns the carousel. At last, I choose a slippery dolphin simply for its appealing lavender-opal shine, but when I sit, I know at once that something is wrong.

Between my knees, the animal's sides move. It is breathing.

They all are.

Suddenly, I am not seated on some fanciful carnival ride, but enmeshed in a cold grip of horror. These are living, respiring animals staked by the Circus's power to this carousel. All around me I see wild eyes darting and rolling, and I know that these are Mirror Folk and misbehaving performance animals who were impaled in service to the carousel.

The moment the great wheels of the carousel begin to grind, I stand, gripping one of the brass posts, my heart thundering and stomach queasy. I already want to be off and away, and the ride is only just now beginning, the carousel's plate-bones shifting, the column starting to turn and the mirrors flashing past one another. I swallow the heavy surge of mouth-moisture that always precedes nausea and hold on tightly as the tinny calliope music begins to whistle from deep within the body of the carousel.

Nothing comes of it at first. Two revolutions pass, and I feel as normal as one can when surrounded by bayonetted prisoner-creatures. It isn't until the third time around the circle that the mist rises and drifts, whipped up by our momentum, skimming across the carousel's floor. When the fog grazes my ankles, a sickened, choked feeling rises within me, as if it's seeping into my pores.

Something darts along the mirrors to my left, certainly not my own gently-swaying reflection. I twist to look.

I am there, looking back at me. But I'm not me, not really.

The fog chases me away almost at once, and I let out my breath. I don't know what I've just seen, this mirror-Tessa, but now I'm pressing into the crossed scars on my palm so harshly that tears spring to my eyes.

Faster and faster the carousel goes, and faster the music plays. Dizziness makes my knees swim and my mouth sweat even more. I sag against the brass pole, fighting to keep my feet as the mirrors dance and ripple beside me.

And then I look closer, and for the first time, I see my reflection while I'm wearing the headband.

I almost smile with relief. It's still me: Tessa in a dress, the same skin, the same eyes, the same freckles. Her hair is the first thing I notice that's different, even wilder than usual, not tamed the way I always wore it at the Morrow Daily. The smile on her face is changed, too—cool and confident, edged with sass and mischief under beguiling brown eyes. She looks like the sort of person you'd invite into your home only to have her steal your genuine silver cutlery. But then she'd return it, because the fun was in scaring you, not in actually having those things.

And why in the world did I think that? But I believe it's true. Even when I realize how odd a thought it is, I can't shake it.

I plant one hand on my hip, keeping the other wrapped around the pole, and the Tessa in the reflection does the same. But then, lazy and grinning, she unwraps that other arm and curls her fingers twice, beckoning me. When I don't move, she bends slightly and urges me closer with a jerk of her head.

And when I obey this time, dazzled and dizzy, the image behind her starts to shift form. The carousel's reflection vanishes. This other Tessa steps back and back again and melds into the scenery behind the glass. She turns up her gray hood, smothering her face in shadows until only that wicked smile remains.

This is me. This is the first of the memories I must confront.

And it is not a memory I recall.

CHAPTER EIGHTEEN

*J*essa LaRoche walks the streets of Barrow Downs, gray hood cast up to hide a smile so knife-sharp, she'd be collared for illegal weaponry if the night watch caught her. But that stride suggests she's not afraid of them, or of anything else. Her gait sways with the easy confidence of a woman who can survive anything, but she can hardly be older than seventeen. Ill lime and maroon hues paint her skin as she approaches a Rift, and she doesn't hesitate. She walks directly into it.

Tessa follows the flood of people through the heart of the Chaos Circus. Hood laid back, she drinks in the sight with wide-eyed wonder and a smirk to devastate. She moves with purpose through the fog, to the tent-spotted plaza and one in particular where no one else goes. She enters its dim confines where a man sits at a high table, laying out a deck of playing cards. She swings her legs casually over the guest's bench and leans her elbow on the wood. "I've heard all about how this is done. The person touches your hand, and you show them the future. That's all it is?"

"Hardly. Glimpsing the future comes with a price."

"Most things in this Circus do. Well, I'll play your game, Lord Harlequin," she says with a seasoned gambler's drawl. "But I'll name my own price. When I beat you, I want to know how to become immortal."

The man raises coffee-dark eyes to her. "No one wins my game, Miss—?"

"LaRoche. And don't worry, I'm used to shocking and amazing people just like you, the future-seer and fortune-teller. You were recruited from Barrow Island less than a century ago. Your act is to peer into the future, but by seeing it, you've already changed it. Go ahead and look at mine, if you dare. I promise it will surprise you."

Lord Harlequin lays back his tasseled dark hood. But he isn't Lord Harlequin.

He's Nicolai.

A dark room, backlit by a stage light. Tessa sprawls on a settee, arms folded behind her head, eyes closed. Lord Harlequin sits on a chaise across from her, brow furrowed in a familiar look of confusion. "Tell me how you did it. How you evaded my foresight. Why couldn't I see your future? That has never happened once in a hundred years."

"Perhaps your gift isn't as strong as you think it is, Lord Harlequin."

He blows out a frustrated breath. "Are you still here just to torment me?"

"I've told you, I'm studying the rides. Once I'm ready, I'll pass the tests you told me about."

"Such brazenness. You intrigue me, Miss LaRoche."

"Likewise. That's how I was able to beat you, after all. I've done my research. I know all about your Circus and its players—Maligna, Rouge, Lore, even Dread, and that Wish Granter. I just need to learn how to beat them."

I can feel myself running now, my legs unlocking, I'm dashing along the twisting carousel as I chase the next vision through the mirrors, this impossible, inaccurate portrayal of my life, as if I lived any of this, as if these memories could possibly be true...

Tessa sprawls in Moe's lavish parlor, snacking on a feast of cakes, her legs kicked out across the tailor's lap. Moe helps herself to tea and biscuits and they laugh at some joke about the Mortal Lands. The ease of their friendship is impossible to deny. Tessa wears Moe's designs, wears her threads with pride and pomp. Her hair is longer now—time has passed. She possesses an ease that the Circus seems to take note of.

It wants her, but it's never truly had her.

Tessa and Nicolai perch atop one of the balloon carriages of the great wheel. They share a box of peanut butter truffles and look up at the stars.

"Strange," Nicolai says. "I've never met anyone else so keen on adventure. Especially not from Barrow Island."

Tessa shrugs. "My parents are dead. Nan abandoned me. What reason do I have to stay in one place when there are two enormous Lands to explore, with places no one else has ever been?"

"Then you aren't interested in holding a job, like most mortals."

She laughs. "Who has the *time?* I know how to scrounge for meals, and I haven't had a roof over my head in years. I prefer a life with nothing to tether me down. There's so much to explore that you couldn't go everywhere, not in one mortal lifetime."

"And that's what you want. To go everywhere."

She pops a truffle into her mouth. "To see *everything.*"

"So did I, but not without my siblings. It's an intriguing life, but lonely, adventuring across the Mortal and Mirror Lands on your own."

Tessa stuffs the truffle into her cheek and eyes him sideways. "It wouldn't be if I found someone who loves adventure as much as I do. Someone to share it with."

Tessa strolls through the Circus, munching on candy floss, eyes tracing the spin of the great wheel, the revolution of the swings. Beside her, Nicolai crunches an apple, his posture more relaxed than before. There's an easy intimacy to how close they walk. In between bites, they're discussing things—Barrow Downs, Nicolai's siblings, Nan, and Tessa's mother and father.

"When will you go back?" Nicolai doesn't sound as if he wants her to go.

"When are you going to say you want me to stay?" Tessa bats her lashes at him, then laughs. "I'm only teasing, Nic."

"And if I did say it?"

She halts, licking floss from her fingertips as she studies his face. "Then I would reply that I could wait a bit longer to go. There's so much to see here, after all. So much to explore, so many adventures to have. There's a thousand things I haven't experienced yet, but I will. Once I'm immortal."

Hand in hand, Nicolai and Tessa look out from the basket of the floating balloon across the endless expanse of the Mirror Lands at dawn. Their silence is just as easy as their conversations have been. It's clearly not the first time they've done this. And they're both smiling, perfectly at ease.

They're waiting for something.

And that's when the sun rises in full, arrayed with a great burst of gold and streamers of pastel pinks and yellows, and Tessa sighs with pleasure. "Mirror sunrises are so much better than Mortal ones."

Nicolai laughs, and turns to her, offering a small black box. She takes it with a grin and opens it, and out comes a fine silver chain and a perfect balloon pendant.

"So you'll always remember this place, whenever and wherever you go," Nicolai says, "and remember what you told me about how it's better if our Lands think we're strange than cruel."

"I don't think I've owned anything this fine since I started to live on the streets," she admits. "Thank you, Nic."

He clasps it around her throat and presses his lips to the column of her neck. It raises all the miniscule hairs on my nape now just as it did back then.

"Speaking of going places, I have an idea," Tessa says. "And you're going to love it."

They're in the usual room at *Red & Gold's*. They're shouting at one another.

"Just because it's never been done before doesn't mean *we* can't do it!"

"I am telling you, Tessa, it's too dangerous. Two people completing the tests together, one of them Deathless—the Circus won't like it. It won't allow it."

"So, you're afraid. Afraid to take the risk. Or maybe you never wanted to leave this place with me. Perhaps the great Lord Harlequin just can't fathom spending an eternity exploring the Lands with a girl from the gutters," she spits. "Well, I'm going to do it anyway, and I'll become immortal like I always wanted, and I'll spend the rest of forever haunting you, you spineless, ungrateful, unfathomable bastard!"

"I wish you would! I just relish the thought of enduring your horrendous eating habits, your taunts and insults, matching wits with you for an eternity, and your clever mouth—"

Tessa steps up to him, chest-to-chest, as close as the night we swam in the moat. "What *about* my mouth, Nicolai?"

He grips her chin. "You know damned well *what*."

"Then do something about it."

And he does.

I nearly tumble to my knees as the force of that kiss blows through me, mist and hot wind spiraling together. I can feel the bruises on my lips afterward, I can taste the gold dust that littered my tongue and numbed my mouth wherever his touched—

I drag myself up the golden stairs to the second level, chasing the memories as they swivel around the column of glass.

"You want to do *what?*" Moe grates out.

"We have it all sorted." Tessa sits on Nicolai's knees on Moe's chaise lounge, his arm flung so casually around her waist. "We're going to take the trials *together*. When we win, I'll wish for immortality."

"And I'll wish for our freedom from the Circus," Nicolai finishes.

Moe's jaw hangs aslant. "Is that possible? A Deathless wishing themselves free from the Circus?"

He shrugs. "I doubt many have had the urge to go. You've always said I was anomalous that way."

"We're going to find out for certain," Tessa grins. "And when it succeeds, which I suspect it will, we'll be able to explore the Mirror and Mortal Lands together for eternity. No tedious servitude to Barrow Island's workforce, no enslavement to the Chaos Circus. An endless existence of adventure. We'll turn over every stone from here to the Horn Mountains and across the wide world beyond them."

Moe shakes her head. "Darling, I don't like it. No two people have ever tried this before."

"That's why it's going to work!" Tessa exclaims. "The Wish Granter must grant *any* wish, Libertine said. He's bound to the laws of the Circus."

"There are ways around these laws."

"Not this one. Not with him. Trust me...I did all my research before I ever came to you, and I've learned even more than that while I've been here." Tessa stretches forward to kiss Moe's cheek, where a single artificial tear is inked on her skin. "This is what we want, Moe. And you know that together, Nicolai and I can do anything."

The way he looks at Tessa when she says that—the same way he looked at *me* during our swim—I feel as if someone is kicking the wind out of me, again and again. I stumble to my knees once more and pull myself up by a wolf's shivering shoulder. I keep staggering along as the images shift and burst, panel after panel of glass taking on strange new dimensions:

Nicolai and Tessa dancing in a ballroom dripping in rubies on black chains like blood-drops from an obsidian roof; then dashing side-by-side through a verdant emerald maze; then standing brashly on the chained seats as they whirl, and diving from one to the next in pursuit of something; then working their way free of ropes binding them to the same tree as fire bears down on them; then smashing their way through a whole hedge of mirrors, fighting toward one another by sight and shouts alone.

Nicolai and Tessa in their bed in *Red & Gold's*, his arm around her waist so tightly as if he's terrified she'll slip away. Her smile is full of confident contentment as she presses tightly into the curve of his body and drifts off to sleep.

The next memory feels different. It feels wrong.

There's so little to it, but it thumps and shudders with agony. It flickers and fizzles in and out, and I grip the brass poles and thrust myself forward faster and farther to keep pace with it. I fight not to lose it. But it's so different. I see this memory not just in the glass, but through my own eyes.

I see the world upside-down, the great pinnacle of a tent striped crimson-ivory above. Nicolai's hand is below my head, the other on my belly. Terror poisons the bitter brew of his gaze. He twists away from me, looks over his shoulder toward—toward—

"You broke the rules, Nicolai." The voice is quiet, neither malicious nor benign. It's the impartial wind sighing between ancient trees. "There can never be two."

Nicolai shakes his head and presses harder on my stomach. Blood surges up into the cracks between his fingers. "Hold on, Tessa, hold tight to me..."

I feel every stich of fabric in his sleeve coming undone in my grip. "*Nicolai...*"

There are no words for the pain I feel. None at all but his name.

"Tell me how to save her!" he roars.

"You know how."

My head touches the floor. I am so cold, cold all over, until his lips touch mine. A single bead of golden warmth erupts inside this endless, frozen ocean of agony inside me.

"I'll come back for you," he vows against my mouth. "No matter what becomes of us, Tessa, I will always come for you. Forgive me."

Then I smell fire. Then I hear shouts. I hear Nicolai bellow in anger and pain.

And then...
Then I die.

I am dead.
Dead.
Dead...

Life and breath flood into me, but they push something out as they come. I scream and scream as if I'm being burned alive, and everything I was, all that I am, starts to spool out of my grasp. I can feel this moment, this wavering, horrible instant when the past I didn't remember and the one that I do collide.

Rain on my face. Arms around me. The familiar carriage rumblings and the thick smog smell of Barrow Downs wreathe this memory. It doesn't come from the glass. It lies in my own mind.

Something hits wood, over and over. Kick, kick, kick.

"It's going to be all right." That's surely Nicolai's voice, the splendid dark sound I've grown to…to…

Garish white light floods us. I hear familiar shouts. I smell the horrific artificial cleanliness of the Splendor House for the very first time.

"Tessa, listen to me…these people will help you, they'll keep you safe, they'll give you the care you need…"

"What is this, what's all that blood? Who are you, Sir? Miss, do you know this man?"

"I don't!" The scream shreds my throat. "I don't know who he is, who any of you are, let go of me, get away from me, I want my Nan, I want…I want…"

Until now, I didn't know the name I was searching for back then. But now I do. I wanted Nicolai. Even though he was right in front of me, and I didn't recognize him. And I didn't recognize him in *The Alibi Shop*.

But I did. A part of me did.

My knees slam against the carousel's edge. The ground tips and spins below me, and I don't know if the ride has halted or not, if this is vertigo or suicide, but I want to jump. Wave after wave of inconsequential memory slams into me, and only my fingers latching over the edge of the second tier keeps me from flinging to my death as the ground whooshes by on yet another revolution.

No prize is worth this anguish. No wish is worth the terrible illness I feel, the betrayal, the shock, the horror of what I saw. I coil up to launch myself to freedom from this heart-splitting grief.

And then a streak of defiance sears through me, so potent it knocks the breath out of me. I have come this far. I have endured all of this—and for what? So that the Deathless can laugh over my body when it splatters on the grass? So that Madame Memoir can accomplish what the others failed to do? So that the Circus can finish what it began that first time it took notice of me?

No. No, I can't give them that satisfaction. I won't be another victim like my Nan was, buried so deeply that the memory of me is erased in a few short years.

"Get up, Tessa," I rasp, and I sound like the girl from my memories. I grab the haunch of a Mirror Folk horse and slowly gather my feet. Bent over and shaking, I grip tight as the ride spins and spins, as more and more memories spill from the glass and fill my head. Glimpses of black, rain-slicked streets, the pangs of an empty belly, the feeling of Nicolai's hands on my waist and in my hair, the sound of laughter between him and Moe and me rattling the chandeliers above us.

I'd forgotten them. I'd forgotten so much more than I ever knew.

The churning in my middle ebbs, stops. I pry open my wet eyes and see that the ride has come to a halt, and though my toes graze that platform's edge, I have not flung myself to my death. But as for whether I've gone mad...

No, madness is nothing compared to this. I stumble down the stairs like a tipsy sailor fresh back on land, and Madame Memoir waits at the bottom. Her eyes betray neither resentment nor surprise that I survived as she offers me the key and the card. I tuck both away in my bodice without looking closely at them.

I don't step off the carousel the same girl who stepped onto it, not at all, and I hurry to the road instead of the park.

I break my promise to Nicolai.

*   *

I hardly know where I'm going, but my feet have a mind of their own. Somewhere along the way it begins to rain, and my dress is soaked and clinging to my every curve when I come to a halt outside the impressive pillars of Moe's shop. I wish I didn't know why I came here, but I do.

I test the handle, and the door is locked, but not for long when I remember what this scar on my palm can do. My hands have already formed such tight, trembling fists that the scab has torn, and blood eases down my palm. With one press to the latch, the bones of the Circus taste my presence. The door clicks open with such mocking ease. I slip inside and think to call out, but there's no need. Moe has sensed my presence too, and here she comes toward me, carrying a fine candelabra in her hand. It spills warm fragments of light along her black silk robe embroidered with cranes that take flight from one hem to the other, flustering and ruffling their wings in agitation. The same agitation lines Moe's wide eyes and sets the stern rose-gold of her lips as she holds up the flames to see my face.

"Tessa? Goodness, it's the middle of the night, darling…most mortals are asleep at this hour! You can't possibly need another dress?" Her eyes dart along my drenched frame, and she wrinkles her nose. "On the other hand, perhaps you do. Where's Nicolai?"

Where indeed? Back in the park. By now he must know the test is over, and I didn't come to him. Perhaps that's what he's feared all along if I learned the truth. Perhaps it's why he wept as I slept, when he thought I didn't see.

I wish his anguish didn't matter to me. I wish I didn't remember how I felt for him then, all tangled up in how I feel now. It's too much at once, the young and the old sensations colliding. I'm so dizzy I sway, and Moe catches my arm. "Tessa! What's that scoundrel done now?"

"It isn't him. It's me," I choke out. "I'm here because I remember you, Moe…I know you were my friend."

Yes, I've not only encountered Deathless before…I've befriended them. I've cared for them. I cared for Moe, and I cared for Nicolai.

Moe's eyes widen, but her lips form words I know—a familiar mantra between us: "The best and most beautiful of all friends, of course." Moe sets the candelabra on the floor and grips both of my shoulders now. "Look at me, darling. Tell me what you remember."

The room spins as if I'm still on that carousel, on the whirling edge of my own death. As if I will never stop turning.

"I remember everything."

CHAPTER NINETEEN

*O*nce I've donned clean silk pajamas, Moe summons
Corriene, and none of us speaks again until she's brought a
pitcher of tea and a platter of tiny lime cheesecakes. I ask
her to stay, and she does. I know I've asked her to before, and now I know
why: she reminds me of the orphans crawling through the shadows in
Barrow Downs, the ones like me. I don't want to see her overlooked.

We gather on the lounges, nibbling and sipping. It's a stilted silence,
which I know now is rare for us. Or at least it was before.

My head throbs. I know now I'm not mad, but it feels as if I'm moving
that way. Perhaps the carousel is still working its dark power over me.
Perhaps I'm going to be sick. I set down my fourth cheesecake, finding I'm
so full of chaos that I can't fit another bite in my belly. Moe watches me
with those piercing, lovely eyes.

"So," I say, with all the brightness of a sun-edged sword, "I've been
here before."

Moe sighs and sets down her cake, too. "I wondered when he was
going to tell you. He was so worried it would break your mind.
It's...difficult to know what the Circus's power will do to mortals in some
instances. Your kind are fragile in many ways. So very strange."

"He didn't tell me anything. I saw it all on the carousel." I squeak my
finger around the rim of my glass. Corriene lays a hand on my shoulder.

"What precisely happened to me, Moe?"

"You died." Her bluntness stops my breath. "The Wish Granter let your plan play out, but he always intended to put a stop to it, I suspect. When you reached the tent, he ran you through and left Nicolai a choice: wish for your life, or wish himself free from the Circus. Nicolai chose you."

That golden warmth buds in my chest, just as it did in my memory. "He did that?"

Moe shrugs. "He couldn't stand to be without you, the first person in a hundred years to truly understand both his mortal memories and his Deathless deceptions. But the wish went wrong. Wishes often do. Oh, they give you what you want, make no mistake…but there's usually a catch. It's the power of the Chaos Circus, it can't help itself. A last little trick, woven into the gift."

Her entire shop creaks and then settles. We look up at the loadbearing beams and columns, and Moe's fingers clink restlessly against her teacup.

"Not that we usually tell the mortals that," she adds.

I chafe a corner of my sleeve between my thumb and forefinger. It's expensive and fine. I used to love these sorts of things before…I remember that. The more exquisite and lavish, the better. Anything that put distance between me and those horrendous garbage-eating years, I would take it.

"So Nicolai wished me back," I murmur, "and I returned without most of my memories."

Moe nods. "You were inconsolable, so Nicolai returned you to the Mortal Lands. He thought your own kind could help you."

And that had been the end of it. All my dreams of immortality, my visions of eternal adventures with Nicolai at my side…gone. I'd forgotten him, I'd sunk back into resenting Nan for leaving me, I'd been consumed with seeming normal.

Now I know that normalcy hadn't mattered before. I'd been an outcast at nine years old, one of the many blights on the darkest roads of Barrow Downs. My scrapping, starving kind, skating on the edges of death and neglect, had been hidden from the eyes of tourists who came to indulge in the Rifts and the Mirror Lands. No one on Barrow Island had ever thought I'd amount to anything. I'd been cast out, forgotten, strange, *mad* from such a young age that I'd never cared what anyone else thought of me. I'd never had to.

To coinless orphans and friendless rogues. That was a toast we'd made, Nicolai, Moe, Corriene and I, in this very parlor. And not only us, but...

"Libertine." His name hisses out of me. "He was a part of this. He knew me then, too."

Slowly, Moe nods. "You did rather threaten his life if he didn't let you and Nicolai into the trials. He warned you of the dangers, of course. We all did. But you both were confident you had it all sorted out. Libertine was most worried for Nicolai, I think. He's the one who recruited him off the streets of Barrow Downs, after all. I think he feels responsible for his wellbeing."

He certainly hadn't seemed concerned when he'd pulled Nicolai into the Feast...unless he'd been trying to help us. Unless he'd known that seeing Nicolai would both calm and convict me, that it would be the push I needed to sort out the clue. The notion feels right to me, and I bury my face in my hands.

So many layers to this I hadn't known, so many friends and enemies dancing in the darkness around me, that impenetrable shroud of my forgotten memories. I feel as if I'm drawing back row after row of curtains, seeing glimpses of a palace of lies stretching beyond it. I hold my head in my hands so it won't spring off my shoulders and go rolling away. "I can't think. My mind is splitting open."

"Well, it's quite full of a lot of things now."

"I don't know how to be the old Tessa. I feel like I'm her, but I'm also me...and we aren't the same. I can feel her boldness, but I'm afraid of it. I see her dreams, but they're different from mine...or at least, they were. It's as if I'm being torn between two Tessas. Does that make sense?"

"No," Moe says. "But quite frankly, mortals rarely do. You're such odd, contrary, charming creatures. With all the freedom you have, you enslave yourselves to the whims of the Circus. With all your potential for goodness, you're selfish instead. And yet, as harsh as you can be, you often choose to be kind. You love the unlovable. You even care for us, and I've always liked that about you, darling."

A fist clenches at the base of my throat so all I can manage is a strangled, "Thank you."

"You need a good, long sleep." Moe gestures around us. "My couches are yours. I have no clients tomorrow, as usual, so you can rest as long as you need."

I'm no more fit to wander the Circus tonight than a drunkard is to drive a horse cart. But I know I can't stay, and I know why. I pry myself up from the lounge. "Thank you for the tea, but I'm afraid I must go. I have things to take care of."

"Are you leaving the Mirror Lands?"

"No. Or, at least, I don't think so." How could I give these Deathless the satisfaction of having chased me out? I know that's what they want. If the Circus took my memories, it certainly hasn't returned them as mercy. It hopes to drive me away.

Stubbornness clamps my bones tight at the hinges as I march out of Moe's shop and down the road toward the Circus proper. It's stopped raining, and the streets are beginning to hum with life as mortals seep from galleries and drinking niches to peruse the rides and booths again. A fine, humid haze curls around my feet as I slip into the crowd, headband firmly in place. I angle myself toward the park.

I don't make it that far.

"Madame Mystery!" The hiccupping shout comes from one drunk man in a sea of them, but I'm truly alarmed at how quickly the call is taken up. The headband may conceal my true features, but I still look one way to each of them, and they recognize me by now. The tide shifts, the focus of the crowd turns from the Circus and onto me. Suddenly I'm at the center of everything, and the old discomfort takes hold as the people crush in at my sides.

"How did you do it? The masquerade—the boxes—the Feast!"

"When is your next test? Will it be open to the public?"

"Come drink with us, I'd love to hear the stories!"

The old Tessa would've taken them up on such an offer, I know it without question. She would've regaled them with stories for as long as they refilled her champagne glass. But I don't want anything to do with their praise. I don't want them to be so taken with the trials, with poisoned wishes and life-altering outcomes. I don't want them to be like me.

"Make way." I tuck my shoulders and start to nudge through, but they close in front of me—a hot, meaty wall of skin and sweat. The reek of spirits punches me across the face so hard I gag.

"The drinks are on us!" A giggling woman latches onto my arm. "Tell us how to beat their games! I would so *love* that wish, why, I'd never want for another thing in my life…"

"Is it true they can make your rivals drop dead in a moment?"

"Can the wish really bring back the dead?"

Tears stab my eyes. I extract my arm. "I'm sorry, I have somewhere to be."

"Is it the next trial?" A man's palm descends on my shoulder. "Take us with you, we'd love to watch!"

I don't mean to, but I'm afraid at that moment, I burst like a firecracker.

I remember exactly how to do it: how to brawl like street scum. I grab his wrist and separate his hand from my shoulder, twist nimbly and slam my knee into his tendermeats. He crashes down, lowing like a shot ox, and the people pull back in one hypnotic tide—then rush back in, and suddenly they're all grabbing for me at once. They say they're trying to calm me, but it certainly doesn't feel like it. It's absurd that I'm hitting and biting at them in my silk pajamas like some ridiculous bedtime show, but there's nothing entertaining about it. I feel as if I'm back on the streets of Barrow Downs, fighting for my life. And I may remember how to do these things, but my muscles can't keep up with my mind anymore. They've atrophied as I've forgotten.

When one of the men takes my arm and twists it up between my shoulders, hollering at me to stop kicking, I obey—not because I want to, but because pain slams through my torso so swiftly it blinds me. Nauseous, I buckle forward, the cobbles swinging up toward my face as if I've leaped from a carousel after all.

And then the pain is gone, and the hand is gone, and a crackle of golden energy booms through the street, flinging all the drunk mortals backward. I stagger straight and twist to gape at Nicolai pressing up behind me, his arm extended, the ropes of hot energy popping between his spread fingertips.

"Touch her again," he seethes, "and I'll see to it you're all tossed through the Rifts and banned from ever setting foot in the Mirror Lands again. *Do you hear me?*"

Shocked, frightened mumbles are the only consent. They back away from us with fear in their eyes, but I can't bring myself to feel guilty about that. I was afraid, too, and they handled me like an effigy to pass around, as if I didn't have any feelings. Maybe they do belong here, I think, in this Circus that also treats mortal lives like a game.

In seconds, they've all scurried away. Nicolai and I are alone. I don't ask how he found me, now that I remember the promise he made.

"You didn't come to the park." There's no accusation in his tone. There's no force behind it at all.

"You must have foreseen that I wouldn't, Lord Harlequin." It's not quite that he flinches at the name, but his bearing does shift. "You always were my favorite of the Deathless. I studied you. I chose you, didn't I? Because I knew so much about you."

He offers me nothing but a long, troubled look.

"You knew what I would see tonight."

"I suspected, yes," he says. "The Circus hasn't found a way to break you yet, so naturally they would like to see your own mind land the crippling blow."

"It nearly did." I make slow, painful fists. My fingers are swollen and sore from holding onto the brass posts and metal edges of the carousel for dear life. "All wishes come with a cost. The trials aren't worth it. Isn't that what you said to me?"

His silence infuriates me more than if he'd become defensive.

"Why didn't you tell me?"

"You would never have believed me unless you saw for yourself what the Circus could do. You would have insisted the Splendor House did this to you."

He's right about that. The Tessa who shrank in the shadow of her mentor would never have dared entertain the notion that her lost memories were the result of some enchanted wishing gone awry. "Could you have showed me? Showed me with your powers, somehow, and protected my mind from breaking?"

Something strange flickers in his eyes—the same look from *The Alibi Shop* again, as if he's trying to convey a deeper truth with that look. "Yes."

"Then why didn't you?"

"It's complicated."

"Don't condescend to me, I'm not a child. This isn't about complexity, it's that you feel guilty for what happened. Because you wished and brought me back broken, and then you abandoned me in the Splendor House."

"I thought that mortals could do better for you than I could." His eyes sharpen as my words suddenly sink in. "Tessa, you aren't broken."

"No, not anymore. I'm stitched back together now like one of Nan's dolls." My laughter is ugly and mirthless, cruel only against myself. "The carousel showed me *everything*. I know I've been to the Circus before, and I know why. I remember all the research I did on you so that I could outwit your Circus game. Years of studying while I ate out of trash bins and ran with the smaller gangs in Barrow Downs after Nan left me."

I finger the headband settled across my hair.

"That's why all of this, isn't it? You're hiding me from them, like you did that first night, so they won't know it's me returned to the Circus. It's why you don't want to be seen with me. Because you helped me before, and we failed." I don't wait for him to answer. I remember. I already know. "What a silly little fool I was, believing I could have it all. That girl deserved what she got."

Nicolai's jaw clenches, and the power pulses around him. "Don't say that. There was nothing wrong with you as you were."

"There is everything wrong with that Tessa! She put us in the Splendor House, and I despise her for it!"

It sounds absurd, but it's true. I do hate her. She was brash, bold, and too reckless. She squandered our life away to that place, to that nightmare I can't run from.

Nicolai shakes his head. "No. Don't despise yourself. You didn't do it alone. If anything, you should despise *me*. I encouraged you. I didn't protect you like I promised to."

Furious, I draw myself up to my height. "I know that. I know how you failed, how you broke all your promises. I hate you twice as much as her. Twice as much as *anybody*."

His jaw cracks open, and his eyes go wide. Pain slashes into the streaks of Circus light already stamped across his face. I know he didn't expect me to say it. But I have. I can't stop saying things now.

"You kept secrets, and you were going to let me use the wish to mend *your* life. You never even suggested I could wish my memories back, or that I could wish to be unbroken."

"Because you aren't broken, Tessa!"

"You don't live in my mind, so how can you know that?" I toss my hands in frustration. "This is pointless. None of this was for my own good. You didn't care about my life when you brought me back to this Circus, if you ever have."

"That's not true." Nicolai steps closer to me, the heat of his power engulfing my body and putting an end to all the ridiculous, tense shivers of this damp and unbelievable night. "I searched for you and watched over you in Barrow Downs. I was only there to be accused of those murders because I was in the Mortal Lands looking out for your wellbeing. And yes, I brought you back to the Circus...but not to take the trials for me. I hoped that being here would spark your memories. That you would remember how even at your lowest of lows, you were never a creature kicked aside by the likes of Metters. You would put them all in their place. I wanted you to remember who you were before."

"And if I don't want to be that Tessa?"

"Then don't be. But you deserve the right to choose between them, not to believe your life's only ever been one way."

The hot wind drops out of my sails. He's right. I do deserve to know about the old Tessa, to choose whether I'd follow in her footsteps or forge a new path. I've always felt something was missing from me, ever since I left the Splendor House. But I never expected it to be *this*, or for it to be revealed by a Deathless of all things.

"This is why The Wish Granter wants you gone, isn't it?" My voice is so soft that I feel the buildings on the street lean in slightly, keen to overhear. "Because you broke the rules. And because you despise him for killing me."

Nicolai's power banks low to his body, and he nods.

So. This is what I'm truly up against. Past and present colliding, and in the middle of it, me: the reason Nicolai and The Wish Granter hate one another. I am the upset of the balance. Because I know, as clearly as if he's told me himself, that The Wish Granter believes he chose wrong. He should have taken Nicolai, not me. He should have removed him from the Circus when it was an easy choice.

How will the Circus twist my wish if it's for Nicolai's safety and freedom? I can't do it. I can't curse him with a wish as he cursed me. And

I tell him that.

He nods again. Slower. Resigned. "I suspected as much. It's the wise choice. You shouldn't insinuate yourself any deeper into this struggle between us. It will end badly for everyone involved."

I hate that it sounds like giving up, like cowardice of the highest degree from me. And I hate that he sounds so hopeless—as if he's accepted that this only ends one way. How was last evening's swim so long ago? How does the hope I felt then seem so far away?

I turn to go ahead of him, then hesitate. There is one pressing question the visions didn't answer—something I suspect only he can explain. "Why couldn't you see my future?"

Nicolai comes up beside me. He doesn't look down when he says, "Your mortal gift is unpredictability, Tessa. You came to this Circus with so many plans that even my power couldn't see which one you'd choose. It's how you've kept yourself alive since Barrow Downs: you always have more plots than people around you who can ferret them out."

And I suppose that's still me—flighty, unpredictable, and uncertain of which future I'll choose. I wish he didn't sound so proud of something that all but seals his fate.

We walk back to *Red & Gold's* together, as tense as that first night we came through the Rift. I can't think of a single thing to say to him, not with every memory churning through me in a raging torrent. Every touch, every kiss, every intimate secret whispered in the solitude of our room. Every second that his fascination with me turned to something deeper. The very moment that I realized Lord Harlequin was more than a story, more than a favorite doll on Nan's shelf—he was a man who'd given up everything to save his family, and lost them, too.

I go straight to the bath and scrub the night's horrors from my skin. Nicolai makes no sound from the other room. I can't imagine if he's pacing or weeping or sitting there staring blankly across the room. I feel badly for us both, but I can't give him anything he would want, not when I feel so hopelessly entangled in this thorny mess. I prick myself and bleed everywhere my thoughts turn.

I must stop thinking about this, stop dwelling on this past that I suddenly and painfully remember, so instead I drape myself against the tub's edge and retrieve the sharp obsidian envelope Madame Memoir gave me. The steam has loosened the seal already, and it's easy to open. In silence and solitude, I read the last clue:

Look all around, on every side
The beast is here—nowhere to hide!
How will you fight? What can you do?
The thing you fear the most is you.

CHAPTER TWENTY

*T*he House of Mirrors is my final test. This time, I don't need Nicolai to tell me a thing about it.

"The House of Mirrors is like Lady Lore's maze." I reflect on this previously-forgotten knowledge as I tug on my ankle boots and button my waistcoat. I slept poorly the night before, but I won't let that stop me. I want my wish, and I want to be done with this. "Usually one must find the exit to win a prize, and every wrong turn costs a day of mortal life. But for the trial, of course, it will be different."

Nicolai turns my headband around in his hands. "Lord Dread prides himself on making the most hideous visions appear in those mirrors. Don't look at any one for too long. That's how he traps you. Scathing glances only. You're good at those."

"Thank you." I infuse my tone with all the tartness of cherry compote, and he makes some undefinable sound. I glance up at him.

Seated on the opposite bed, Nicolai is clearly at a loss, and I have no desire to deliver him from the awkwardness. I wait for him to speak again, and his voice is strained when he does: "Don't succumb to the vision. Remember that this is real. Use your hatred of me, if you must. But don't give over to the things he shows you, because they will *not* be true."

I nod. I can't say that I don't hate him. I don't know what I feel. I was awake all night polishing off my newly-restored memories, turning them over in the ocher light seeping through the triangular window, and I'm still no closer to making sense of myself. Everything is so snarled and hopeless, and I can't think about any of it now, so I just finish lacing my boots and put out my hand. Nicolai surrenders the headband.

"I'll be here when you return," he says. I've already asked him not to come. There's no sense complicating this further by risking Nicolai being noticed while walking me yet again through the Circus proper. "Be careful, Tessa."

I nod, feeling more and more like a broken doll crumbling on its last threads, and I slip out of *Red & Gold's* by myself. This time, when I walk the cobbled paths, no one reaches for me. In fact, the mortals will hardly look my way. But I know now that this is nothing special to me. Things have been like this for a very long time. I simply set my gaze forward and stride to the long, deep building that is the House of Mirrors.

Nothing about it feels harmless. The entrance is domed with the gaping mouth of a clown: grisly scarlet lips peeled up in a sinister grin, eyes hooded and narrowed, dark as graves with their thick black banding and the stripes above and below the hairless lids. The wrinkles in the cheeks are ghastly. He knows a secret I do not.

Lord Dread reclines at the entry booth, leer as broad as his attraction's. His sleek dark hair is bound in a tail down his back, and his broad shoulders lift and settle in a short sigh. He surveys me with his arms crossed and his shoulder dipped to the clown's cheek, sharing a private chuckle at my expense.

"That was quick," Dread says. "Already recovered from last night's event?"

I'm suddenly unsure if he means the carousel or my encounter with the mortals, and I don't know which is worse. If word has spread about the latter, then the other Deathless know that Nicolai got involved—again. Whether they're aware Tessa LaRoche has returned or not, the Circus is bound to take notice that Nicolai is aiding another mortal wisher.

I can't afford to show Dread my fear. I tuck my hands behind my waist and clench them around each other there, pressing into the scars on my palm with all my might—a habit I'm beginning to realize came from before. "If I hadn't recovered yet, I would not be here, would I?"

Dread clicks his tongue. "They always grow so overconfident at the last trial. This is where they usually fail."

I gnaw at the inside of my cheek and imagine I'm chewing up fear so I can spit it at his feet. "Is the last trial that I must endure your prattling, Sir?"

His smile shifts from satisfied to downright nasty. "I'm going to enjoy listening to you scream when the mirrors tear apart your mind, Madame Mystery."

What an utter and abhorrent bastard. I nearly tell him he is, but he interrupts me with a clap. The clown's grinning teeth click apart, sliding up and down, and a tongue-pink carpet unfolds from the black chasm beyond. A saccharine and unfriendly mist curls out of the throat of the mirror house, caressing my face with its tingling breath. If fear had a smell, it would be like this: sickeningly sweet and of savory odiousness, all at once.

I'm suddenly glad that I remember the old Tessa. I may need her brashness and courage if I'm to survive this test.

I force myself to pay Lord Dread not one more glance as I slip inside, but I feel the brush of his power as we cross paths. He's muscled and tall and intimidating enough, but it's the sheer might of his bubbling black energy that sets my hairs on end. He feels almost bloated with the stolen years and terrors that seep from the pores of this place, and now I remember that the guile of any Circus attraction grows stronger the more it feeds on the emotions of the people who partake in it.

Judging by the sense of it, the House of Mirrors may be the most powerful of all the attractions in the Chaos Circus.

A wicked, wild jester's giggle echoes through the black nothing beyond the clown's mouth as soon as I cross the threshold, and its teeth clamp shut behind me. Engulfed in shadows, I wait for my final test to begin.

It starts with calliope music played out of tune, discordant and grating. A glowing orb ignites overhead, shedding a thin pool of white light no further than the tips of my boots. Sucking in a gulp of courage, I sidle forward into the dark.

It's difficult to maneuver at first. I'm afraid to put out my hands, afraid I will brush up against something large and hairy or scaled, something dripping blood, or even just another person. Anything could be out there in the blackness. I divide my time between watching my feet and glancing ahead, just as wary of pits opening before me. I didn't give myself long to study the clue, but I know to expect Dread's mirror house to be a house of horrors regardless.

I send my gaze up from my feet again, and this time I am face to face with a person.

I shriek and stumble backward, averting my eyes as soon as I recognize that terrified face. It's me. I've reached the hall of mirrors.

The light overhead becomes many lights, shed on tall upright panes and bouncing erratically all around. I'm dizzy, confused, turned around before I've hardly started. I press my palms together and settle them against my lips as I take short, cursory glances at the mirrors. Right away, I can tell there's something wrong with them.

My reflection is strange, each and every one. Sometimes I'm not wearing the right clothes. Sometimes my skin, my hair, even my eyes are the wrong color. The settings all ripple out of blackness, turning to mountains, to meadows, even to Barrow Island.

I tuck my shoulders and start forward blindly. I know that unlike the usual maze, wrong turns won't cost me years of my life here. My challenge is different, whatever it is. I haven't decided that yet.

Oh, that ghastly music is making my ears bleed, sending sharp pain digging through my temples. Every so often it's broken by another mischievous cackle that whips past me with substance, stirring the darkness. I always twist to follow it, wondering if something is here with me, if Dread himself stalks my footsteps to mock. But I never catch more than a flirt of sable fog disappearing around a mirror's edge.

These mirrors are everywhere. I exist within a prism, and beneath the shredding tune of the calliope, it seems they whisper to me. A thousand Tessas press their palms to the glass and beg me to look here and there, to let them out. Wherever I search for the exit, they're waiting for me, watching with strange eyes and faces that hold roughly the shape of mine, but it's as if they've been painted by artists who didn't know me at all.

In the fist of shadows with that grating light following me, I finally stop and consult the card again. It feels wrong to stand still, and I can hardly breathe from exertion and nerves, but I must. There's no going forward, just around in circles at this rate.

"The thing you fear the most is you," I recite under my breath. Am I my own obstacle here? Well, if Lord Dread expects me to break a mirror and take my own life with the lethal shards, he's going to be sorely disappointed. I'd sooner kick out the clown mouth's teeth than do that! But the notion seems as hopeless as finding my way through the maze, because when I try to retrace my steps I find I'm desperately entangled. The House of Mirrors certainly didn't look this size from without, but within it could be endless, fathoms upon fathoms of blackness only broken by gilt-framed mirrors that distort the true image.

Panic claws my throat. I slip the clue away and move faster, skidding through room after room and row after row of mirrors. All my reflections shout after me and pound at the glass, begging me to look, but I do not. I dare not.

Finally, panting and panicking, I come to a halt. There is no door. Not ahead, not behind. Only mirrors.

"Tessa."

That voice...so familiar, so soothing. The sound of hundreds of bedtimes rocked to sleep in soft, strong arms. The sound of porridge food fights and learning to read by the fireside.

"*Tessa.*"

The tone that always made me confess if I broke one of her valuable dishes, or if I sneaked out to the rooftops of Barrow Downs to watch the riots, hoping for a glimpse of my parents.

I won't really look, I tell myself. Just a slantways glimpse.

But even that is a mistake, because with one glance, I know it's her. I recognize Nan by the dark braid that goes down her back, peppered with silver threads. She stands at the tallest and broadest mirror of all, on the other side of it, and her palms touch the glass as if she's searching for a way out. And I'm not so sure she isn't. This is the first mirror that hasn't shown my reflection, after all. Did Nan try to conquer the House of Mirrors, only to become a slave to it?

I edge over to her without looking directly into her face.

"Tessa." Her voice breaks with longing, her hands shoving the glass as if she could push through and reach me.

"Nan." My voice breaks, too. I realize that, like Nicolai, I don't really hate her for what happened, and I don't blame her for the life I now remember I spent on the streets after she was gone. I would take her back, if I could. I *will* take her back, this very moment.

I lay my hand over hers, against the glass, still not looking. I can almost feel her warmth beyond it, like sunlight touching the smooth surface. "I'm here, Nan. I'm here."

"Tessa." Her voice is suddenly not hers, but I still know it: chilled and professional. "It's time to come back to reality now. Where were you?"

I open my eyes to the polished ivory office of Missus Fiona Chambers. I'm back in the Splendor House.

CHAPTER TWENTY-ONE

J leap back from the glass. It isn't a mirror, but a window. It's not Nan I see reflected there, but myself, in the starched white smock I wore day after day during my confinement in the Splendor House. I blink and blink and shake my head, but the vision doesn't dispel. I spin from the window to face the sharp whites and rich darks of Fiona's desk and bookshelves against the alabaster walls.

"What—where—no," I stammer as she folds her hands with endless, patronizing patience.

"Tessa," she has that indulgent tone I've always hated, as thick and syrupy and difficult to swallow as treacle, "you were daydreaming again."

"No, no, I most certainly wasn't!" I start to pace on the pristine floor. My slippered feet know every inch of it so well. I shut my eyes and tear them open again and again, but it doesn't wake me. "I was in the Circus, I was with Nicolai..."

Fiona frowns. "Nicolai. Our newest orderly? Tessa, I know you've taken a bit of a shine to him, but even if he was the slightest bit interested in a girl with...mental challenges, the House forbids relations between staff and patients."

A bit of a shine...staff and patients...a girl with mental

challenges...the *House*.

The door opens behind me, and I turn with a gasp of relief. "Nicolai!"

He swaggers in with his eternal strut, enigmatic eyes a bittersweet sanctuary in this unexpected nightmare. He carries a small white cup in his hand and I think he's going to offer me a sliver of Circus magic to whisk me away from here. He's come to set me free.

Unless he put me here. Unless he brought me to this place, just like he did last time. And that memory introduces doubt to my heart, even moreso when Nicolai passes me with no hint of his usual smirk. He sets down the cup, and inside I see two sky-pale capsules gleaming. Then he departs without paying me a second glance.

"Handsome, I know," Fiona says with a sort of purring undercurrent that makes me bristle, makes me want to spit that he's *mine*, though I haven't decided yet if I want him to be any such thing. "But you don't need the distraction of romance when you're trying to get well, Tessa."

"I *am* well!" My shout rattles the noble portraits on the walls. "You should see what I've done since I came to the Circus, the trials I've overcome on my own wit and wiles!"

Fiona frowns, and her pen rises like a guillotine, poised over the paper—poised to rend my neck with destructive words about my mental state. "What sort of *trials*?"

"You know exactly the sort." I delve into the front of my smock and withdraw the cardstock, flinging it onto her desk with smug triumph. "Explain *that*, if you can."

Fiona scrutinizes it briefly. Then she raises her eyes to mine. "Of course, I know these riddles. You've written them every day in poetry class. I must say you're quite good, I suggested to Missus Eve that we ought to double up your time in that class since it seems so beneficial to your recovery."

"Don't play this game with me, you know I didn't write these!" I snatch the card back and turn it over, ready to prove her wrong. But...that *is* my handwriting. The pitiful scratch and the strange loops and curls on the end, all mine.

My hand starts to shake. The cardstock wobbles.

"Tessa," Missus Fiona says gently, "I understand how difficult this is. Lapses back into psychosis are very common, nothing at all to be ashamed or frightened of. We'll simply adjust your dosage and soon you'll be making great strides again."

"But," my voice is tremendously small, "the Circus…"

"The Chaos Circus is what we call a mental fort. It's where your mind goes when it ceases to cope with reality," Missus Fiona says. "In this case, I'm afraid we dug a little too deep in group discussion, and that's what caused the lapse. You didn't want to think about how your parents were killed in a coach crash…"

"Riftless riot. It was a riot."

"Tessa." Missus Fiona's voice is stern again, allowing no nonsense at all. "It was a coach crash, the night of your sixteenth birthday. You were inconsolable. Your Nan brought you here when you threatened to harm yourself and her. There are no Rifts to some ethereal Mirror Lands, there is no Chaos Circus, nothing called a Deathless…and while Nicolai is very real, I can assure you that he is a new figment to this story you've told yourself. *This* world is reality, Tessa. You must wake up to that."

Now she stands, high as a behemoth, and I shrink back. I want to argue, yet my tongue shrivels. How can I be certain I didn't just dream up the Circus? How can I be certain of *anything*, with the poem-card in my hand, and that orderly walking past me as if he didn't know me at all?

Lapses back into psychosis…

What if I really am sick? What if I'll never be well?

"Come with me." Fiona slides a matronly arm around my shoulders. "Back to your room. Mona misses you…yes, that's right, Moe, your roommate. You and she can peruse her wardrobe while I adjust your prescription. Afterward you'll have a restful sleep, and you'll feel much better. You'll remember what's real and what isn't."

A restful sleep. I know what that is. It's the topple over the edge of madness into a dark vat of nightmares. It's the comatose state they send me to when my flights of fancy become uncontrollable. It's meant to rejuvenate my mind like normal sleep, but I can't control it and I'm never truly asleep when it happens. I'm paralyzed and floating in the terrifying dark, unable to move my limbs or scream when hideous, slick notions and nightmares wrap around my body and choke me.

"No." I scuff my slippers on the floors, but they're so slippery I wonder if the orderlies keep them this way just so we can't fight back. "No, I don't want to go to sleep!"

"It's just a short nap, Tessa, and then you'll be all right."

No. This isn't happening. I'm in the House of Mirrors and this is just an illusion, it must be, because this is what I fear the most...I fear that I really have lost my mind.

I struggle, but Fiona's arm around me is no consolation, it's a straightjacket. She steers me through the stark silver halls of the Splendor House, toward a door I despise. I never hated any particular doors before I came to this place, but this is the one behind which they administer that strange, merciless drug that sends me to the darkness.

I won't let them put me there. I will not.

I crumble forward suddenly as if in despair, and Fiona stumbles at the change in our already-mismatched heights. I seize her lapse in grip and twist, putting my foot into the back of her leg and shoving her down to the floor with a satisfying *crack* of knees on hardwood. Then I cast off her arm, and I run.

Seconds later, from somewhere high up in the House, a bell shrieks, sounding just exactly like a wicked clown's laughter. I pump my arms and legs faster, tearing past several orderlies who gape at me in shock before they give chase. But I've been running since I was nine years old—from tailors where I stole clothes to survive the winter, from bookshops where I took charts to amuse myself during lonely nights, from old Mister Cortese where I stole fish to tide me over until my next meal. They never caught me, and neither will these people.

It feels as if the very fabric of reality is rending apart around me, the House grasping at me with clawed hands to slow my stride as I swing around a corner and smash straight into someone.

Familiar hands latch onto my elbows. "Miss LaRoche?"

"Nicolai!" I grasp him back, nails biting into his forearms. "I know this will seem utterly absurd, but this is not real—you're not an orderly, you're a part of the Chaos Circus, and we...and we..."

I can't bring myself to say it, but I hope he can see it in my eyes.

He stares at me for a long moment. Then one side of his mouth curls up into that devastating smirk. "I'm well aware, Madame Mystery. Why do you think I'm here?" He casts me suddenly behind him. "Go! Run! I'll meet you in the attic."

My faith in him is implicit. I dash down the corridor and hear him directing the real orderlies away. My heart soars with trust, with a warm rush of feeling I can't quite believe is...is *love*.

But maybe it is. Maybe I loved Nicolai the moment I saw him again in *The Alibi Shop*, and it's taken me this long to remember it.

I sidle and sprint past stations of orderlies over the following half-hour, that mad cackle of a bell still chiming every few moments. Then it's up the long twist of stairs in the bell tower of the House, wrapped around its pinnacle like a candy stripe on a peppermint cane, straight to the attic.

Nicolai is already there. He stands facing the triangular window, his back to me. When I shut the door, he turns. His face is guarded.

"Are we going to jump?" I ask. "Can you use your power to keep the fall from killing us?"

Nicolai pushes his fingers back through his hair in that way I find so disarming. "Tessa, this has to stop."

I tilt my head. "I don't...I don't understand."

"All this talk of magic and Circus power. You aren't helping yourself. They'll keep you here forever if you don't learn to control that tongue."

I blink and blink, but it doesn't clear the blur before my eyes. "What are you saying, Nicolai? You know what's real...that's why you helped me escape just now from the others!"

"I hoped that if I had you somewhere confined, I could talk sense into you." His eyes flick to my hands. "No one needs to be hurt."

I follow his gaze and stiffen. I'm holding a knife. Where did I get a knife? Why do I recognize it?

Then I remember: it's Fiona's. She laid it into a latch on the windowframe of her office to protect herself from unruly patients. Was that why I was at the glass today—to steal her knife?

"Put down the weapon, Tessa." Nicolai raises his hands and steps forward.

"I can't," I whisper, "I won't let them put me to sleep again. You don't know what it's like...what I see there..."

"I'll try to convince Missus Fiona not to send you under." He continues to advance. "But you must calm down, Tessa. It's the only way."

The only way they can subdue me. The only way they can control me.

"This isn't real." The knife rattles in my hand. "None of this is real. I *know* what's real."

"That's right. *I'm* real." Nicolai rests his hand on my wrist.

I look up into his face. "No. You aren't."

I turn the knife around and push it into his chest.

It goes in so smoothly, like cutting soft butter with a hot blade. Nicolai's eyes widen. He hiccups with agony and jerks forward, and I step back as blood spews from his heart. I let him crash to his knees, watch him crumble onto his side. He grabs at the blade with weak hands, then sinks into a stupor. Then his eyes fix, and he moves no more.

I wait, and wait, and wait to wake from this nightmare. But nothing happens.

I clap a hand to my mouth. There is blood all over it. *His* blood.

Footsteps strike the stairs. I hunt wildly across the attic and see the bronze frame of a mirror half-buried under a cloth against the wall. I jam it under the knob and scurry to the other side of the dead body on the floor as someone hits the door. Then they start pounding on it.

"Tessa!" Fiona shouts. "Tessa, I know you're in there!"

"It's not real," I hiss, "it's not real, it isn't." I'm not here, this blood is not on my hands, I didn't really do what I've just done.

"Is Nicolai in there with you? Have you hurt him?"

Clowning laughter bursts from my lips. "You might say that!"

The pounding stops. I hear the world gather its breath.

"We can still put this right, Tessa. I can fix you. Open this door!"

"No!" I howl. "No, you had no right to do this to me. And I don't believe you anymore that I deserved it! I wasn't mad, I was hurt and frightened. But you didn't try to help me, you tried to cure me the same way you cure all your patients. I may be odd, I may be silly, but I am *not* insane, and I never was, and I won't change myself to please you, or anyone on Barrow Island ever again!"

"Do you think you have any right to make these claims? You've killed someone!"

My breath catches.

She's right. Nicolai is dead. Dead at my feet.

I killed him. My actions brought about his death.

I sway forward and kneel beside Nicolai. Blood stains his front...so much blood.

I say his name. I say it again. He doesn't move, of course. I brush those unruly curls from his brow and catch the reflection of my movement in the mirror. A cold wash of fear and hatred moves through me as I regard my own face, freckled with blood, my hands coated in it from murdering Nicolai.

I stare. And I stare. And something slides into place in my mind.

The thing you fear the most is you.

This is me. This is selfish. This is unsure. This is my choice to let Nicolai die rather than face what's real around me. Rather than to wish for him to be free.

Before my eyes, the Tessa in the mirror shifts, her form growing darker and darker. Her eyes adopt serpent slits. Her nostrils collapse into her face. Blood burns bright as crushed berries on her palms, slick between her fingers. A wicked smile, as wide as a clown's mouth, peels up her cheeks in ridge after ridge. Her jaw elongates to fit all that sinister glee.

She is destruction and consumption. She is the Tessa who will take what she is owed, no matter the cost to others. She is hurt and vengeful and so very, very afraid. She is reckless and bold. She is the part of myself from my memories that I hate.

She is the ugly part of me that I've run from, the madness and wildness that I've stuffed down deeper and deeper. She is how I see her. She is what I fear, because I know what she will do next.

The door cracks open with a thunderous boom, flinging the mirror across the floor and cracking the glass in a spiderweb. Orderlies swarm inside, led by Fiona. I let them grab my arms because I am too stricken to fight, watching colorless fingers peel the glass aside like a curtain. Dark Tessa is climbing out again, unrestrained by the wisdom gained in years and suffering, in forgetting.

She needs my caution. And I need her courage.

So when they lift me up, I fight back one last time. I kick and flail as they drag me. I must get to that mirror. I know what I must do.

But I'm at the door now. I can't reach it.

Dark Tessa has risen. She blots out the light. She lifts the knife.

"Tessa!" I scream, and the whole room shudders to a halt. "Break the mirror! You must break it to save him! To save *us!*"

She hesitates, turning red, lidless eyes to me. I nod so frantically a crick forms in my neck.

She is me. She cares for what I care for. She loved before I knew what love was.

She will do this.

And then she does. She brings the knife slashing down into the punctured glass, and the mirror erupts in a roaring wind, sucking all of us inside it. The same cyclone blasts Dark Tessa to mist, and as it passes through me, I let it seep into my pores.

I don't let her consume me—I consume *her*.

And there I know I will find the balance between the wariness I've learned and the brashness that will win me this game.

My hands drop boneless at my sides. I step back and look all around the frame of the mirror plastered into the darkness of Lord Dread's house. The reflection is not me anymore. It's Nicolai, bloodsoaked in a heap in that attic.

I grab the mirror's edges and kick the glass with all my might.

It shatters just as easily as the knife went through Nicolai's heart. A gentle, cool spring breeze wafts into the broken frame, and beyond that I see Circus lights. I see freedom, and I step into it with my head high and my hands shaking like autumn leaves clinging desperately to a high-up branch. I step out of the mirror frame and onto the other side of the House of Mirrors, far down its long porch from the clown's mouth. Lord Dread awaits me there, reclining this time against an awning support post, his face inscrutable. "What an interesting thing you fear the most."

I extend a rattling hand. "The key."

He unloops it from a chain around his neck and gives it to me, but not so simply. "Who would have thought a mortal most feared the demise of the Deathless."

He leaves me there as he struts back to his booth. I stare after him with my heart thudding in the base of my throat.

Is that why I saw what I saw? Is my worst fear, deep down, that Nicolai will die? Am I truly afraid to be alone, to lose again what I've nearly lost once already?

But that was what unleashed Dark Tessa after all, wasn't it? I'd conquered my fear of Fiona. Conquered my fear of the House itself.

Neither of those things showed me a way free of the mirror vision. Neither one brought her out. But when I drove that knife into Nicolai, and accepted what I'd done as murder, that I'd killed him...

I clutch the obsidian key so hard its shaft bites into my scabbed palm. And when I step off the porch, I begin to run.

* *

Nicolai greets me in the doorway of our room as if he sensed my approach. By the way tendrils of power snake through the room, I suspect he may have been reaching out to find me. His face is haggard with dread just now beginning to give way to relief when he sees I'm not dead and haven't quite gone insane. "You were gone for such a long time, I thought—Tessa?"

I slam the door behind me and throw the key onto the bed. He searches my face, and smirks. That *smirk.*

"I take it you missed me?"

And I do something then that the old me might've done, the girl from the memories of a carousel who had the heart of a lioness, and an unbreakable spirit to match it. I march right up to him, grab the back of his head, and relish the pleasure of seeing the smirk melt from his face when I startle him, before I bring his mouth down to mine.

And my lips know him, even if the rest of me had once forgotten. They mold to him as my body does, as my hands thread into his dark hair and seek a spot at his nape where some part of me knows he likes to be touched. I anticipate the sound he will make before he makes it—a soft, covetous growl, and my chest tightens in response. This is a dance. These are learned motions.

This is a disaster, and I know it even as I stretch up into his mouth and my toes curl in my boots. Because I've willfully forgotten again every other boy I've ever kissed. I know now why I'm so afraid to lose Nicolai, just like the mirror made me see. And I do not know how I will do this thing, how I could ever go and make a wish and pretend he is the same stranger I met a week ago, and that his fate doesn't matter to me.

Not now that I know I still love him.

CHAPTER TWENTY-TWO

*J*he moment feels both endless and far too short, as if we're racing toward something inevitable, our hearts stumbling and throbbing through this thing in rhythm. It's him who breaks the kiss, who rests his brow against mine.

"I don't want to finish this," I mumble into the folds of his collar. "I don't want to face him again."

"I know." A pause. "I could finish the trials again, make the wish for you."

"It would never work, he wouldn't allow it. And besides, I've done all the difficult parts, why should I let you claim the glory?"

His laughter gets trapped deep in his throat, and his hand settles in the small of my back. "What did Dread show you?"

"What I fear most. What I think I've always feared." Maybe this has never been about the necklace—that gift he gave me. Maybe I'd always been so desperate to win, deep down, because his life was at risk. "You kept your promise. You came to find me. Now I must keep mine and finish it."

He lets me go, and I walk to the bed, where I stashed the other four keys. I line them up: gold and rose, porcelain and blue, silver and black, brass and cobalt, obsidian. I truly have earned them. Each one took away a piece of me and replaced my fear with fire.

But I can't shake the feeling that the worst is ahead of me. That I must prove myself still.

"Tomorrow night, I'll go," I say. "Today, I just want to walk. I just want to think."

Nicolai holds open the door. "As you wish."

* *

I am absolutely convinced that time is a cruel, sentient thing, that it knows when it's being watched and moves all the faster like a skittish pony. I returned to the inn at dawn, and yet the day streaks by in shades of vivid chiffon blooms and bright emerald grass, and clear blue skies. We walk in disguise, sit on benches, consume pastries and observe the mortals.

I tell him about the vision that Dread showed me. He scoffs.

"I sincerely doubt if I could really trick you into going anywhere with me—even a scandalous attic. You're too clever for it." He bites powdered sugar from the backs of his knuckles and frowns at a couple leading their child down the road. I remember now that he hates to see children here, that he believes their parents often use their numerous and glorious remaining years as leverage in the games.

I pluck thick, cloudlike whips of chocolate frosting from a cupcake. "I don't know if that's true or not. The Splendor House changed me, Nicolai. Memories or none, I'm not the same girl you knew."

"Perhaps." There's no animosity in his tone. "But it matters little. You're still extraordinary, Tessa. You must be, for an immortal to have fallen in love with you twice in one ridiculously-long lifetime."

I put my elbow into his ribs. "You've always been charming."

"And you've always thought I was, even when you didn't remember who I am."

I make a face. There's no denying that.

I think a bit about love as we wind back through the curly paths toward *Red & Gold's* while dusk starts to march across the Mirror Lands. Ever since the Splendor House, I thought no one would ever love me. Now I remember that several boys did, or at least professed to. Boys I ran with in the streets of Barrow Downs, hunger-panged and gaunt like me; hardy fishermen always smelling of too-strong cologne to fight the perpetual haze of dead sea creatures on their hands, who taught me to fend for myself with a rod and a hook; gentle baker's sons with unruly hair and flour-dusted hands and powdered-sugar smiles who fed me when the tide pools were empty; electric boys with cool eyes and rakish grins who would flash into my path sudden as lightning, light me up with their kisses and wild touches, and then vanish back into the gutters where we all struggled to survive. I'd never known if they lived or died after our paths crossed. I'd tried not to care.

And I know that Nicolai is different from all of them. I know that the shine of his power settled into my life, and stayed. And this must be the difference between love and infatuation, I think: that though I've changed, Nicolai isn't bothered. To care for something—not because of what it can do for you, like a child brought to a Circus to be devoured, but in spite of what it can't—because you care for it more than yourself, so you remain, even when it goes through the ugliest shifts and resettlings, the deepest lows. I've faced my valleys and I'm climbing again, and still Nicolai walks beside me, banded in golden light and swaggering with hands in pockets, deceptively calm.

But inside him, a storm is raging. Because he loves me, and he is going to watch me walk to the Big Top tonight and finish this for us both.

At *Red & Gold's*, I topple straight into the bed. I haven't slept at all since the House of Mirrors, and suddenly I'm exhausted. It feels as if my body hopes to delay the inevitable, and I let it. I haven't thought a wink beyond opening those doors, after all. Above my head, the iron buds cringe shut, fearing the future.

"Tomorrow," I mumble. "Tomorrow night, I'll go."

If Nicolai protests, I don't hear him. I'm fast asleep in seconds, no time for pacing or fear, but I'm beginning to hope that those long nights are behind me, anyway. I sleep dreamlessly and wake to a bright room. I've slept all through the night.

We have one more day. It isn't enough.

Night comes so urgently, I know the Circus is fiddling with time again. We've barely returned from a distracted perusal of Sweet Street, where most of Lord Mull's goods are pedaled off on the unsuspecting mortals, when the sky grows dark. I change out of my dayclothes with automaton hands, a distracted metal girl with her gears wound too tightly.

I fumble into the serrated dress, smooth out the black and red plume of the skirt more than it needs smoothing. I adjust my leggings and wiggle my toes in my boots.

I want Nicolai with me tonight, but we both know he can't be. So our goodbye is here.

"He'll give you one last test," he says. "It shouldn't be anything too complex."

"Complexity is relative." I tame down my skirt, but it poofs right back up.

Nicolai steps forward and hands me the keys. His eyes are the darkest, strongest, bitterest brew. "Remember, Tessa. Our ringmaster is unpredictable in the most dangerous ways if those suicides on Barrow Island are indeed true."

"I know." I stretch up and press a kiss to his cheek. "I'll see you after."

I leave it at that. Neither of us really knows what *after* will look like.

There is a stark air of eagerness about the Circus once I reach the Big Top. The great silver bridge spans the moat like the tendrils of a dream, and when I step onto it I see that it's glass, that I can peer through straight to the dark moat. I gather courage from the memory of swimming there, of frolicking at the ringmaster's feet and encroaching on his refuge without his notice or consent. I do not exist to be stomped on by the Metters and Fionas and Wish Granters of the Lands. Tonight, I will show him so.

The Big Top is such a grand thing up close, and the moment I touch its striped canvas hide I know it's not mortal material. It's tough as armor but light and smooth as silk, and there's some resistance to it. I couldn't just force my way through.

There is a door set where the fabric gathers back. It's painted in swirls of bronze and cobalt, so that's the key I use. Clever of them to have given the keys all out of order. It discourages the wisher from sneaking a peek at the tent too soon.

I step inside to a sharp grade from spring warmth to winter chill, and shudder. The first layer of the tent is dark, its curve lined with empty covered wagons tipping on rotten axels. It's clear they've been here a very long time, perhaps since the tent was first erected. I hurry to the next door, straight across, and enter the second loop.

And it goes like that: I slide through graveyards of iron cages, smashed steel rings, broken poles, severed wires and more. I think now that they're a warning, that they're meant to intimidate me, and I hate that in some fashion they do. It's a distracting effort not to think of past wishers whose bodies broke like these things did, who might have been eaten by whatever clawed its way from one of the cages, rending the bars apart like damp noodles.

I nearly run to the fifth and final door, porcelain key in my fist. I jam it into the grand lock, and when the two halves split apart it's with a great sigh from the other side. I know at once that this is the heart of the Big Top itself—a wide room thickly clothed in gauzy gray shadows, lacking any sort of the ghoulish light that gave me at least a hint of clarity in the House of Mirrors. I could as well be in a cave or on the edge of a precipice. Somehow, I feel it's both.

I swallow, then call out, "Hello?"

The Big Top must have been waiting for me, for my voice. When I speak, a high, thin spotlight flashes on, scours briefly across the slope of cloth up to the pinnacle of the tent, and descends rapidly along black stands all the way down to a lonely figure poised halfway across from me on the sandy arena floor.

My heart skips at the sight of his tall hat, his waistcoat and tails, his knee-high polished boots and his cane. He stands with feet shoulders-width apart, looking very much like his image on Libertine's rostrum. The poster I was so certain was watching me.

The Wish Granter.

I tap my palms to my thighs for a count of five. Then I muster my wits and walk toward him.

"I did what your Circus demanded." My voice seems quite small and thin in this place, the tent soaking the strength from the words. "I've done your trials, now I'm here for my prize."

"I know why you're here, Tessa LaRoche."

There is no accusation in that quiet, melodious voice, no condescension or condemnation. Yet I halt as if he's slapped me, and chills retreat from my hairline to the base of my spine, burrowing their way down my legs.

"You've come to undo me," he adds.

"I'm sure I don't know what you mean."

A glint of silver unravels in his palm. I suck in my breath as he unleashes my necklace, letting it sway from his fist. "Your desired wish, to know which Deathless stole your necklace."

Libertine. If I ever see that treacherous lion-faced fool again, I'll throttle him with my bare hands.

"But this is not only about the necklace," the ringmaster goes on. "You know it's far more complex than that."

I'm growing tired of hearing that word. Perhaps it's aggravation that makes my voice pert: "You're referring, of course, to the people you killed. Or rather that you forced to kill themselves."

There's little sense hiding what I know. He can taste my fear, I'm sure, and if he can't, then the Circus is whispering into his ear about it. That's something else I remember from my many, many years researching this place: the ringmaster communes deeply with the power that holds this once-city hostage.

"You cannot destroy the ringmaster, Tessa." He states it as calm fact. "The Circus would crumble without him."

"But if he kills a girl and takes away her memories, or if he frames an innocent man for murder, that's all right." The fear is fading. Old Tessa, Dark Tessa, is clawing her way out in every indignant syllable, and I have no desire to stop her. Our fury and disgust make us one.

"I should not have killed you. I should have killed Nicolai, but I was too frightened of what would become of my Circus if I murdered one of the Deathless. And look at it now. It hangs askew, drunk on angry whispers, because here you are again. I knew it was you the moment I saw this gift. And I think you know, too, that you should never have come back."

"Well, and *you* should never have come to Barrow Downs to lead the watch to Nicolai. I know you were the witness that tipped them off. I know everything."

The Wish Granter is silent for too many heartbeats. Around us, the Big Top shallowly breathes, and so do I.

"Perhaps I should not have. But my actions do not change the fact that everything is still out of balance," The Wish Granter continues at last. "Because you didn't solve this by yourself, did you? You had help again."

The shadows lock me in, humid and crowding. We stare at one

another by the garish spotlight's glow.

He knows. He knows of Nicolai's involvement as surely as if he walked beside us, swam beside us, watched us from the wound in my palm.

"So it seems we have both committed injustices." The Wish Granter shifts subtly. "But you are here, and subject to the power of this Circus. I will set the balance now, for the sake of us all. It will be finished."

Unlike me, The Wish Granter needs no knife to do this murderous deed. It's his power that carves toward me, a deadly white scythe screeching out all at once, and there's no way to deflect or dodge it.

Just like last time.

And then a solid shape materializes before me, blotting out the sickle of power.

In a flicker of gold, Nicolai is suddenly between us.

It happens so quickly I don't have time to fathom where he came from, whether he was here all along. I can't even say his name.

The ringmaster's magic slams into Nicolai, and blood erupts across his body.

CHAPTER TWENTY-THREE

*N*icolai! *Nicolai!*"

My screams sound as if the world is ending, and perhaps it is. I claw at his shoulders and back as he falls past me, but I'm too weak to hold us both up. We crumble to the floor, and I tear open his coat and the halves of his vest to the white shirt below. It's already rouged with blood.

I bite my lower lip so hard it bleeds, too. "Oh, no."

A swell of sudden sound roars in my ears. I think at first that it's dizziness, that I'm going to faint. But then lights flare up all around us, and the Big Top comes to life. It's absolutely packed, floor and stands, with mortals and Deathless. A prismatic tide of their collective energy collides in the air as they look down on this horrific display. I twist on my knees to look across the three great rings and see The Wish Granter silhouetted against a backdrop of flaming hoops, tightropes, and leashed animals, both Mirror and Mortal, snarling in rage and hunger. A webwork of pinnacle-high trapezes extends across the chasm of the far-below floor. There isn't one net.

"You can't do this!" I scream.

"It is all that can be done. He aided you. He interfered. Now to set the balance, *you* will decide his fate." The Wish Granter offers his hand to me.

"All you have to do is touch my hand, and you can save him. If you fall, you fail. If he helps you, you fail. And if you fail, I will not save him."

"Tessa," Nicolai chokes. "Tessa, no."

I don't know if he fears he'll die and come back without his memories like I did, or if he's afraid for me. And I find it doesn't matter, one way or another. The Wish Granter has given me no choice. He's stolen the possibilities from me. I can't wish for condemnation for his crimes against the Accord if I must also wish for Nicolai's life. And if I fail...if I fail, the ringmaster of this detestable Circus will have precisely what he wanted: Nicolai will be dead, and the blood will not be on his hands. It will be on mine, because I couldn't save him.

And I know he will not give me another chance to take the trials and wish for both Lands to be made aware that he framed Nicolai for murder.

I turn back to Nicolai, and I know he sees what's coming. Resignation twists his mouth, and he jerks me close and presses something into my hand. This time, it *is* a knife. He knows I must be able to defend myself against this last test, and that I lack his power, but I'm powerful in my own way.

His blessing is in the blade between us.

I lift Nicolai's hand and mine, twined around the polished handle, and kiss his bloody knuckles. "Keep your eyes open, Nic. Watch me."

"I'm not going anywhere."

Oh, I must wish him healed, so that I won't feel badly about slapping him over the head for that cheeky retort.

I stand and stride toward The Wish Granter, and a smile with neither cruelty nor pity curls his lips. This is all part of the great show to him. It's to the entertainment of his audience.

This is the balance.

I hear the snap of a rope going taut, and just before my fingers graze his, he's lifted away from me. In one lithe movement, he launches up and sails backward, coming to rest on the zenith of the contraptions: a narrow post with a platform barely three feet across. The crowd hushes as his cane taps the wood, the resonate sound of a death knell. Even the animals cower in silence. The Wish Granter skims the brim of his tall hat in silent salute to me, then smoothly folds his hands on the cane's head and inclines slightly on his polished boots.

"Begin." His soft murmur carries like a thunderclap.

I look up at the gauntlet before me and know that for my necklace, I would have turned back. I would have given up here and now.

But this is not about my necklace. Not anymore.

CHAPTER TWENTY-FOUR

*T*hink! my mind rages.

Move! my feet command.

Nicolai is already dying. If he crosses into that dark oblivion, I will never reclaim him the same as he is now. And he may hate me forever for that.

The crowd resumes its sound, begins to cheer. I breathe and release, in and out, curling and uncurling my fingers around the knife. I reach into the old memories now at my disposal. I call on Dark Tessa, that toughened creature from the gutters who bit and scrapped and clawed her way to survival, to this Circus, for the immortal life and the chance to share it with someone who mattered. Someone who shared her dream.

That dream-sharer, that just-right someone, is bleeding to death behind us now. So I let her out, and the havoc of sound drops away. Everything before me in the gauntlet slides into sharp focus, and suddenly I see patterns. They're everywhere. This is like the alleys where we fled from the watch's dogs, their slobbery jowls chomping at our heels. This is like the rooftops of Barrow Downs, where we fled from the shopkeepers when we stole our next meal. We had no net then, either, but we survived. Our body knew how. It still knows.

We grin together, not in any amusement, but to show The Wish

Granter that we know we can do this, and we *will*.

Then we move.

The sand compresses and reshapes in the imprint of my boots as I run straight toward the beasts. The crowd gives a rising, sonorous cheer, and the animals lunge to the ends of their chains, scraping the hot air with their wicked, curved claws in anticipation of sinking them into my skin. I tally them in my head: a bear, a tiger, some gilled Mirror feline with webbed toes, a fiery red lion, and an elephant that trumpets nervously off to the side.

I'm not concerned about the elephant. It's not as likely to sit on me as the predators are to tear me apart. These creatures who are between me and the narrow rungs that climb up the posts to the maze of hoops and wires above...

My feet churn faster. My blood boils. The teeth and claws flash closer.

Dive! Dark Tessa shouts, and I do, tucking into a forward somersault under the red lion's claws. I roll back onto my feet and dart out of reach of the mesmerizing gillcat's open-palmed slap. But that puts me in reach of the bear, and its hooked nails tear at my skirts, fat lower lip drooping as it snarls in my face.

It doesn't get through. Its claws bounce uselessly off the fabric.

A collective gasp goes up from the audience, and I hear an unmistakable, smug shout of glee. My eyes cut briefly to the stands and now that I've heard her voice, Moe is absolutely impossible to ignore: on her feet and screaming, the light revealing her hair, lips, and eyelids all painted a comparatively conservative wine-red. *My* color, my favorite color, as she well knows.

There's panic in her eyes for Nicolai. But her raised fists are for me.

The bear rises on his hind legs. If he can't scrape me raw, it seems he'll smother me. I hold my ground a moment longer, hearing the stir of long fur and hot breath behind me. Then I leap aside, and the bear comes down on top of the tiger instead. A squealing, harrumphing mess of tumbling beasts follows, and dark shapes slither out of the sidelines to intervene— handlers, I think, the ones who usually put these poor beasts through their paces. I turn and run as they approach, and the gillcat and lion give chase.

They're so much faster than my out-of-shape body and I know that if they catch me, eventually they'll find a place to stick their teeth that isn't covered by Moe's armored designs.

I must make chasing me worse than starving. So I veer hard right toward the flaming hoops on cinderblock pedestals and hope that without a whip cracking over their heads, the enormous cats will balk at the leap.

The ring is unbearably hot even from a distance, but I must do this. I push up with all my might and lunge through, ringlets singeing, my belly protected from the flames only by my enchanted dress as I tuck and roll back onto my feet. The gillcat loses momentum skirting the jump, but the lion comes through like a fiendish nightmare, soaring above me, paws extended, jaws agape. I cringe backward, and his great feet slam into the sand just beyond me, sending him skidding in a comical tangle along the floor. He strikes the end of his chain with a cry.

The audience groans. I leap up and start running again. I'm out of reach, I think, and there's nothing left but precious taupe sand and the rungs before me.

And then I feel claws smack into the backs of my thighs, shredding the leggings, then my skin. It's the only pain I feel—a swelling hot burst, and then numbness as my body chokes down the agony so that I can keep moving. And I do, so quickly I think I may trip like the lion did. I lunge and take the lowest rungs, propelling myself up to safety before I dare look down.

It's the tiger that caught me, the noose of its broken chain swinging between its front legs as it claws uselessly after me. I can't feel anything but pity as I stare into its ravaged face. It's hungry, not cruel. The cruel ones are the handlers snapping the whips to corral it. I know the Deathless could feed these animals a good meal every day, but they choose not to for their show. Their silly, soul-stealing show.

Grimacing, I push myself up the rungs to the first narrow platform and crouch to catch my breath. A dim sizzle of pain is all I feel of the scratches, but I know I have little time before they'll start screaming. I try not to think of infections or blood poisoning or any number of things I read about in the books at the Splendor House. I can only spare thought for the aerial feats before me: the rings and handlebars, the silk ropes, the series of platforms barely as wide as my two feet, the tightrope…perilous, but as a whole it doesn't seem so bad.

So, naturally, they make it worse.

I don't see them bring out the fire-breathers and knife-throwers from the Menagerie, but I feel them. The air heats below me, shimmering with mirages of the steep plunge and the upturned faces, and then a streak of flame whips between all the trapezes, and the audience goes wild. Meanwhile my heart plunges to the floor, whispering as it goes that it will see the rest of me there soon.

But it can't. It can't, because I can see Nicolai's shape below, still stirring in pain, trying to sit himself up. Trying to watch me. Failing this test is not a possibility, just like starving to death in Barrow Downs was never a possibility. It simply means I must do the impossible.

I grit the knife between my teeth and rise. I wait for the next cycle of fire to gash the air, leaving a heated trail of embers in its wake. Then I leap into the gauntlet, reaching for the patterns between the flames.

My arms begin to throb at once, my shoulders rebel and threaten to dislocate. They are so very, very out of practice with all of this. But desperation bludgeons them into submission, silencing the pain so that I can cast one hand in front of the next, in front of the next, over and over. I swing from hoop to hoop, pausing here and there to let the fire go by, or casting myself forward at greater speed when I feel the air start to swim with the coming flames. Sweat soaks my collar and ruins Moe's lovely creation, but I don't think she'll mind. I suspect she'll demand this dress back and hang it among the portraits in her parlor for all to see. If nothing else, I've restored her good reputation tonight.

I reach the second post without catching fire, but now it's the ropes I must contend with. So many silky ribbons strung from the bracing beams above. I flex my aching, swollen fingers, which creak like an old crone's claws at the second knuckles. This will not end well.

I don't realize I've paused too long for their tastes until a knife skins across my upper arm, opening a wound that hurts surprisingly much. I gasp and waver, and hear shouts from below. One is gruffer and weaker than the rest, but I hear it the loudest—hear the way it cracks around my name.

I grab the edge of the post's skinny platform to steady myself. I bat the water from my eyes and push down fruitlessly on the wound, hoping to stanch it at least a bit. From the corner of my eye, I catch the gleam of another knife soaring, and I don't wait for it to find its mark. I lunge from the platform to the closest banner, graceless and unbalanced, and grab with the wrong arm. The wounded one.

There's no strength in my left hand. Down and down I skid, buffeted by the groans from the mortal onlookers. I think the Deathless are laughing but it's difficult to tell over my own frantic breathing as I grab and grab and finally latch onto the twist of silk with my right hand. I hang and spin, slowing my thundering heart, waiting for panic to loosen its tight grip on my chest. Then I shake out my left hand and curl it slowly around the banner, and I start the grueling climb back up to where I was.

It's wasted time. The fall could cost me everything. And outside the broad cocoon of mauve silk that flutters around my body, I hear knives whistling by, the Deathless hurling them blindly at the banner like striking into a barrel of fish and hoping to land true.

Well, I am not a fish, and I will not swim about waiting to be impaled. I keep climbing even when blood drips from my elbow and tears drip from my eyes. I climb up into the rafters above, where their knives can't reach, where they fall far short. I crouch on the beam and haul up the streamer as I back away, stepping over the trapezes again. Someone shouts at the fire-breathers to bring me back down where I can be seen.

Little do they know I have every intention of being seen.

I twine the silk cord around my injured arm in a tourniquet, grip it with my right hand, and leap.

The fall is exhilarating and terrifying, jerking a scream to the backs of my teeth where I bite into it like a delicious tart, relishing the power not to show them my fear. The banner jumps when it catches, and then I'm sailing forward between the rest of them, a jungle of vermillion, shamrock, ginger and flax streaming past. There's a soft intake of breath from below as I soar straight through the gauntlet and toward the third platform. I stretch out my boots and skid to a halt, bringing up my knife to cut the cord off at my shoulder, leaving the tourniquet in place. It soothes some of the pain in my arm, and I peer ahead.

I am so close, just the tightrope left. The Wish Granter waits at the end, and he hasn't moved. The bursts of fire from below illuminate the contours of his hat, the silver curls on his sable cane, and the brass buttons on the gloved hand he extends to me. He's truly going to let my strength decide if I succeed or fail.

It won't be failure.

I slide out of my boots, biting down on the knife's blade when the gashes on my thighs whine and tug at their frayed edges. Fear snatches my throat when I look below the tightrope. I know I've done these sorts of stunts before, but I'm not certain I still have the strength. And I will learn the most difficult way possible if I don't.

I sidle out onto the rope, and to my relief, my feet know what to do. They center me, my toes curl, my body sways to find balance. Arms outstretched, I begin to make my way toward the man who can doom or save us.

But this is not as easy as it once was. Even Dark Tessa knows that. And as the fire-breathers move into place below, I realize my mistake. I'd foolishly expected The Wish Granter to allow me this challenge without distraction.

When the first gout of flames shoots up, I drop. The people's moans turn to cheers when I manage to grip the wire, but I feel it slit open my palms. My poor left hand, with its two scars already. Now it will have a third. Tears slide down my cheeks as I stomach the pain, swallowing it like the most grisly and horrific bite of anything ever consumed. Then I sidle along the rope a ways, until a knife sings past my side, telling me that this will not do.

I curse the entire Circus and its ringmaster as I boost myself back onto the wire, rise, and seek my balance. The Wish Granter watches so keenly, and though his presence may not feel malicious, it is mocking. I can see the unfurled edge of his half-smile, and it goads me on. I start to pick my way back down that wire, leaning completely into the strength of Dark Tessa and all the memories she embodies, all the things we did to survive.

Step by sidling step. Closer and closer to The Wish Granter's outstretched hand.

And then I hear a great, screeching trumpet that bursts against my ears, and all of a sudden, I remember the elephant. The creature I ignored. The one I thought was of no concern because it had no fangs or claws.

I'd forgotten the strength of its massive body.

I don't dare look down, but I can imagine what's happening by the elephant's cries and the snarls from below. The handlers haven't cornered the tiger yet, and, emboldened by hunger, it's turned to larger and tougher prey. The elephant lumbers to escape from it, and it smashes into the third post—the one behind me.

The tightrope bobs. It goes out from beneath me, then comes back, and I fall to my knees on it.

The elephant smashes into the post again so hard it breaks off with a sickening *crack* of separated wood. The wire jerks down and then smashes up, unseating me again, flinging me one way as the post plunges the other. My injured hands slap at the frayed wire as it lashes past, quick as a snake disappearing under a rock—and slides out of my grasp.

"How disappointing."

Those are the last words I hear before The Wish Granter vanishes in a plume of smoke. The audience, the animals, the handlers and the Deathless all disappear in the eddying current of his power, and I fall, fall, fall as the ropes and silks and trapezes do. A slow and graceful descent, as silent as collapsing backward into one's own grave. All I can hear is a roaring in my ears that is not the wind whistling past me.

I failed.

How could I have failed? How could I have forgotten the elephant, and now—now—

Death reaches for me, but its gruesome hands never touch. A flare of golden power slaps them away, and my descent slows. Instead of the cold sandy floor, I crash into a web of warm energy and sink through it, settling light as a feather on the ground. Twisting to look around, I see Nicolai propped up on one hand, the other extended. Power gutters and then winks out between his fingers. He sinks back with a groan—the sound of giving up, of a final task completed.

All at once, I feel pain everywhere, popping silver stars across the sooty chasm of the Big Top and the dusty wreckage of the gauntlet that I failed, failed, failed. Not only did I fall, but Nicolai used his power to keep me alive. We failed twice over. I don't know how many more times we can fail together, but I think we've used up all our chances now.

I try to stand, but break down on bleeding legs. I feel the mayhem of pain gnawing on my muscles now. I feel it everywhere, in both arms and down my hands, and even in places I wasn't struck, as I drag myself through the semidarkness and the wreckage of the fallen gauntlet to Nicolai's side. He's spread out on his back, one hand pressed into the gashes that mar his chest. Blood surges up between his fingers and runs down his sides.

"I'm sorry." I join my hands to his and feel his icy skin and the slowness of the bloodflow, as if he has little left to give. "I forgot the elephant. I'm such a fool."

"No. You were magnificent." His voice is hoarse, a harbor tide fading in and out of pitch. "Never forget, Tessa, how magnificent you are…never forget yourself again. Promise me that."

"*Magnificent?* Nicolai, I failed!"

"You survived. I don't care about the rest of it."

"Well, maybe *I* do, you absolute goof! Maybe I put myself through all of that just now because I can't let you go any more than you could let go of me."

His chuckle bubbles with blood, and his fingers wrap my wrist so tightly as he raises his head to peer at me through pain-stricken eyes. I know that look…it was there the day he touched the clock, that moment he wouldn't share with me.

This is what he saw. This hour of his death. He knew how close it was, and yet he followed me to the Big Top anyway. To keep me safe.

"You asked me, at the moat, Tessa. You asked me what I saw when you wore the headband." His other hand rises to brush the burned, frazzled ringlets behind my ear, to cup my cheek. "Nothing. You. I just see you."

I gather him into my lap and pull up his head when it lolls against my belly. It's all awkward, my grip on him, his lean figure sprawled on my short legs, but I won't let him go. He slides his hand into my hair, and that is the only invitation I need to kiss him. Though he tastes of blood and darkness, I kiss him and kiss him. The desperate, defeated boy from Barrow Island, the Deathless who dreamed of adventure, the man who traded his humanity for the hope to save his brothers and sisters…I couldn't save him, but I will not let him die alone.

And so I kiss him until the hand in my hair goes slack. Until our breaths no longer mingle. Until he dies, kissed, and held, and loved.

With him goes my heart. And with him goes the world.

Which is not a broken heart speaking, it is not the helpless cries of love defeated, spiraling down like a torched feather into the dust. It is no exaggeration that when Nicolai takes his last breath, the world itself stops breathing, too, and begins to decay.

THE CHAOS CIRCUS

The Big Top falls to dust around us, carried away on a strong breeze. The dazzling halo of color that is the Chaos Circus beyond the bridge, beyond the moat, is disintegrating before my eyes, the shrill screams of exhilaration and delight falling out of tune. The calliope music I've grown so used to is no longer playing. And even as I cling to Nicolai's cold, dead body, it too turns to embers, floating away.

Chanting a litany of *no, no, no*, I try to grasp at him, the last sizzling flakes of his power hanging on the air, but they pass through my hands.

And then they pulse. And then they bloom, and the strokes of his enchanting might swirl around me one last time, flooding the world in gold. I reach out for something to hold onto. I reach and reach through empty air for a final touch, a last taste of him.

His power closes over me, and I shut my eyes.

CHAPTER TWENTY-FIVE

*J*essa, you little fool!"

I suck in a breath, sharp and harsh as a sob. Then another. My eyes fly back open.

Sangria wood. Pearl booths. Amethyst coils of inner-lit jellyfish lights spooling from a high, long ceiling. The flickers of watchmen's uniforms and Mister Metters' tan coat on the corners of my vision. I jerk backward, and my hand slips from the grasp of strong, smooth fingers, the heat of sweating skin soaked into the metal of my balloon necklace, which is still offered out to me.

That, and so much more, by the one I thought I'd lost just now, and forever.

Nicolai.

I almost do sob then, as I trace the contours of his face with my eyes. I want to rip open the front of his coat and look him over for wounds. I want to leap forward and press my lips to his, but I'm frozen still, stunned like I've hit my head. Understanding is slowly making its way out of my tight, shaking limbs and into my whirling mind.

The glittering dust of golden power flecks his dark eyes, settles like new freckles on my skin, and as our gazes meet, I know.

I am looking at Lord Harlequin, I am feeling the currents of the future-seer pass in and out of my body, hot and cold at once.

I know what I just saw.

Gong!

None of it ever happened. Or at least, it hasn't happened yet.

He's just showed me everything that will transpire when that clock is finished chiming. Clever Nicolai, finding a way to show me back to my memories without telling them to me. It's a perfect strategy to protect my mind from the utter chaos of knowing: instead of coming to this speakeasy and saying it all, he's taken my mind down the roads of the future, to learn at my own pace. About what's happened in Barrow Downs, the suicides, The Wish Granter...and what's to come.

I wonder how long he planned this, how long he spent drawing me to this place tonight, so that I would touch his hand and see that future.

It seems we didn't fail, after all. Because now I am standing here, having just taken his hand only moments ago. And yet I remember everything that has happened in the past, and everything that will happen next.

The Wish Granter is crouching in one of the booths even now, recently come back from checking on the suicides of the past winners. He will leap from that booth in a moment, and he will steal my necklace and make his escape through the Rift. If I chase him, I will take the trials. I know because now I've seen it, just as Lord Harlequin saw it.

Gong!

"The House will hear about this!" Mister Metters howls. "You're finished at the Daily! This is the end of you!"

In Barrow Downs, it is. But if I take Nicolai's hand again, if I step into the future I saw, perhaps we can change it. Perhaps we can find another way for him to be exonerated and free from the Chaos Circus. Free from The Wish Granter.

Perhaps we'll still have our adventure after all.

Gong!

Nicolai waits, hand extended. He is here, he is still alive. But if I go with him, he will not survive unless we're strong enough to change the very course of fate—betting the risk of my future, which he could never see before, against this one where he is certain to die.

"Tessa!" Metters growls. "*Tessa LaRoche,* come back here!"

"Tessa."

It's all Nicolai says. It's all I need to hear.

My fingers flutter. I see nothing but Nicolai, and the choice before me, which he offers without impression or pleading. He simply waits for me, as he waited all this time.

Deep within me, I feel Dark Tessa stir and test the winds of fortune. I feel her sense an adventure, and her smile finds its way onto my face as I hold Nicolai's gaze. It's a grin that is wild and wicked and free—just as we could be, if I dare to take his hand.

Gong.

ACKNOWLEDGMENTS

There are so many people I should thank for their help with this book—too many to fit here. *The Chaos Circus* was a strange, magical foray into a story I've wanted to tell after years of obsession with state fairs, carnivals, and the circus: something that blended these things into one. But the process of moving this story from years of daydreams to a published work wasn't easy, and I only survived it thanks to the support of so many people:

First, my amazing husband: for the (thankfully inaccurate!) *Far Cry 5* theory that sparked the idea for *TCC*, for listening to me rave about the beginning and the end, for sitting patiently while I figured out the middle, and sticking around to hear me read it out loud. For loving me unconditionally. You are the greatest adventure in my life.

To my family, both blood and in-law: for listening, for brainstorming, for encouraging, for reading and giving feedback and always supporting this dream. It may not look how we imagined it, but it's everything we dreamed. Especially to Dustin, my alpha reader, and Mom, my beta reader. Couldn't do this without you two. <3

Special thanks to my sister, Maggie, for showing love and making me feel like a real author for the first time in my life. I can never thank you enough. Matched set for life. <3

To my writing family: Atty, Chief, Joy, Jen, and Holly. For every conversation, every rough spot you got me through, for knowing my language (not just my insane typos) and speaking it back to me when I lose my way. You were the piece of my life I didn't know was missing until I had you. Thank you for the beta reading and the magic Discord brainstorms and for loving Tessa and Nic just as much as I do.BAnd a special shout-out to Atty for being my critique partner, for telling me what did work and what didn't, for putting months of work into this story so it could be its absolute best. No story feels right until it has your seal of approval anymore.

To all the friends who encouraged me, but especially: to Meagan and Annelisa for all the art and dream-chasing, and for the Chicago trip right in the middle of drafting that got me over the writer's block. For loving me good and true. To Christina for having the heart to reach out, for helping bring my babies to life through art—for loving my book and becoming a lifelong friend. To Miranda and Cassidy for devouring this book and SCREAMING at me – love you two, and sorry! And to Jeff, for asking me "How much of you is in Tessa?" All of these moments have meant the world to me. As all of YOU mean the world to me. <3

To Dussy, Danny, and Jerry, for taking the road less traveled to the backwater carnival that truly gave this story its wings. I'll never forget what that day meant to me. <3

To Pam, best of wives and women—for being there all the time, for the photoshoot and the design help, for reading the manuscript and enduring the food torture, for diamond paintings and IT Crowd marathons and Hamilton jam sessions and never letting me throw away MY shot.

To all my writing friends on Instagram, Facebook, and Twitter, who fangirl and encourage and give nothing but support, always, and everyone else who shares the struggles, the insanity and the sheer joy that is writing. Special mention goes out to Holly, Heather, Breeann, Becca, Brittany, Christina, Devin, Katie, Meaghan, Maverick, M.K, Lina, Craig, Jay, Jamie, Never, and Red. You all mean so much to me.

To the authors who taught me through example that this indie publishing thing can be done with success, and how to do it right. You have paved a path that many, many indie authors will walk behind you. For that, we could not be more grateful.

To Maja Kopunovic, for taking my breath away with that first draft of the gorgeous cover that truly captured Tessa's tightrope walk between two worlds. For seeing the story within my short briefing and bringing a face to this novel. And for becoming not just the artist who brings ALL my books to life now—but a friend who continues to see my heart.

And last, and greatest, to God: for the wake-up call that showed me where I was going wrong, and for guiding me back to the path I now know is right. Your plans are always greater – I'm just following Your way. Thank you for redeeming everything I thought was lost. Lead on.

CHECK OUT THESE OTHER R. DUGAN TITLES
AVAILABLE AT ONLINE BOOK RETAILERS EVERYWHERE!

THE STARCHASER SAGA

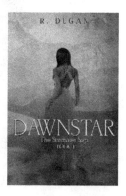

ABOUT THE AUTHOR

Renee Dugan is an Indiana-based YA/NA author who grew up reading fantasy books, chasing stray cats, and writing stories full of dashing heroes and evil masterminds. Now with over a decade of professional editing, administrative work, and writing every spare second under her belt, she has authored *THE CHAOS CIRCUS,* a horror-lite fantasy novel, and *THE STARCHASER SAGA,* an epic high fantasy series. Living with her husband, dog, and three not-so-stray cats in the magical Midwest, she continues to explore new worlds and spends her time in this one encouraging and helping other writers on their journey to fulfilling their dreams.

CPSIA information can be obtained
at www.ICGtesting.com
Printed in the USA
FSHW011637280121
78023FS